The Last Winged Hussar

Sarah J. Waldock

ISBN-13 9798637221790

Dedication

Firstly, to Sabaton; without their great song 'The Winged Hussars Arrived', I would never have got interested in who the winged hussars were, and this book would never have been conceived.

Secondly to Aleksandra Leśniewska, Master of World Literature, without whom this book would never have been completed because I would have given up in despair of getting matters Polish correct

Thirdly, to the Polish people of the world

Lastly, thanks to the Lone Ranger for inspiration

Other books by Sarah Waldock
See end of book

Sarah Waldock grew up in Suffolk and still resides there, in charge of a husband, and under the ownership of sundry cats. All Sarah's cats are rescue cats and many of them have special needs. They like to help her write and may be found engaging in such helpful pastimes as turning the screen display upside-down, or typing random messages in kittycode into her computer.

Sarah claims to be an artist who writes. Her degree is in art, and she got her best marks writing essays for it. She writes largely historical novels, in order to retain some hold on sanity in an increasingly insane world. There are some writers who claim to write because they have some control over their fictional worlds, but Sarah admits to being thoroughly bullied by her characters who do their own thing and often refuse to comply with her ideas. It makes life more interesting, and she enjoys the surprises they spring on her. Her characters' surprises are usually less messy [and much less noisy] than the surprises her cats spring.

Sarah has tried most of the crafts and avocations which she mentions in her books, on the principle that it is easier to write about what you know. She does not ride horses, since the Good Lord in his mercy saw fit to invent Gottleib Daimler to save her from that experience; and she has not tried blacksmithing. She would like to wave cheerily at anyone in any security services who wonder about middle aged women who read up about gunpowder and poisonous plants.

Sarah would like to note that any typos remaining in the text after several betas, an editor and proofreader have been over it are caused by the well-known phenomenon of *cat-induced editing syndrome* from the help engendered by busy little bottoms on the keyboard.

This is her excuse and you are stuck with it.

And yes, there are two more cat bums on the edge of the picture as well as the 4 on her lap/chest

You may find out more about Sarah at her blog site, at:
   http://sarahs-history-place.blogspot.co.uk/
   Or on Facebook for advance news of writing
   https://www.facebook.com/pages/Sarah-J-Waldock-Author/520919511296291
   Or particiapate as a beta reader and get an advanced look at Sarah's work in draft form at
   https://mywipwriting.blogspot.com/

Glossary for Winged Hussars

Bohatyr
A hero of legendary abilities, something akin to the knights of the round table. Plural, bohatyry

Burmistrz
Mayor

Chorąży
Ensign

Czamara
high length coat worn by the clergy and merchants.

Dworek
Manor House

Hetman
General; there were 4 of them, 2 Polish, 2 Lithuanian.

Hussar
Polish hussars were heavy shock troops, wearing wings on their backs of wood and leather with feathers of various kinds set into them. The most plausible explanations I have found for these are [a] to scare the wits out of other horses [and their riders] and [b] to create enough resistance to discourage a horse from going full tilt, thus ensuring that they could manage a second charge. Unlike many cavalry, the Polish winged hussars were able to stop short, wheel, regroup and attack again. They were disbanded in 1776 as obsolete.

Kontusz
the outer garment of a szlachcic, a rich long coat often much braided on the chest and sleeves, and often with slashed sleeves to allow the arms to be worn outside the sleeve which is left to hang. In winter, lined with fur.

Kontusik
A female version of the kontusz, usually hip length but can be shorter or longer.

Mazurek
Mazurka

Pan
Address of a szlachta, 'sir' or 'lord'[nowadays, Mr.]

Pani	Address of married szlachcianka equivalent to 'lady'[Nowadays Mrs.]
Panicz	Address of a young szlachcic, meaning 'young master' much like the archaic English 'Childe'
Panna	An unmarried szlachcianka [see also Waćpanna]. [Nowadays Miss]
Poczet	a towarzysz's unit of men, a lance of men and their support staff
Pocztowy	retainers, members of a poczet
Polonez	The dance, Polonaise
Porucznik	'lieutenant'; the one who does the work for the rotmistrz, probably would be called 'captain' in the west.
Queen of Poland	The Mother of God
Rotmistrz	translated captain, militarily a company commander and probably closer to a major in a western army
Rynek	Market square
Sejm	Polish-Lithuanian Commonwealth Parliament
Sołtys	Village mayor
Starosta	Sheriff; also an administrative position, nominated by the king, and the king's representative.
Szlachta	Nobility. In theory all szlachta were equal, but some really were more equal than others in terms of wealth and prominence.
Szlachcic	Nobleman
Szlachcianka	Noblewoman
Tok	A leather sleeve or shoe depended from the saddle pommel in which the foot of the lance rests. A Hungarian loan-word
Towarzysz	Companion/brother-nobleman-warrior, maintains a poczet for a Rotmistrz, an officer.

Ulans	Polish light cavalry, replacing the hussars entirely after 1776.
Waćpan	archaic address form for speaking to a szlachcic.
Waćpanna	archaic address form if speaking directly to an unwed szlachcianka, about equivalent to the English 'Burd'
Wojewoda	a district administrator or governor
Wójt	a subordinate administrator
Złoty	Unit of currency, 30 groszy = 1 złoty. After the money reforms in 1772 the coin 1 talar was worth 8 złoty. At the time £1 was worth around 8 Złoty ie 1 złoty ≈ 2/6d [half a crown]. This at a time when a clerk is paid around £75 a year which was slightly less than the yearly cost to keep a horse even in a livery stable. Each of our hussars is going around on the 18th century equivalent of a Jaguar E-type.
Żupan	A szlachcic's garment, a long tunic high at the neck and buttoning down the front, worn under the kontusz.

Pronouncing Polish

First sit down and eat plenty of stuffed dumplings in soup, breaded pork cutlets and quaff mead or wódka until you feel enthusiastic.

Second, listen to Sabaton's 'Winged Hussars' to get in the mood even more, optionally sing Hej Sokóly.

And third:

W is always pronounced v
C is pronounced ts except before i when it is ch
Ń is ny
Ł (aka 'dark l') is w
Ż is zh
J is y
Sz is sh as is Ś
Cz is ch and so is ć
Ą and ę are pronounced in a French manner, and are approximately –on and -en
Ch is as in loch.
R is rolled

I think that accounts for most of the main ones used. The main one to remember is w as v, and otherwise with a consonant cluster try to imagine being a bee.

Note; being Scots is an advantage.

Chapter 1
1776, Poland

He absently wondered at the paradox that his feet should feel so heavy he was almost stumbling, and yet his head was so light he was afraid of falling as he went down the stairs from the audience chamber.

Automatically, he made his way to the stables to his big red-chestnut hussar-horse, whose stable name was Ogień na Skrzydłach, Fire on Wings, but who answered to Ogień.

"Well, my old friend, we are no longer wanted," he said, bitterly. "Not even in the ceremonial role we have been shuffled into lately. A chance to join the Ulans, and retrain as light cavalry – in a subordinate position of course. And with a lighter horse. You could beat any Ulan horse standing, my friend, and keep going longer."

Ogień whickered gently and nuzzled his master. They had been together boy and colt and knew each other well. The big chestnut was as rich a colour as his master had ever seen, matching the curly locks of his rider. Perhaps it was one reason they were so close. Judging by paintings, he closely resembled the stallion out of whom the family horses had been bred, almost a century ago.

"It's a sad business, my lord," the voice of Jan Nowak came from the loose box where he was currying the horse. "They told us we can transfer to these Ulans. I won't abandon you, my lord, whatever you choose, but I won't stand by to see anything happen to Ogień."

"Jan, I will not transfer to the Ulans, and Ogień is my brother in arms," said Wojciech Płodziewicz. "I will not be ordered around by some youth with half my experience; I who have won the right to wear wolfskin rather than spotted cat when I was scarce more than a stripling myself."

"What will you do, my lord?" asked Jan. He was

almost as tall as Wojciech, with a thatch of straw-coloured hair, and a neat beard and moustache.

"I ... am not sure," said Wojciech. "Jan ... it is your son who is my steward."

"Aye, my lord, and loyal as I be, even if some of the young fools amongst your servants want to serve Ulans. I've served you since I took you off your father's Husaria Horse when you could scarce walk; aye, and put you on your first pony the next week, years before you were even breeched."

"It is their right to do so, as I will not be able to maintain my *poczet* of lancers any more; to accompany those of my retainers who transfer will see them looked after properly," said Wojciech. "I ... let us ride home."

"They took your armour and wings," said Jan.

That stirred Wojciech to anger.

"They had no right," he hissed.

"No, my lord; but they took them anyway," said Jan.

"Our country is doomed," said Wojciech. "The winged hussars are the last bulwark of stability. With the games between Catharine of Russia and our king, Stanisław August, her puppet, who dances when her hand pulls his ... strings ... we have lost some of the Polish-Lithuanian Commonwealth already, and nobody seems to care. What is the good of electing a king only to be ruled by Russia? And now he favours ulans and arquebusiers over heavy cavalry. I have broken arquebusiers before."

"Yes, my lord," said Jan. "What will you do? Become a mercenary? Settle on your lands and marry to gain an heir? You are the last Baron Płodnadolina."

"I am also a soldier and have known nothing else," said Wojciech. He drew himself up, with a toss of his head and a glance down his roman nose which put Jan strongly in mind of the horse Ogień. "I am Porucznik Wojciech Płodziewicz, of the Skrzydło Escutcheon, of Płodnadolina, a noble heritage, but it is for nothing and my ancestry means nothing if my duty is wrest from me. I am, however, beginning to formulate an idea. There is dissent amongst the nobility, and such leads to unrest, and a failure to keep the peace. But let us ride home, and I will speak with Jaromar Nowak my steward."

"Aye, my lord and our family is tied to yours and we are of your banner," said old Jan.

"I need loyal men who understand me and will know why I have to do what I have to do,"said Wojciech.

"Whatever you do, my lord, if there is a place for me at your side, I will take it," said Jan, firmly.

Wojciech sent word for his steward to join him in his study, and went, while he waited, into the family armoury at Castle Płodnadolina. He had often been taken by his father to see the armour of his great ancestor, Wojciech Płodziewicz , the first baron, who had been raised to the position for his valour in battle. He had modified the coat of arms of his family, for only a noble could be a winged hussar, to blood red. The wings he wore and his armour had become so stained in battle he had commemorated it in his own armour thereafter, and Wojciech smiled at the tales his father had told him of their ancestor. The winged hussars were known as 'Angels of Death' and Wojciech had called himself half in jest the 'angel of blood.' He had been part of a group of 200 hussars who had been sent ahead of the main force, to damage the Turks' lines, and they had not been expected to survive. The first baron's mount had been killed under him, by having a leg blown off by a grenade, and this had served to enrage the angel of death to the point that, having shot his agonised steed, he was later found with the bodies of twenty Janissaries piled around him as he swung his four-foot sabre with a maniacal grin avenging his horse.

Here in the armoury was held that first Wojciech's

famous red-gold gilded scale armour, the helmet and the face guard set with ruby-red enamel. And his wings; the curved sticks set with feathers, to denote his status as a winged hussar, dyed as red as blood, fearsome emblems of a fighting unit which was renowned for winning even against overwhelming odds. The first Wojciech had ridden down upon the Ottomans and routed them at the siege of Vienna, riding at the side of Jan III Sobieski, the king, when the baron had been a king's favourite.

But that had been when kings had done the job they had been elected to do.

He knew that the armour would fit him. He knew the first Wojciech's measurements by heart for they were the same as his own. Six foot two, a thirty-six-inch waist, a chest of forty-eight inches, and ten inches more about the shoulders. The Płodziewicz men were blessed with slender waists and a naturally strong physique. They all had piercing blue-grey eyes, and curly hair with a touch of red to it. The first Wojciech had had a bright auburn hair, if his portrait was to be believed. Wojciech had slightly darker auburn hair, but the red had run true.

He returned to the study where Jaromar Nowak was waiting for him. Jaromar was about Wojciech's own age, some years short of thirty and a younger copy of his father. Raised alongside his future master, and educated as well, he had grown up as Wojciech's crony and confidant – and loyal follower into any trouble.

"My lord! My father has told me the bad news! What are we to do?"

"How much of the property is entailed on a new generation?" asked Wojciech.

"The castle and the home farm and the village," said Jaromar.

"Good; that leaves plenty which can be sold," said Wojciech. "What I want you to do is to sell anything which can be sold, including any geegaws save my ancestors' armour and portraits. Raise as much as you can, in cash. Purchase small properties all around the borders, and place caches of money and dried foods in each of them. Do not do it in my name; do it in the name of Jan Kowalski or some such common name, and be sure there is stabling for each. No, let me take a pseudonym, I already bear the name of one saint of Poland, so I will keep that; it is common enough. I will be Wojciech Skrzydło. Keep a horse for yourself, one for your father and of course Ogień, and the mare with the last foal he sired; have someone care for the mare and foal somewhere quiet."

"My lord – your other chargers ... you would sell them too?"

Wojciech considered. A hussar had at least two mounts, in case of losing one in battle. Ogień was his favourite, having learned the art of war alongside the horse, when he was a colt.

"Keep Wicher, to live up to his name of being like a gale of wind for Jan to use. If you feel you can handle one of the other two, keep one, if not, sell them both, and take an ordinary riding beast. It were a shame to lose trained war horses, and they will not want them for the Ulans."

"Szybki is the lightest; they may take him. I have ridden Blyskawica as a youth, helping my father."

Wojciech nodded.

"Yes, that is possible, and then Szybki may still have work. Oh, I will need a couple of sumpter beasts. Do you gossip much?"

"No, my lord! Of course not!"

"But others gossip and you hear it?"

"Aye, my lord, though I try to discourage it."

"When they speak of me drinking too much, look sad and angry but still discourage them. Let word get out. And when you have disposed of all my property and found me safe houses, then procure for me a body; the body of a man hanged for armed robbery about my own

9

size and age will do."

"I ... yes, my lord," said Jaromar.

"Once you have the body, and I have a list of the properties, disappear to one of them. You are unwed?"

"Yes my lord."

"Have you a sweetheart?"

"No, my lord."

"Anyone you wish to take into hiding with you?"

"No, my lord."

"Good. Over the next few weeks, you will remove the portraits from the gallery and cache them in the house you choose for yourself; you are their steward and guardian. Likewise, the contents of the armoury, and my personal effects. You will buy brandy by the barrel, and will be more open about that, but tight-lipped about the order."

"And gunpowder; will I leave any in the armoury?"

"You think of everything, Jaromar," said Wojciech.

"I will always be there for you, Wojciech," Jaromar permitted himself the informality.

It was sad, everyone agreed it, that the handsome young baron should have turned to drink, and ruined his own life because of the parliamentary decree to end the winged hussars. Women at court cried bitter tears that the most eligible bachelor in Poland-Lithuania should be killing himself slowly with drink.

The fire in the baron's personal quarters was put down to too much brandy and a naked flame; and it was caught too fiercely for anyone to put it out by the time the alarm was raised. The kegs of brandy he insisted on keeping close to him made the flames too hot to pass, and it was a fortunate thing that a keg of gunpowder in the nearby armoury blew up when it did, making it impossible for the flames to cross from the family part of the house within the walls to the stables and barracks.

Fortunate too that the baron had been in a towering rage from his drinking and had roved through the house, shouting at the servants and driving them out of doors, and telling them not to return until the morrow. Most wept genuine tears at his decline, but could not deny that he had not been a pleasant master to work for of late, morose and surly, and disinclined to listen to tales of woe or weal from his people, as he had done before.

The fear of fire in the stables made the grooms evacuate such horses as remained, which were led by Ogień in a stampede away from home, as if he knew that his master was dead, and was determined to join him, said a wall-eyed ostler, generally held to be a seer for his eye's ability to look elsewhere than upon the world in front of him.

Nobody had seen three figures slip out of a postern; and none had heard the whistle which summoned Ogień and the horses which looked to him as their herd master. The steward and the head groom were missing; but their absolute loyalty was known. They must have tried to get to the baron, and took the route through the armoury and had been blown to kingdom come by the gunpowder in there. Masses would be said for their souls.

The wall-eyed ostler was named Jerzy Fiszer and he was loyal to Jan and to Jaromar as well as to Wojciech. He quietly packed and left, collecting the horse which was his to use from the dale where Ogień had led them, to join Jaromar in one of the residences which had been set up. His wife, who had been supposedly visiting relatives, was already there. Jaromar Skrzydło was setting up a comfortable haven for his father and a supposed brother when they needed it.

The funeral was magnificent; the king attended, and the coffin was surmounted by the wood and feather wings which Wojciech had worn proudly before his world had fallen apart. Men who had known and liked the Winged Hussar cried unashamedly, as did a generation of young women, whose innocent nightly dreams had been of getting their fingers into his unruly curls.

The more worldly wise ones also dreamed of getting their fingers into his curls, but their dreams were better informed. And none seemed to be able to boast that they had been his mistress.

And now the funeral was over, those dreams were dashed. Rarely had there been such an outpouring of grief. The baron was dead; the barony reverted to the crown, for all the good it did the king, being but a damaged castle, a village and enough land to feed the inhabitants.

One hundred miles from the funeral procession, Wojciech was attending to the leatherwork of his ancestor's armour, to make sure it was in good repair, supple and comfortable. Each feather on each wing was checked to make sure it was secure; a few had needed to be replaced. Red breeches and red-dyed boots with a red dolman completed the image.

"I want to strike fear into the hearts of all wrong-doers and oppressors," said Wojciech. "They called my ancestor the *anioł krwi*, the blood angel; and as such I shall be known. And if any know the stories of him, perhaps they will think my family has a ghost to avenge the slight to the winged hussars. But what they think, I care not. Is the ornamented face guard enough to hide who I am?"

"Save perhaps to an old comrade," said Jan. "But it is by the armour that one's colleagues are recognised in the first instance. You must not stay to chat, however, my lord."

"Indeed; I must do what I must, and leave," said Wojciech. "And I must decide upon my first target."

"There is an ethnic half-Russian Wojewoda, or

governor, who oppresses his people with taxes," said Jan.

"Then we must travel quietly to his district, and Ogień must put up with the indignity of being dyed black until we are ready to strike," said Wojciech. "Jan, my friend, I will need a selection of disguises, and I should have asked Jaromar to arrange such things at the various houses."

"I will write to him and see it done; in the mean time you will have to make do with me making whiskers for you out of horse hair."

"I have no doubt Ogień will permit it, and I will survive," said Wojciech, gravely.

"No, my lord; you will have whiskers for now from Wicher's tail and the same dye I use on Ogień will be in your hair," said Jan. "He will mind less if you suffer the same indignity."

Chapter 2

The wealthy merchant and his man were too wealthy for Wojewoda Władimir Trąbka to interfere with; the quality of his black steed and the fine clothing spoke volumes, even if the dark-haired bearded man did not surround himself with retainers. There was an arrogance to the way he sat on his horse which suggested that he had friends in high places. Trąbka had seen the man pass down the street, and sent out messages to his henchmen to leave the merchant alone and to hope he passed through Żyznaziemia quickly.

"These whiskers tickle," muttered Wojciech. Many szlachta wore facial hair, but Wojciech's family found growing beards difficult and eschewed the straggly and unimpressive whiskers they might manage. It troubled him more than to be wearing a czamara, a thigh length frock-coat, shorter than the kontusz he was used to.

"Don't fiddle with the whiskers," said Jan, severely. "A fine thing it would be if they fell off! And it took me hours to get that curl into your moustache to give it just the right air of prosperity and position to prevent anyone from interfering with you."

"I will have to learn to take more subordinate roles at some point," said Wojciech. "You are right, though, with the upturned ends I feel like some pompous fool in parliament with nothing better to do than wax his moustaches and polish his jewels."

"Good; it's the way I planned you to look. You need a role in which some natural arrogance is reasonable, since for now you cannot act subordinate if your life depended on it, as it might well when you learn how to do it," said Jan.

"You are right, old friend; but I must start somewhere. How miserable all the people here seem to be!"

"Aye, and as your supposed servant I have heard more than you have seen, and more than I would have seen merely as your agent. Wojewoda Trąbka taxes everyone at five percent more than the taxes demanded by the state, and pockets what is over and above what he has to pass on. I know what the taxes should be, and so do some of his people here, though he has tried to keep the peasantry ignorant of it. And if any complain, he sends his bullies to beat them."

"Perhaps it is time to start reducing the numbers of his bullies."

"I thought you would say that," said Jan. "A miller is holding out against the taxes, for he has moved here from another province, and knows what he should pay; it is expected that the enforcers will fall on his mill early tomorrow morning to teach him their brand of lesson. The mill is a watermill and is overlooked by a small eminence, which is a perfect place to wait."

Wojciech gave a small, fierce smile.

"Just like when Jan Sobieski led his men down upon the Turk at Vienna, in 1683," he said.

Early morning saw Wojciech and Ogień waiting on the high ground overlooking the mill, concealed in a light spinney. Wojciech had cut branches to set in the ground in front of him as well, the razor-sharp hussar battle-axe making short work of the thin branches he used. Birdsong as dawn broke and the miller's cockerel crowing his own morning hymn to the sky made it seem like just one more day.

The miller thought so too, and got up to go to wash under his own pump, before doing the heavy chores for his wife, while she prepared the first meal of the day.

It was to be interrupted.

Wojciech waited for the half-dozen men to convict

themselves, still and silent, Ogień equally still but with a quivering enthusiasm to be in action again. With the dye washed out he seemed to know that he was back to his normal role.

"What are you doing?" demanded the miller as they kicked over the hen-house. "Hey! I'll have the law on you!"

"We are the law," sneered the leader. "You owe more tax."

"I paid my taxes; I know what's due," said the miller.

"You forgot the breathing tax; it's a tax you pay to keep breathing easily," said the leader. "First time you default, we only break your ribs and show your women who the real men are around here. Second time you stop breathing for good."

The miller seized the axe he had plainly been using to chop wood.

"You're nothing but brigands!" he declared.

"He wants to die today," said one of the others.

This was enough, and Wojciech touched a light heel to Ogień.

The big red horse thundered down the slight decline, and the leader screamed once in terror before he died with Wojciech's lance through him. Wojciech swung the broken lance skilfully to catch another on the side of the head, before dropping the lance and drawing his own axe. It was not a fight for the finesse of the sabre, and moreover as the miller appeared to have taken one of his adversaries down, it was as well to have all marked with axe, so the blood angel might be blamed not the miller. Ogień, trained as well as he was, turned on his own length to allow Wojciech to decapitate another of the ruffians, with a neat backhanded stroke, leaning out of the way with effortless grace from the worst of the mercifully brief fountain of blood from the man's neck. It was the secret of the success of the winged hussars;

horses trained so well they were back in the fray before they had left it, something many heavy cavalry found hard.

The other two had pulled out weapons by now, one with a musket, one with a knife. Wojciech swung his axe underhand and released it in a throw which culminated in the chest of the musketeer and neatly cleaved his upper body as it continued to tumble. The miller despatched the last.

Wojciech dismounted.

"I ... that was magnificent, my lord!" said the miller.

"My advice is to get your family away, neighbour," said Wojciech. "They may seek vengeance. All being well, you can return soon." He heaved up the man he had hit with the butt end of his spear, the man groggy but regaining consciousness, the lance being lightweight, and it being Wojciech's strength which knocked him out.

"Cur, take a message back to your kennel and the master of it that his actions have awakened the vengeance of the blood-angel. If I see you again, you will die," said Wojciech. He watched the man on his way, then he knelt, crossed himself, and prayed for the souls of the dead brigands, that they would learn enlightenment in purgatory. The miller doffed his cap and joined him. Wojciech nodded approval; then he swung himself easily back onto Ogień's back and was riding away while the miller was still calling his thanks.

"Well, the news of the blood angel spread," said Jan, as he restored Wojciech's whiskers, back in the house they were renting on the market square of the town, Pomarańczowemiasto. "Apparently you arose from hell, flames flying from your hell-steed's flanks, overcoming your foes with the stench of sulphur to defeat them the better."

"Really?" Wojciech laughed. "Well if you see about

getting red and orange dyed silk we shall attach streamers to Ogień's barding for another outing, they will ripple and flicker in the breeze of Ogień's charge and add to the illusion."

"You're enjoying yourself, aren't you, my lord?" said Jan, affectionately.

"I am," said Wojciech. "I now have a purpose."

"The Biały Dworek is buzzing like a hive that's been kicked over," said Jan. "You were wise to tell the miller to get out for a while, because he and his family are easy targets to take vengeance on."

"Something has to be done; I wager Parliament has been informed and choose to turn a blind eye. He is half Russian, so probably it is some plot of the Russian woman, and of course our king will not go against her."

"What is your overall plan, lad?"

"To kill all his strong-arm men until he has to appeal to the crown for troops, and then someone will ask why," said Wojciech. "Complaints from the peasantry may get ... lost ... but when there is a serious breach of the peace needing more troops, and it is not the peasantry rising but the ghost of a winged hussar doing the killing, questions will be asked. Find those who have whispered against him, and let them know that help will come but that they are to do nothing and trust; but to bring word of any situation in which violence is likely to be used against one of their own."

Jan nodded.

"I can do that," he said. "What do you think Władimir Trąbka will do next?"

"If he's like many tyrants who have had their own way too long, he will first accuse the survivor of lying, and may even have him beaten for running away and lying. When the others do not return, however, he may send someone to check. If that person reports truly, they will report a hussar spear tip in one of the dead, and injuries only possible from a battle axe on two others. A felling axe does not do the same amount of damage. Oh, and I found two muskets – the one I killed first also had one. I thought we might as well add to our armoury. My own side-arm is finely-crafted but has not the range of a musket."

"No, my lord; but it carries its own surprise in being multi-barrelled. Nobody will expect you to be able to fire it again after having discharged it once."

"No, and it is to my advantage in a tight spot," said Wojciech. "As to what Trąbka will do when he finds out that his men have been killed depends much on his personality. He might decide it was the miller and friends pretending to be an army of hussars. He might think that it is a band of renegades. He may know enough to recognise that one hussar could cause that much damage to ruffians; I had no hesitation, six men of their calibre would have caused me no trouble even without aid from the miller. Indeed, twice the number would merely have inconvenienced me. But if he wants to retain fear he has to do something. And I suspect his response will be to take hostages and threaten them."

"That ... is not good," said Jan.

"We will have to rescue them, if that is the action he takes," said Wojciech.

"You're quite insane, my lord."

"You have said this before."

Jan sighed.

"I have all my medical kit with me," he said. "You've needed me to patch you up before; I have no doubt I will need all my experience."

"Would you rather have a pension?"

"Never, my lord!" said Jan, fiercely. "Who else has been a second father to you?"

"Warmer than my sire, too," said Wojciech. "He taught me to do my duty for my country and respect for the king; you taught me to do my duty for the love of my people and comrades."

It was not long before the Wojewoda responded.

His soldiery rounded up a dozen people from the market place, and notices were posted.

"The murderers of my men have until Monday to give themselves up, or those I have seized will be hanged; and twelve more every Monday until I am given the traitors."

"I need a chorąży, an ensign, and too a stableboy to ride and run messages," said Wojciech, irritably. "When we rescue these people we will have to smuggle them out to a safe house and to do that I need Jaromar to send me in pack ponies with people prepared to melt out of town so that those rescued can ride out in the open as my men with goods."

"I'll go myself," said Jan. "Try not to get into trouble while I am gone."

"I thought I might scout around the Biały Dworek, and see where they are kept," said Wojciech.

"Don't get caught," grunted Jan.

The girl known as Irenka Trąbka was staying out of the way of her uncle Władimir. She was horrified by his hostage-taking but nothing would be solved by speaking to him about it; it would only make him worse. She took herself to her own room, and went out onto the balcony to gaze out on the lovely gardens and the peaceful mountains beyond.

She did not expect to stare into the piercing blue-grey eyes of quite the most beautiful young man she had ever seen, with curly auburn hair and the body of a bogatyr, a legendary hero, dressed in homespuns. He had no business to be in a tree overlooking the house! He stared back, seeming dumb-struck by her.

"You're not really Romeo, you know," she said, in her own language.

He responded in Latin; and the cultured Latin of the Polish court.

"Maiden, I know not thy tongue; speakest thou Latin?"

She reverted to Polish.

"I am not sufficiently well-versed in Latin to speak in it," she said. "You are no peasant boy."

"You are surely no connection to the monster Władimir Trąbka," he responded.

The girl was lovely; a cascade of strawberry-blonde hair, or as Wojciech thought of it, cream roan, and eyes as green as April leaves. He had the greatest of difficulty finding words to say, for his chest knotted at such beauty in the hands of the Wojewoda.

"Alas, he is my uncle," said the girl. "I think of myself as Irene Easterby, but I suppose I am Irenka Trąbka, and so my uncle calls me. My mother may have been forced to marry my father, but she did not count it a true marriage."

"Why ... your father then is the disgraced diplomat who abducted an ambassador's daughter!" stammered Wojciech. "I remember the scandal, though not all the details; I was eight years old. But it is not right that he names you as though you were married."

The way she said her name was subtly different to the name Irina which he knew. Eiyreenee? It was pretty.

"Why do you think my father skulks under the protection of his half-brother?" said Irene. "And what do you mean about my name?"

"I had no idea he did," said Wojciech. "An unmarried maiden should be Irena ... Irenka ... Trąbkówna. I do not like it that he implies you are ... not a maiden." He blushed to use her name and to make so infamous a suggestion.

She frowned.

"I do not put anything past my uncle," she said. "I

can see I need to take more notice; it had not occurred to me. And my father never goes against him, despite being so much older than his brother. Now, may I be direct, and ask why are you here?" Irene was frankly curious about why a beautiful young man with eyes which pierced her soul should be up a tree. He did not know who she was, so he was not a wildly crazy suitor trying to rescue her.

What a shame.

"Do ... do you know about the hostages?"

"I know about them; and nothing I could say will sway Uncle Władimir," she sighed.

"Do you know where they are held?"

"Under the barracks in the prison," said Irene. "In the pit; it is a room without windows at the centre of the prison."

"I thank you," said Wojciech.

"You are a noble, whatever your garb, your speech betrays you; if he has taken a retainer of yours by mistake, you could probably make him give them up."

"Waćpanna Trąbkówna, I count all the oppressed of this province as my retainers until your uncle is deposed or dead," said Wojciech, with steel in his voice. "But he will not accede to any requests I make, nor will I do so. Where is your mother?"

"Alas, she died last year, pining still for England whence she was riven so cruelly," said Irene. "Well, technically, she was taken from Russia, but she was expecting to return to England and have a Season and marry an Englishman."

"Do you wish to go then to England?"

"Yes, for I have relatives there, who are aware of my existence, for when my mother and I lived on my father's country estate, loyal servants smuggled letters for us. They are not, however, well enough off that England does more than send diplomatic protests."

"I see. I will make no promises I do not know if I

can fulfil."

"No; and you must get out of that tree and be out of sight ere the guard I see comes round the corner."

"My thanks, my lady," said Wojciech, slithering out of the tree with haste and enough grace for Irene to watch in admiration.

He had given himself away on his first attempt to dress down; but he hoped the girl would not give him away.

The hostages could not be rescued from the prison; he must try another way.

Chapter 3

Wojciech encountered a small boy curled up on the edge of the berm about the barracks. He was bloodied and bruised and sobbing. He had auburn hair, which gave Wojciech a fellow feeling for him right away.

"What ails you, child?" asked Wojciech.

"My ma is in there; she's one they took," said the boy. On inspection, Wojciech reckoned him to be about ten or eleven years old, if small for his age. "I asked to see her; she is not well. They laughed at me and beat me."

In any civilised society a hostage was sacred; but Wojewoda Trąbka would not honour that.

"You had better come with me," he said. "My master needs a boy in the stables as I have to go out of town. What is your name?"

"Feliks," said the boy. "I'm worried about me ma."

"What is her name?" asked Wojciech.

"Marianna Ślusarzowa," said Feliks.

"Your mother is a locksmith?"

"No, but my father was," said Feliks. "I was his apprentice, but a lock he repaired for one of the Wojewoda's men was picked by a thief, and so he was hung, because they said that either he was a bad locksmith or he had opened it himself." He was crying again. "Mother does what she can, takes in washing and sewing and it is killing her."

"I will see what I can do," said Wojciech. "Are you happy to care for my horses in the meantime?"

"Yours, or your master's?" asked Feliks.

Wojciech cursed himself for the slip.

"Feliks, do you know any ostler who doesn't consider that the same thing?"

Feliks managed a wry chuckle.

Wojciech saw him to the stable, arranged a bed of straw with some blankets in the hay loft, and went to don his disguise as the merchant. Jan had shown him how, and the aggressive moustache was ready curled to put on. Shortly thereafter, Wojciech was strolling up to the Biały Dworek

Wojciech went to see the Wójt, being the official most likely to have any say in releasing prisoners. It took a half hour wait to see the man, one Jerzy Krzak.

"The hostages include my washerwoman and seamstress," said Wojciech. "I want her back."

"Her name?"

"Marianna Ślusarzowa," said Wojciech.

"You know there is a question of the family's honesty?" said Krzak.

"You know that I live near your mistress?" said Wojciech.

"She is not my mistress, we are just good friends," said Krzak.

"Of course, and you help with her financial difficulties," said Wojciech. "Now, those administrative fees for releasing Marianna Ślusarzowa; I was thinking around forty zloty[1]."

"That should cover most of the paperwork," said Krzak. "Wait in the antechamber, and I will have her brought to you."

Another wait; but a careworn, ill-looking woman was finally dragged to Wojciech.

"She had better not cause any trouble," said the man who brought her.

Wojciech looked Mrs. Ślusarzowa up and down and raised an eyebrow.

"I can see why you would be afraid of so villainous-looking and vicious a ruffian, neighbour," he said with heavy sarcasm.

The man flushed.

[1] About five guineas in English money of the time. That'd be around £700/$1000 now

"Her husband was a thief, and doubtless her spawn is too."

"My husband was not a thief!" Mrs. Ślusarzowa found her voice. "It is not his fault that some town thief was able to break in; there are no locks which are impenetrable."

"I trust your honesty, Ślusarzowa, which is what counts," said Wojciech. "Come."

He led her away.

"I do not know who you are, sir, or why you have released me," said Mrs. Ślusarzowa when they were out on the street, "but if it is in some mistaken belief that I can break locks, I must disabuse you."

"Oh, I had not thought it," said Wojciech. "But I encountered your son, and as I am an indifferent housekeeper, and my man is away, I thought I should ask you to be my housekeeper."

"But ... why me?" asked Mrs. Ślusarzowa as he ushered her into the house.

"Because you owe me a favour, and therefore you will be loyal to me, and keep my secrets," said Wojciech. "I find myself in need of living here longer than I intended, and that means I will need servants, and that means I need loyal servants. You may go to your son; he is in the stable, and you can send him to your home for any belongings you want. Here are twenty zloty to purchase any immediate needs for yourself and the boy, and a further twenty for provisions, and you will apply to me as needed for more."

"Yes, sir," she said, bemused.

Wojciech left her to settle in.

After a couple of hours, Wojciech made his way to the kitchen, where he found Marianna Ślusarzowa preparing a meal. She tried to curtsey.

"Don't let me discommode you," said Wojciech. "I need to know what other people were seized with you, and what the procedure is when there is to be a mass hanging."

Mrs. Ślusarzowa sat down and started sobbing.

"Oh, sir, I am so grateful to be with my Feliks, but I do feel guilty for being safe when the others are not! None of us are criminals, just ordinary people who were at market!"

"I know that, Mrs. Ślusarzowa," said Wojciech, gently. "But I need to know what sort of people there were, and if you can tell me the customs which are likely to be followed. I can't see about rescuing people if you don't tell me."

She stared.

"Rescue? Surely that is impossible?"

"And if Trąbka also thinks so, it means he will not expect it. Come! I need to know if there is a point between the prison and the gallows which will be vulnerable."

"No ... no, they will be brought by cart, with soldiers riding at each side," said Mrs. Ślusarzowa.

"So we are left with the gallows itself. Where will it be erected?"

She gave a hysterical laugh.

"Just across the square from this house," she said. "In the market place."

"And will the townsfolk help the soldiery or the hostages?"

"The hostages."

"Then I will give you money to see to the purchase of several carts which are to be filled with vegetables – save that there will be barrels and crates under the vegetables to make a chamber, with a hole into which to creep. If you know any of the relatives who will help, they can be getting the prisoners into the carts."

"But carts cannot be driven out of town in a hurry!"

"No, and nor will they be; we also need a number of horses, and your skills as a seamstress to make rough dummies to go on them, and they will be let loose to clatter out of town, so that any soldiers able to make pursuit will do so. I will see to getting horses. And I will also make sure that the soldiery is dealing with too absorbing a spectacle to take much notice of the former prisoners."

"I ... why, sir, I find I trust you," said Mrs. Ślusarzowa.

"Good; I feel I can also trust you, and I pray to the Mother of God that I am right to do so."

"And what will I do?" asked Feliks, slithering into the kitchen like an eel.

"That depends if you can be quick with a knife to help cut bonds on the hostages," said Wojciech. "And if they will be left in the carts and taken out one by one, or all taken out."

"They will be taken out and all stand on the platform to be hanged three at a time," said Feliks in a hard little voice. "Thus they hanged my father with other men, criminals or maybe like him, unlucky."

"Thank you, lad," said Wojciech.

"I know you ain't a merchant; you don't have stuff," said Feliks. "And if the horse which smells of dye ain't a warhorse, I'm a Russian. I'm your man, my lord."

"Well don't go throwing around 'my lords' when I'm wearing these whiskers," said Wojciech.

"No, sir. Why, sir, was you the groom too? I thought he talked a little posh."

Wojciech laughed.

"I will have to learn to alter that."

"I can help," said Feliks. "People didn't ought to hang people on suspicion because they can't be bothered to look further, no and they didn't ought to demand more'n is fair in taxes."

"And that's why I'm here," said Wojciech. "To stop Władimir Trąbka."

"I'll do all I can, my lord, but I don't know a whole

lot about horses."

"Ah well, it was an excuse to get you safe and to get your mother out; and now I can formulate a plan," said Wojciech. "Now I know you also have a pressing and personal reason for vengeance I will be able to teach you more. And you will be in charge of getting those hiding in carts out and down into my coal cellar through the trapdoor onto the street."

Feliks nodded.

"I can do that, my lord," he said. "And though I have never stolen, I wager I could help you through locks should you need it. I was going to slip a skeleton key to ma if they'd only let me visit her in prison."

"Alas, they probably already worked that out," said Wojciech.

"Yes, I suppose so," said Feliks.

"Now; to whom I am giving succour, please," Wojciech looked at Marianna Ślusarzowa.

"Yes, there is old Paweł Paszek, the shoemaker, my lord," she said. "He is not doing well in that hole. Then there are the Górski brothers, Jan and Mikołaj; Mrs. Stolarzowa, whose husband could knock together the chambers for the carts, my lord, he will be out of his mind with worry."

"See him and I will pay him well for it."

"He will do it for nothing."

"I will not have him out of pocket. If it can be dismantled in an instant and re-made another time I will pay him extra."

"Yes, my lord," said Marianna. "Then there is Tekla Stawska and Janek Sitko, who were to have been married this very day. Do not trust Tekla's father, as he is a man who loves money more than anything else; Tekla loves Janek but I think she'd marry Paweł Paszek to escape her father! Janek is a good, solid young man, for all that he is an artist, he can turn his hand to many things, and had been lending a hand to Piotr Stolarz in his carpenter's shop. Prokop Kowalski is Piotr's apprentice but he is no older than my Feliks, and he was given permission to go out with Tekla and Janek, just his bad luck! The Widow Jedynakowa and her only child, Marina are there, the widow, like old Paszek will need more help getting into carts. Last are Jan Sadowski and his wife, Elżbieta, who were selling fruit when they were taken. She is expecting her first child," added Marianna.

"How, er, ... I mean, does it incapacitate her?" stuttered Wojciech, embarrassed to ask such personal details.

"Not enough for it to show, my lord, though they cared not when she told the soldiers; said it was one more potential traitor not growing up."

"Bastard! Oh, I beg your pardon," said Wojciech, colouring at having sworn in front of a woman.

"You ain't said anything the rest of us haven't thought, save that there's them born out of wedlock as are better people," said Marianna.

They ate, Marianna having finished cooking while they spoke, and then she and Feliks went out on their various missions, and Wojciech went in quest of horses, not concerned as to their quality, to be stabled at the inn until needed as diversions. He also scouted for a barn out of town in which to become the blood angel and rush down on the proceedings, fulfilling the name of the winged hussars as angels of death.

He had to hope that neither of his new servants would betray him; but he trusted his own judgement, it having been proven in his choice of men before.

He hoped Jan would be back before Monday; but if he was not, then Wojciech would have to do the best he might on his own.

Chapter 4

Jan arrived with a string of pack ponies.

"The packs are full of different clothes for anyone you get out. It's a crazy undertaking and why is there a boy in the stable?"

"That's Feliks; I bribed the wójt to get his mother out to get information. I know now who is in there, and therefore who to trust, to help get their family members to safety."

Jan sniffed.

"Well, I can't say you've ever been wrong, my lord. Is that hammering in the cellar?"

"Yes, Jan, it is; the carpenter Stolarz is making a false wall with battens and stretched linen, to which Feliks will add a coat of lime, for an artist to paint it to resemble the wall. In case the house is searched, I want the prisoners hidden behind it. It will take time to search, and I have gesso for the artist, which will dry quickly."

"It has a certain insane genius," Jan admitted grudgingly.

A barn on the outskirts of the town owned by the father of the Górski brothers and gladly donated to anyone who thought he could rescue them would do to change, and rinse the dye out of Ogień and get ready. A selection of boys known to Feliks would send a signal as the tumbrels arrived, by the expedient of whistling. None knew why they did this, but had agreed to do so in any case.

It had been Feliks' own idea when Wojciech had suggested firing a rocket.

"That will put the soldiers on alert, my lord," he said. "A whistle may not carry as far but several whistles will carry one to another."

Wojciech had to hope the boys would do their jobs; but Feliks vouched for them. The hussar spent the night in the barn with Ogień, ready to position himself to charge as soon as the whistles blew, out of sight of the self-proclaimed constables who were roaming the streets from first light. Wojciech did not know, but spears and bayonets had been thrust into the carts, to be certain no peasant army lurked within them. The platform was erected in front of the townsfolk, and a last proclamation read to demand that the renegades be given up.

Wojciech did not know it, but it had been his warning to the miller to make himself scarce which had convinced a wavering man who was the miller's friend that his sister and her daughter would stand a better chance relying on the mad szlachcic than on hoping that by turning him in the hostages would truly be saved.

Irene looked at her uncle in horror.

"You want me to watch hangings? Why?"

"You are too nice, my dear; you need to be hardened towards these animals."

Irene shuddered. It was as well that her uncle and her father had no idea how close she and her mother had been to some of the servants in her father's country house.

"I just think it is wrong to hang ordinary townsfolk for the deeds of another."

"Oh, but I am not hanging them for the deeds of this unknown who calls himself the Blood Angel; I am hanging them for the failure of their families and friends to hand him over," said Władimir Trąbka, with a nasty smirk on his face. "And if he is not handed over after this, I will hang another dozen next Monday. They will soon get the idea. And you will watch it and learn, Irenka."

Irene knew that there was no point pleading or crying or refusing. If her uncle told her she was going to watch, she would be there, and nothing would stop it. And she must hide her emotion because he would enjoy her horror and revulsion.

She went wordlessly to change into a carriage gown.

Feliks lurked under the completed gallows, hidden by carelessly-left ends of wood, left not so carelessly by Piotr Stolarz, who had been made to build the platform and gallows for the unjust execution of his own wife and apprentice, whom he loved like a son; and the carpenter had managed to make screens for the cellar overnight, and protective caves inside vegetable carts as well as to hide a way up onto the platform under cover of building it. Feliks and Jan had only to kick out two pegs for a part of the scaffold to fall away and form a chute like a grain chute and push the prisoners down that whilst milord distracted people. Feliks grasped his shrill pea whistle and waited, thinking about what milord had said to him the day before, right before he slid out into the darkness with Ogień and who knew what equipment in heavy bags.

"Feliks, you and Jan are the real heroes of tomorrow; and too, Piotr the carpenter. Sometimes in a battle it is necessary to hide your true intent with a diversion. I will be providing the diversion whilst you and Jan do the real work. It is up to me to be the one they look at. And the flour so carelessly spilled from the sacks on that pack pony will also play its part. It's a bit like a charlatan at a fair who puts a bean under a cup and invites people to bet where it is. He uses misdirection to make people see what he wants them to see. All eyes will be on me, and that's the way we want it."

"What if they shoot you?" Feliks asked, round eyed.

"My armour can take a musket ball if it is not fired too closely. It may have scales on the outside but that is decoration."

Feliks nodded.

He was looking forward to seeing milord's diversion, but he swore to himself that he would turn away as soon as he had seen milord approaching, and not be one of those diverted.

The prisoners in their tumbrels reached the scaffold. The priest rode with them, intoning prayers for the dead, ready to take last minute confessions and give absolution. As he saw his current charges as martyrs, he had little trouble with that. Mounted soldiers rode on each side of them, and on each side of the open carriage in which Wojewoda Trąbka, his brother and niece rode. They were in cleared streets on the far side of the market square, away from the crowd, the scaffold between them and the people. The people cowered back by the houses about the square, fearing to approach the gallows too closely lest they be accused of helping any to escape; a notice had been pasted up to tell them to leave the centre of the square empty. The notice had been posted by Jan, but nobody knew that, and the soldiers nodded in approval. The street behind was blocked with waggons and cavalry. The same side as the inn where various ponies waited, with the men who had brought in the train of 'goods' to Wojciech's house. They had their own task, and Feliks firmly put it from his mind. He blew his shrill whistle, and heard the next boy along blow his. He thought, because he was listening for it, that he heard the third.

The boy's ears strained, until he heard hoofs, cantering. And then, the pace increased as the big red horse swerved into the main street, hoofs ringing on the cobbles like some thunderous bell sounding a bizarre death knell. Ogień thundered down the street, and Feliks caught a glimpse of the golden and red figure on the big husaria horse, red wings waving and clattering with the movement. The hoofs hit the flour in the road, raising a massive dust as the streaming pennant lowered, the lance set.

Feliks shook himself, dragging his eyes from the mesmerising spectacle of the winged hussar, and climbed up the ladder to the scaffold. Jan ahead of him. But then, Jan had seen Wojciech in action before.

The horse neighed as the crash of spear meeting man broke the shock of the troops, and they began fumbling for weapons.

Feliks' little knife flashed, cutting bindings in the thick cloud of flour, and he kicked out the pegs, pushing the hostages down the chute. Jan ceded way to him to go first as they followed the bewildered captives down, and they grabbed an arm each of one of those preceding them to drag into the crowd and thence to the barrows. It would be a long wait, but better a long wait, said Jan roughly to one he thrust amongst vegetables, than a short life. Somewhere where there was a sound of clashing steel, Wojciech was keeping the soldiery occupied in this world or the next, and then the big red horse was flying overhead onto the gallows itself.

"Flashy bugger," said Jan, proudly.

And then the sound of galloping hoofs as the ponies burst out of the inn and galloped off. Four were ridden by those trusted men sent by Jaromar, who would leap off them as soon as they were out of sight and make their own way out of town.

Predictably, the cavalry turned to follow them, but it took time to turn frightened horses in narrow streets, and these were not elite cavalry, but soldiers who could ride. Then the warhorse landed amongst them and set off in the same direction. The mounted soldiers set off after the ponies which must be carrying the fugitives, since they had riders, and the monstrous figure who was escaping as well.

That most of the riders were bolsters filled with hay, wearing cloaks, they would not discover until they caught up with the ponies; and so great is the power of human suggestion that they believed all had carried real people, who had plainly got off and taken cover with friends. It would be a while before they completed a house-to-house search on the way back into town.

Wojciech would swear that Ogień was laughing with joy as his lance struck home, going right through two of the soldiery there to hold the townsfolk back, and wounding a third. To kill two with one lance was not unheard of; to wound a third was a bonus. Flour and dust swirled about him, and he drew his sabre to cut down anyone who came near him. A slamming blow to his chest meant that one of the soldiers had the presence of mind to get off a shot; a steady man, but he had no chance to reload and Wojciech steadily, if regretfully, rode him down, saluting the brave man with his sword as he went by, swerving Ogień at the last minute so as not to trample on a brave man. The startled look in the fallen man's eyes showed that he understood and he raised his hand in a clumsy return salute.

Ogień knew what was expected of him. He aimed a few vicious kicks at soldiers as they passed through them. Ogień was quite happy to trample on fallen bodies, something a horse will not do unless trained to war. And then he was bunching his haunches for a jump, and Wojciech could almost believe his wings had carried him up as Ogień leaped onto the platform of the scaffold. It creaked alarmingly under the combined weight of an armoured man and a war horse. However, it gave him the chance for a quick glance around; most of the surviving soldiery were disoriented. And then Wojciech looked down on the other side, the direction in which he was going, straight into the green eyes of Irenka.

Irene sat in the carriage, closed in on herself, trying

not to cry as the hostages were forced at bayonet-point onto the scaffold. A singular, shrill whistle rang out, and her uncle stiffened, but nothing appeared to happen.

And suddenly there was the sound of a horse galloping; dust flew up in clouds on the other side of the gallows, and she could catch glimpses through the woodwork of a horse. Shrill screams broke out and the sounds of battle could be heard. Suddenly, the great horse was soaring onto the scaffold, it, or the fantastic figure on its back wearing wings; surely they could not fly? And then he was looking down, and Irene gasped.

The steel-bright eyes were the eyes of her visitor in the tree.

Her uncle jumped to his feet, drawing his pistol. Irene cried out and sagged against him, ruining his aim as she let herself fall, seeming to faint as the red horse flew right over them towards the road.

One red feather fluttered down and landed in front of Irene. Surreptitiously she moved to cover it, groaning to make it seem that she came out of her swoon.

"Fool wench!" cried her uncle, striking her across the face as he heaved her up and threw her onto the seat. "I might have got that bastard!"

Irene covered her face, seeming to weep as she stowed the feather in her bosom. Her fanciful thoughts aside she would keep the feather forever, as a reminder of what could only be one of the fabled winged hussars, the angels of death. She had never seen one, nor even a picture, but there had been news in the papers that they had been disbanded.

Apparently this winged hussar had other ideas.

Wojciech saw the Wojewoda fumbling for a firearm, and urged Ogień to jump; and the beautiful Irenka, eyes never leaving him, fell against the fellow in a well-simulated swoon. The bullet whined past him, but he concentrated on landing, causing as much disruption as he could to the frightened mounts of the accompanying soldiery as he did so, and heading in the direction the ponies which had just started off.

With a bend in the road, Wojciech urged Ogień into another leap, one of distance this time, to the left, veering off down another lane, but the leap hopefully concealing the change of direction, landing beyond where a casual look would see.

He noted out of the corner of his eye an urchin dart out with a broom to sweep out his tracks and raised a hand in thanks.

A few twists and turns, and he was heading back towards the barn.

He would have to see to all his own armour and tack, cooling and currying Ogień, as Jan was busy. He took a moment to kneel in prayer, for thanks at the apparent success of the mission, for the survival of the one steady man, and for the souls of those he had killed.

He prayed also to have the means to rescue the owner of a pair of leaf-green eyes.

And then he saw to Ogień's needs as any good horseman should.

In an hour or two, a merchant with a black horse would ride back to his white-painted town residence, staring in wonder at the mayhem, and wondering out loud what had happened.

Chapter 5

"The artist is painting stonework, and the carpenter is making roof supports to mine out of the cellar," said Jan. "I thought that was worth doing; you studied siegeworks and mining, didn't you?"

"I did," said Wojciech. "I had a very thorough military education. How many are ready to slip out with the pack ponies?"

"All are prepared to go, except the artist and his betrothed who want to stay and serve you. He really is good at turning his hand to anything, and she can sew. And Feliks refuses to leave you and his mother won't leave you either."

"Well, I did say we needed more people and that I should not have been so hasty in breaking up all my servants and retainers," said Wojciech. "I was so desperate to free myself and to be officially dead."

"We could hardly maintain secrecy with a *poczet* of five lancers," said Jan, dryly.

"I suppose there is that," said Wojciech, ruefully. "Well, if the other women are happy to be dressed as men to be scruffy looking pony-drovers we can at least make sure they get to safety. I am sorry they have to leave all their possessions."

"Feliks has been running about collecting valuables and any money they have in the house, and I have also compensated them out of your purse since it was you they wanted to be given up," said Jan. "I did right?"

"Absolutely," said Wojciech.

"Piotr Stolarz and his wife and apprentice would have liked to have stayed but the risk is too high. Feliks got him his best tools, and he has asked Janek to use the rest," said Jan. "The only thing Janek and his Tekla want are a priest to marry them."

"There must be one around who has the courage to

wed them," said Wojciech. "I am going to rescue the Wojewoda's niece."

"Definitely insane," said Jan. "And why are you breathing shallowly?"

"Musket ball," said Wojciech, meekly. "It's a nasty bruise on my ribs, but nothing serious."

"Well, that's lucky," said Jan. "And I'll look at that when you've eaten. You can't pull that attack again, you realise."

"One should never repeat the same attack twice," said Wojciech. "You mean, if he seizes another dozen, he will erect *Chevaux de Frise* in the street to prevent a charge."

"Yes, my lord," said Jan.

"Well, obviously he will, any sensible fellow would," said Wojciech. "I would, and I would also have pikemen around the scaffold. I'd also defeat me by having a cannon, loaded with grape, because galloping down this road means the relative lack of aiming power is immaterial. And only have *chevaux de Frise* nearby to slow me up and lead me in to be enfiladed."

"Yes, and it's not hard to make Frisian Horses," said Jan, who preferred not to mess about with the French tongue. "A cross-beam at each end to hold a log across them well spiked with bayonets, swords, spear end or even pointed sticks driven into holes drilled in it."[2]

"Of course, he has to have someone who understands how to make them, and his troops do not seem to be such good quality; but one assumes that he is some level of szlachta, nobility, albeit illegitimate. He seems to be close to his brother, so one assumes they had some level at least of military training, even if they

---

[2] The cheval de Frise [plural chevaux de Frise] is what they had before rolls of barbed wire were invented; essentially spiky bits sticking out from a centre, but easy to improvise according to Jan's suggestion.

are drobna szlachta, petty nobles. Their father at least was placed within the embassy in Russia to have taken a Russian mistress on whom to sire Władimir Trąbka, and in which situation his son was able to abduct the daughter of an English diplomat."

"Oh, *that* Trąbka!" said Jan. "What a scandal it was, and our king swore he knew nothing of the matter, nor where the girl was. She'd be in her late thirties by now."

"She's dead," said Wojciech. "But her daughter isn't, and she wants to escape."

"The niece you mentioned," said Jan. "Well that makes more sense now. I fear her escape is the least of our worries if the Wojewoda seizes more hostages; and frankly, I don't see how he can fail to do so without basically admitting that he's lost control."

Władimir Trąbka was rapidly coming to the same conclusion.

"I will make them pay for making me look a fool!" he howled. "I could have shot him if your idiot daughter had not swooned, but I suppose one can expect nothing else of her, a woman, and with the diluted blood of the effete English too."

"You would take her to see it," said his half-brother, Stanisław. Stanisław Trąbka was much older than his brother, approaching his fiftieth year, and had lines of disillusionment on his face. "How can you expect a woman to face that ... that *thing* leaping right over us without swooning? I knew the winged hussars were supposed to be fearsome, but knowing and experiencing are two different things."

"Coward."

"I was not the one who left a puddle on the floor in the carriage, nor was it my daughter," sneered Stanisław.

"The hoof of that nightmare beast was within an

arm's length of my head!" yelped Władimir. "I ... I spilled the hip flask I had opened to revive the girl with brandy."

"Certainly you did," said Stanisław, smiling nastily. "What will you do?"

"I will have another dozen seized and I will continue to do so until they give up that so-called hussar."

"I don't think there was a lot of 'so-called' about it, you know," said Stanisław. "I may not have had to face a charge of them, but when I was a child in Warszawa I saw them drilling. Only a hussar could have the control of his horse that man displayed. But we know at least that it is not a ghost of a man and his horse from hell; I smelled living horse when it went over the carriage."

"I don't care, I will have him flayed when I have caught him," screeched Władimir.

"You have to catch him first," said Stanisław, not concealing his amusement at his brother's predicament. "Are you sure he has not been sent by the king to test you? Flaying a bandit, you might get away with, but flaying a szlachcic? That's a different matter, even if the king didn't send him. And only one of the szlachta would own a horse like that, and you know it. All szlachta may be equal according to the law, but that's a man who is well above us."

Władimir broke off in mid rant about what he wanted to do to the so-called blood angel. He was a horrid pasty white.

"I ... I cannot believe that he is from the king," he said.

"Well, you had better find a way of stopping him doing exactly the same thing next time," said Stanisław.

"Artillery! We need cannons and grape shot!" said Władimir.

"You'd better borrow something more up-to-date than the ceremonial cannon in the barracks," said

Stanisław. "I wouldn't be surprised if it had crystallised over time; it hasn't been used since the time of the Holy League, and the men drill with it but never fire it."

"Nonsense! I will make a killing ground, and I will have the side streets blocked off, so he must ride into the throat of the cannon and then he will be cut into ribbons!" cried Władimir.

"Tactically sound but only if you have a cannon you know to be well-found and whole," said Stanisław.

"It is!" insisted Władimir.

Irene listened to this, and when her uncle's rant wound down, she went quietly to her room, and took off her kontusik, the jacket worn by a szlachcianka, a noblewoman, often lined with fur, like the kontusz, the male equivalent. She dressed for dinner.

She had to deal with the heavy skirt with its hip-roll in the English fashion and lacing her own bodice by herself since her uncle had dismissed both her companion and her maid when he brought her into his household, and had yet to replace them. There was some positive result from that, however, since Irene had to take her own washing to the laundry and deal with the stains on her rich upper garments, even if all the linens were washed together. Her mother had taught her that a lady knows all the tasks she expects her servants to do, so Irene was quite capable of looking after herself. And as it is inevitable that clothing goes astray in the laundry of a large household, Irene had been making a collection of various garments which might permit her to engineer her own escape. Irene now had the clothes suitable to a page, and had, since seeing the man in the tree – the winged hussar, she amended, wondering why her heart beat faster on thinking about him – acquired clothes suitable for an apprentice boy or stable-hand as well as those of a townswoman and peasant woman. Much of the difference there was in quality. Irene made her own clothes, as any gently born woman must know how to do, and had been making what looked like a kontusik, but was more akin to a kontusz, to wear with the short żupan for her costume as a page. Her own calf-length boots would do well enough for dressing as a well-born boy. She had asked the castle cobbler to show her how such things were made, and paid him for his time and effort. She would have to pick her time carefully.

When she went to dinner, her father asked her sharply,

"Where is your gentlewoman?"

"Do you not remember, sir? Uncle Władimir dismissed her because he thought her too partisan, and my maid too," said Irene.

Stanisław Trąbka frowned.

"It is not seemly that she has no companion," he said. "If you hope to use her to consolidate your power by giving her as a bride, she should have a companion to safeguard her reputation. And a maid."

Władimir Trąbka regarded Irene. She thought this must be how a rodent felt when looked at by a snake.

"You are right; and in case this damned hussar is anything to do with anyone close to the crown, I want you to take her to court. She would make an excellent replacement as an official mistress to the king, ousting Elżbieta Branicka since Magdalena Sapieżyna's rein is over. She is paler but has similar colouring, and she has the dewy freshness of youth."

"Excuse me, but I am here while you discuss something so personal and abhorrent," said Irene. "I do not wish to be the plaything of any man, especially not out of holy wedlock."

"You will do as you are told," said Władimir. "Yes, I will see about a maid and a woman tomorrow; she runs wild, Stanisław, who knows what she gets up to. A companion will keep her in check, and a maid can tell me if she does anything untoward."

Irene felt her blood run cold.

If she delayed any longer, her cache of clothes would be discovered before she could decide which was the best disguise to use. She had to leave tonight.

It was not cold, but nor was it hot as autumn could be felt in the air, so after going supposedly to bed, Irene put on two shifts and the better breeches, as they did not fold up as small. Under-linen and much of her peasant boy garb she put in the long bag she had fashioned which would work as a hip-roll, and would not show with the wide skirt of a townswoman. She put on the decorated corset she had worked on in pretence that it was a decorative cushion, and over it put on one of her light wool kontusiks, which she had lined to look like a lower-class girl's kitlik. A coloured shawl over her head and shoulders completed her costume. She made a bundle of her other clothes after the manner of a washerwoman, and threw them out of a window outside the walls of the Biały Dworek; she must hope to find them later, when she had got out.

She slipped down to the barracks laundry where servants were still working.

"I have come for my husband's clothes, to mend, before he puts them on again," she said, politely, looking down as though respectfully. She was a good mimic, and copied the tones of her former maid.

"And who is your husband?" asked the chief washerwoman, a brawny woman with arms like hams.

"He is Jan Kowalski," said Irene, hoping that at least one Jan Kowalski was a soldier in the barracks.

"Oh, for goodness sake, girl, which one?" asked the washerwoman.

"Why, the one I am married to, of course!" said Irene, glancing up with wide eyes.

"Well, I don't know which one you mean, and I have no intention of handing over clothes to someone I do not know. Here, Dorotka, see she goes out; not saying you are a thief, girl, but clothes do go missing and I don't want to take chances. Have your husband talk to me."

The woman addressed as Dorotka firmly escorted Irene out of a postern, pausing to exchange some chaffing comments with the soldiers on guard.

Irene was much relieved; getting out by being thrown out made leaving much easier. She might creep round the berm and go looking for her clothes at the front of the building. She picked them up and was challenged by a guard.

"Who goes there?"

"Oh! How you startled me," said Irene, once again in the tones of her maid. "Am I not permitted to take a short cut with my husband's clothes?"

"No, mistress, you are not," said the soldier. Irene suppressed the urge to bristle at being addressed like someone low class; after all she was pretending to be low class.

"Will you point me in the way I may go, then?" she asked.

The guard laughed. "Well, you've come so far, nip across the front steps and disappear quickly," he said.

Irene did so, as swiftly as possible, and was soon on the road into the local town. The first stage of her escape was complete!

Chapter 6

The problem was, thought Irene, that she had never really ever thought that she would get away, and had planned out some ideas as a pipe-dream over how to do it, without considering any further.

Well it was the winged hussar's fault that she had dared to take a dream into reality; and she would have to take as much courage in her hands as any hussar.

She had seen him cross himself in battle; the hussars were said to be very devout. Irene was unsure whether she was Church of England, as raised by her mother, or Catholic, according to the doctrine of the church they attended perforce; but God was God, and she knelt at the side of the road to pray to God and to Mary the mother that she should make good decisions, and begged them to protect her from her uncle and father and from other evil.

She felt better when she arose from her prayers. She would start in the market square. Perhaps she would see someone who seemed likely to know the nameless Angel. Fortunately, the Biały Dworek, the official residence here of the Wojewoda, and the barracks lay within the town boundaries; the walls were no longer as defensive as they had been in the warlike past, and parts of them had been robbed out to build new buildings, but gaps had been filled hastily with palisades during the battles against the rebellious nobles.

Had Irene known it, the only reason Wojciech had not joined the Bar Confederation, as the rebels were known, was because he had not felt that civil war was a proper way to convince the king to assert his authority to make sure of his country's independence from Russia. Wojciech was now thoroughly disillusioned with regards to any powers in Poland, but still did not believe in revolt as a way forward.

Irene had forgotten that her uncle had installed a curfew in the town, and it would be long ere it was light. Consequently, she gave a little scream when a patrol of men pointed their pistols at her, and the leader said

"Halt! Who goes there?"

"Oh! How you startled me!" said Irene. It had worked before. "I have washing to deliver; it has taken me all day to do it."

"I'll have to look in that bundle," said the soldier.

"Corporal ... I know the wench, you need not bother," said a voice from the shadows, and a man limped out, his arm in a sling.

"Oh, sergeant, if I had known she was coming to you I'd not have said anything," said the soldier. "Come on, men; doubtless there are more dangerous people around than a ... washerwoman." The soldiers passed on, sniggering.

"Uncouth fools," muttered the newcomer. "My apologies, my lady, for calling you a wench."

"Who are you?"

"Probably a renegade," said the man. "My name is Ryś, Ryszard for best, Góral. And yes, they apply the pun to my surname, and call me 'Lynx' for my eyesight. I suspect I am looking for the same person you are."

"And why should you be looking for anyone?" asked Irene. It seemed pointless to deny who she was as he had recognised her.

"Because my eyes were opened," said Lynx. "I cannot be a part of the forces who fight blindly for an evil man like your uncle any more. The winged hussar spared my life. I fired on him, and hit, I believe; and he rode at me. But apart from knocking me down he did nothing. His horse could have trampled me, which would have killed me; or he could have cut me down with his sabre. Instead, he saluted me, gave me recognition for being steady enough to shoot him. What a man! I would serve him, lady, if I might, but if it is not he that you seek, I will serve you as your bodyguard. I fancy *he* would expect me to do so."

"I do seek him," said Irene. "But ... I am not sure how."

"Come inside the carpenter's shop; it is empty," said Lynx. "Rest until dawn. I will watch over you."

"I ... yes, thank you," said Irene. She had a knife with her, and he would be in for a surprise if he attacked her. She formulated a prayer for forgiveness if she wronged him in wondering it.

Inside the deserted shop, he kindled two candles, gave one to her, and indicated the stairs.

"Go up, and sleep," he said. "I have a blanket down here; I will rest at the foot of the stairs."

"Thank you," said Irene. She hesitated. "Should not you take the bed, and I the blanket? You are wounded."

"Only the most noble of all ladies, blessed by the Virgin herself would ask such," said Lynx, much touched. "It is truly an honour to serve you. But you will go and sleep on a bed; a soldier is used to worse billets than this."

Irene took a few precautions in the carpenter's room. The door opened outwards which meant it could be jammed to keep her in, so she ripped a length off the side of the blanket and tied the door open to a candle sconce. The carpenter had plainly emptied out his pocket onto the commode, and Irene put some tacks on the floor in the doorway, and tied the legs of a chair and the commode together at ankle height across the doorway. It might provide a warning. She observed her handiwork critically. It might not be the best, but it was all she could think of to counter the efforts made against the hapless and usually foolish young women in the English novels her mother had managed to procure.

Then she sank into the carpenter's bed, and if the

palliasse was filled with straw not feathers as she was used to, she was so tired and overcome that she fell asleep almost immediately. She did not undress in case she had to leave in a hurry.

"One thing I am concerned about," said Wojciech, as the pack ponies and their drovers set off, early in the morning, "is that someone will notice that a whiskered merchant is never around when the winged hussar is."

"My lord, if you will forgive me for speaking up, I have an idea about that," said Janek.

"Always speak up; we are a select band," said Wojciech.

"Well, my lord, if I wear your whiskers and make sure to look out of the window or door, that would cover for your absence," said Janek.

"Excellent," approved Wojciech.

"Good plan," Jan nodded. "You're a similar height to milord, Janek, if not the same build."

Janek looked admiringly at Wojciech's wide shoulders.

"My lord is built like a warrior; a bohatyr," he said. "But with a cloak it shows less, and I am not about to try to impersonate a winged hussar in armour. I am no warrior!"

"So I should hope," muttered Tekla. It was a little overwhelming to eat all together with a szlachcic seated at the head of the table, but Wojciech insisted that one meal a day for discussion should be with all of them. Tekla thought it unnatural that any szlachta should be lively so early in the morning, and grudgingly admitted that as well as owing her life and that of her betrothed to this man, she also admired that he was quite capable of shifting for himself.

"I'll be out to the market after breakfast to see what I may find out, aye, and Mrs. Ślusarzowa too; between us we should hear all the gossip," said Jan.

"I wanted to go over to Piotr's shop and pick up some tools, but I saw a light in there last night," said Janek.

Jan nodded.

"As well for you to stay away, whiskered and cloaked or not," he said. "I'll go and take a look."

Irene arose, feeling better than she had done for a long while. There was a chipped jug of water on the other side of her traps.

"Thank you!" she called down the stairs.

"You are cautious, lady; I approve," Lynx called up. "There is food, and I will have breakfast in no time."

Irene washed herself, knowing that sounds in the kitchen meant that she could strip to do so. She changed her shift, and went in search of baskets such as women take to market, in which to re-pack her clothing. Lynx had made a creditable breakfast with cold ham and sausage with bread and butter, cheese and a boiled egg. He had also made a cup of tea.

"Thank you; please eat with me," said Irene, as Lynx hovered, uncertain whether to serve her. "What of the poor people to whom these belong? I did bring some money."

Irene had brought all the money she had been hoarding now for a couple of months, as well as anything she had managed to find in the house she had lived in with her mother. Also all her jewellery and all the jewellery from various bedrooms and stored in the lofts, since the moment her mother died she had been planning on setting off on her own if need be for England.

"The carpenter's wife and apprentice were amongst the hostages; it seems that he has gone wherever they went, the carpenter went too," said Lynx. "There are signs that he came back for some clothes and his tools and any money. I suggest that we consider this a good base whilst we look for the winged hussar. There is more food, enough at least to make żurek; there's stock, plenty of onions and what's left of the ham, some fresh mushrooms, sour cream and the carpenter had set some flour to ferment. We've eaten the last eggs and bread, but that can be remedied."

Irene nodded.

"I can cook," she said. "We can eat it without bread."

"How, if we have no bread to hollow out to put the soup in?" asked Lynx.

"Oh, would you eat it that way? I am accustomed to eat soup out of a bowl," said Irene. Her mother would be horrified, but Irene found herself wondering what it would be like to eat out of bread. "Well, in that case, yes, we will need bread. And it is the time of year to set eggs to be preserved in lime water, but I do not plan to stay here for another six months unless things go badly."

"Now that I did not know; and my apologies to suggest you eat after the fashion of we peasants."

"Food is needed whatever one's social rank," said Irene. "I will eat it as it comes. I am not about to be a nuisance. I was merely surprised."

"You are truly noble, lady," said Lynx. "Now, let us ..." he broke off as the door opened, and Jan came in.

"A tryst," said Jan, disgusted. "You are trespassing."

"I beg your pardon; it seemed unoccupied," said Lynx, smoothly.

"Wait; I know you," said Irene.

Jan let his eyes roam over her contemptuously.

"You couldn't afford me, wench," he said.

Irene flushed.

"You have the wrong idea, fellow," she said, coldly. "And I cannot think that the one you work for would like you speaking so to any maid, whatever her rank."

Jan stiffened.

"Make yourself clear," he snapped.

"Lynx helped me last night when a patrol stopped me," said Irene. "We are both looking for the Blood Angel to place ourselves under his protection and to perform such service for him as we might."

Jan looked again, groaned, and went on one knee.

"My apologies my lady," he said.

"That's all very well, but would you really speak to any girl like that?" asked Irene.

"No, my lady, I thought I had disturbed a trysting couple and I was trying to frighten you into leaving in a hurry," said Jan.

"I see; then your words are understood," said Irene. "Where must my bodyguard take me?"

"Assuming this is no trap of your uncle's ...." said Jan, rising, and looking at her very sharply.

"He is not an early riser and I break my fast in my own room so as not to have to eat with him," said Irene. "I doubt he yet knows that I have gone. I slipped out last night. When he finds out, I doubt he will ask the laundry workers if they saw someone none of them knew, who claimed to be the wife of Jan Kowalski."

Jan looked at her, and nodded thoughtfully.

"Resourceful," he said. "Very well, the pair of you make your way to the back entrance of the big white house across the square, and I will watch to make sure nobody is watching."

"My lady, I am delighted to see you free, but your looks are distinctive," said Wojciech. "Moreover you are undoubtedly a szlachcianka. You did well acting for short periods but for a long time ..."

"That, my lord, is why I have mustered enough clothing to be a page," said Irene. "And when I was growing up, my mother had me take lessons in swordplay, and riding astride as well as on a side saddle, and how to act as a boy in case I had the opportunities to escape which she did not."

Wojciech was rarely rendered completely speechless.

"I ... my lady ... Waćpanna Trąbkówna ..." he stuttered.

"Shall I go and change and you can tell me if I am walking properly like a boy?" asked Irene.

Wojciech pulled himself together.

"Very well," he said.

The slim youth was coltish but definitely boyish. Wojciech threw a book at her as she sat down nonchalantly.

She snapped her knees together as she caught it.

"Well done," said Wojciech. "To manage to catch something and not open your knees to make a lap with a skirt is excellent. And had I not seen you in that peasant girl's costume making sure everything female was ... apparent ... I might have wondered if you had been a lad who dressed as a girl to be harmless, a trick of your mother's."

"Mama was thorough," said Irene, softly. "The captain of the guards was devoted to her, and he trained me as if I was his own son. It is why my embroidery is not of such a high standard as it might have been had I given more time and attention to it."

"Being able to ply a sword is, it seems to me, more useful," said Wojciech. "I am afraid your hair will have to be cut."

"I thought it would," said Irene. "And I cannot really have it in a queue, as it is too close to a plait. I thought if it were tied tightly with thread at the top, and plaited, I might keep the plait and use it to appear to have more hair if I needed to be me. As you say, it is a distinctive colour."

Wojciech nodded approval.

"And then we will dye what is left, and you can run messages like any lad in my household," he said. He gave a ghost of a smile. "I wished for an ensign, but I will settle for a page."

"I could fight."

"No; you could skirmish. You are not trained in the way I have been trained. But I will not insult you in keeping you from doing what you might."

"Thank you. Though I fear with what my uncle plans, you will not be able to fight him again."

"What does he plan?" asked Wojciech.

Irene told him all she had heard.

"And I cannot see what you might do," she said.

"It is not as bad as I feared," said Wojciech. "I have to say it sounds as though the cannon is of greater risk to its crew than to anyone else. Jan, can you still do those horse tricks you learned to help me do them better?"

"I don't know, my lord, but I could try. Diversion?"

"I had an idea; you would not need to get close. Others would have to free the hostages and without a friendly scaffold built to help us as the last was."

"I can do horse tricks," said Irene. "If you mean rolling down to the side and things like that."

"I did mean things like that," said Wojciech. "My lady, it might be improper in me to consider this, but you might just have talked yourself into a role as a temporary winged hussar." He smiled at her slight size. "Well, half a hussar, anyway."

Chapter 7

"You are surely not risking Ogień ... er, and her ladyship ... if that cannon ain't flawed are you?" demanded Jan.

Irene chuckled.

"I am glad to know my place in the pecking order," she said, gravely.

"I wasn't planning on risking either of them," said Wojciech. "If she can do those tricks, she can roll to the side, run along with the horse and choose whether to re-mount or let go. She will let go, leaving a dummy with wings on a cart horse dyed red. And when the cannon has fired its shot, or otherwise, then the winged hussars arrive."

"I'd feel happier on my own horse, but that's not possible. I can do it," said Irene. "Don't the wings hamper you? And the armour?"

"The armour is surprisingly light and flexible," said Wojciech. "And yes, the wings make it exceedingly difficult, which is why your wings will be lighter than usual, and will break off. Even so, I can roll down Ogień's side to pick up something dropped on the ground without him breaking stride, and I can dismount to lie along his side, holding on the saddle's pommel, and too to run alongside him, in giant strides with much of my weight still carried. I can't do the trick of going under his belly with the wings. And I am not as agile at it as some of the Cossacks I've seen performing riding tricks."[3] A shadow crossed his face. "And I learned mostly because I did not want to be at a disadvantage against Cossacks, after the massacre of Humań, eight years ago. I was barely more than a boy, then, so

[3] I've seen re-enactment winged hussars do this sort of thing, as well as cossack display groups, it's mind-blowing.

learning acrobatics came more easily than had I reached man's estate, but a skill frequently practised becomes second nature."

Irene nodded.

"The captain of the guard was theoretically in some way beholden to the family, but he was loyal to us. I enjoyed such tricks. Mama sighed that no English lady would perform such monkey tricks, but her desire to have me safe outweighed her desire for me to be purely ladylike."

"No Polish szlachcianka would do so either, my lady," said Wojciech. "But we won't tell anyone."

She stared at him.

"You are teasing me," she said.

He laughed.

"Yes," he said.

"Good; I would not like you to be too serious," said Irene. "And please will you call me Irene or Irenka? Or give me a boy's name while I am your page."

"Yes, that is important," said Wojciech. "I had a little brother once, though he did not live to be very old; his name was Walenty. Will that do for you?"

"I would be honoured," said Irene. "Your parents were fond of the letter W?"

He gave a rueful chuckle.

"It was just the way it worked out," he said. "Both are family names. So you are Walenty Skrzydło."

"Yes, my lord."

"And you had better call me Wojciech if you are a relative," said Wojciech. "And when we have sorted out your hair, I will put you through your paces with a sword. I will not treat you as a gently born lady if you are determined to be a boy. I will treat you as a boy. You have this chance to change your mind and we will dye your hair and hope nobody realises."

"I am happy with your strictures, Wojciech," she said, blushing at using his name for the first time.

Irene walked over to the carpenter's shop with a message for Wojciech; Tekla was there, keeping watch. She bobbed a curtsey to Irene.

"He's in the cellar, lady," she said. "My, he's a fine one; if I didn't have my Janek, I'd be tempted to try to be his mistress. You don't want to lose him; a szlachcic who enthusiastically engages in manual labour is going to keep that figure and those muscles."

Irene blushed.

"I was not pursuing him in a romantic sense," she said, rather coldly.

"More fool you, then," said Tekla. "You have the opportunity to impress him that you are no normal szlachcianka who simpers like a ninny."

"Perhaps; but in the meantime, my safety and his mission are more important," said Irene.

Tekla rolled her eyes, and Irene could imagine her consigning all szlachta to perdition for a lack of romance.

She went down to the cellar, where a candle burned steadily. Janek was painting a sheet of canvas to exactly mimic the stonework; and there was an opening in the wall opposite this artistic endeavour. Sounds of digging came from the hole.

"He's digging, lady," said Janek. "He will bring some excess earth presently."

"Thank you," murmured Irene.

The sounds of digging ceased and sounds of movement resolved themselves into Wojciech, clad only in a light pair of linen trousers. His bare chest and face were filmed with a light sheen of sweat, and Irene wondered why he moved a bag he was holding so awkwardly in front of himself. She admired his well-defined and muscular chest and belly, muscles rippling in his arms just enough to be rather exciting, without being too muscle-bound. She felt very gauche and tongue-tied. He was looking at her in the same way he had looked on her from the tree, when she had first seen him.

"I ... I have a message from Jan," she stumbled through the sentence, hoping that her voice had not gone squeaky and breathless.

"Oh, he has found a horse?" Wojciech managed to find his voice, realising that he had not previously appreciated what lovely legs Irenka had, when all he was thinking of was disguising her. Her żupan clung rather closely too. "I do apologise for being improperly dressed; digging a tunnel is no sort of job to do fully clad, and Jan is no longer as young as he once was, and moreover I understand about shoring up tunnels ... am I babbling, Irenka?"

"Yes, but it makes my desire to babble less embarrassing," said Irene. "And you should call me Walenty."

"I know I should, but you ought to wear a looser żupan," he said. "I hope you had on a czamara over it."

"I did; I will cut this żupan down front and back and add a decorative stripe," said Irene. "It's one I hoarded from before Mama died and I have ... grown." She blushed. "Is this tunnel to help the next lot of hostages to escape?"

"Yes; and no," said Wojciech. "If someone told you they had descended into the coal chute here, and you burst in and found a tunnel to a well, with a ladder up to outside, what would you do?"

"I'd look for where horses waited to take them away," said Irene.

"Ah, a good point, a few horses waiting there for a while will add to the illusion," said Wojciech. "But that is the obvious way."

"And they are safe behind Janek's painted wall?"

"If all goes well and I have time to finish the mine out of our own cellar, they will be in our cellar with the option to be behind a painted wall," said Wojciech. "Very well, we'll introduce you to your horse this afternoon and you can show me how good you are."

"I don't exaggerate what I can do, my lord," said Irene. "Just because I am a girl ..."

"Just because you are a new warrior who has not yet seen action and who would be checked out by his officer whoever he might be," said Wojciech. "And as much as you might exaggerate, you might play down your skills and I want to assess them, and assess how you adapt to a horse you do not know."

Irene saluted.

"Yes, my lord," she said.

He laughed.

"So I should hope, recruit," he replied. "As you're here, perhaps you can take a few of the bags up and spread them about the back yard, on the vegetable beds. We can spread it out on the floor down here, but getting rid of some would help."

Irene nodded, and took the bag from him, and picked up another she could see. They were heavy! Wojciech had already turned from her to take several planks back into his mine. He was whistling a lively folk dance, and Irene smiled to herself.

She managed three journeys with soil, and then put back on the concealing czamara to return to the other house. She was in time to see soldiers rounding up more people, and dodged back into the carpenter's shop until such time as they had finished.

She slipped down the steps again.

"More hostages taken," she reported to Janek. "Tell him when he comes out."

Janek nodded.

"I will; take care crossing the square, lady."

"Thank you; I will be judicious," said Irene.

"Talk to me about mines, my lord," said Lynx, when

Wojciech came, properly clad, to eat beetroot soup and pierogi for a light luncheon.

"You're wounded; you can't dig."

"No, my lord, but I can learn for when I can take a turn," said Lynx. "And maybe I can prepare things for you."

Wojciech nodded. Lynx had a good point, there was no point wasting time to wait on educating him until he was well enough to help. Irene was listening as well. Jan already knew, and the others ate thankfully in the kitchen while the Szlachta and their immediate servants ate in the dining room. Lynx appeared to be intelligent as well as steady; a good man for Lady Irenka to have as a bodyguard.

A merchant rode out of the town with his man and some young relative. Irene rode on black Wicher, Jan's mount often enough, but really Wojciech's spare warhorse. Irene was thrilled to ride such a quality horse, and appreciated the honour done to her in assuming she could control him, even if Jan was perched on the crupper and ready to take the reins if needed. Irene rode with one hand on her hip, showing off a little that she could ride a horse with her legs and did not need the rein.

They travelled to a small farm. Here a roan horse of some fifteen and a half hands had been acquired by Jan. Irene saddled up with aplomb, and mounted, talking to the horse. The meadow was large, and set back from the road, shielded from view by an orchard. Irene walked, trotted, cantered and galloped round the meadow, finding a gait the horse liked, somewhere between a canter and a clumsy gallop, then she swung one leg over to one side, letting that leg dangle with the other foot in the stirrup, touching down on the ground from time to time, to give the horse time to get used to the idea. Then, with a firm hold on the pommel, she kicked her foot out of the stirrup and swung herself to lie against the horse's flank, concealed from the far side but for her hand holding on, the whole purpose of that move being to avoid being shot by men to one side. Then she was back in the saddle, urging the horse to speed again, the beast thinking, not unnaturally, that with a rider messing about on his back instead of kicking heels into him to make him run that a rest was in order.

The horse was definitely bored by now, and came to a full stop, and threw itself into a roll. Irene felt the motion and rolled the same way, coming off the horse in a handspring before she could be rolled on.

"Now I see why it was so cheap," said Jan. "Are you hurt, little lady?"

"Fortunately no," said Irene. "I thought my wrist was going to go for a moment; I haven't been able to keep up as much exercise in my uncle's house, but it held."

"You can exercise in my cellar," said Wojciech. "We will practise swordplay there as well; it is a fine, large cellar and extends under the yard. I've made a rough vaulting horse down there."

"Thank you," said Irene. "Well, my lazy and stubborn friend, shall we try again?" she took the roan horse by the ear, firmly.

It regarded her thoughtfully and decided that perhaps this one who had not been broken by the usual tactics might just be his master.

Galloping again, Irene came off the side of the horse smoothly, running with giant, leaping strides to be at the same speed, and back onto the saddle again; and then she was down again, letting her feet lower so that she was running, the horse now going on without her as she let herself slow.

Wojciech applauded.

"Well done; if you can manage that with a strange

horse, it should work well."

The horse had come to a stop again.

"He'll want some oats before he'll be ready to play again," said Irene.

"He'll play just enough," said Wojciech. "And with luck will live to go back to pasture and a lazy old age."

"You have the dye?" asked Irene.

"Yes, and he will soon be a lovely red-chestnut," said Wojciech. "Jan will drive him in through the gates with a cart load of barrels to bestow in the barn I am renting inside the town walls. And the merchant and his young relative will ride back into town and pass the time of day jocularly with the guard, and I doubt anyone will even remark that I do not have my servant. Servants are so often invisible."

Irene nodded. She learned a lot from the gossip of servants about what her uncle was up to, since he ignored them completely.

"I'll have a bundle in the doorway where you get down," said Wojciech. "If you wear a blouse and corset under the sort of plain wool jacket a man or woman might wear, you can pull on a skirt with a drawstring and cover your hair with a shawl."

Irene nodded.

People saw what they expected to see.

Chapter 8

A bit of gossip led Jan to a brewery whose premises shared part of a back wall with Wojciech's house. Owing to the problems caused by the Wojewoda, the business was struggling; and rather than purchase the business and premises outright, Jan made an offer. The brewers were happy to lease part of their property, and no questions asked; that little bit extra made all the difference in being able to carry on with their business.

Wojciech and his friends needed to undertake a little bit of demolition of the back wall, where it connected to the brewery property, and to put up high, heavy hurdles to separate part of the brewery yard along the wall. Part of the lease included one of the stables for dray horses, which made transforming into the blood angel easier. Heavy gates in the demolished wall were better than a painting which would not stand up to inspection in daylight. Feliks had sorted out heavy locks supposedly on the other side which were easily unlocked, and Ogień could trot along a narrow passage to the stable, which was a street further from the market place. In emergency, there was also a straight road outside the brewery to one of the breaches in the town wall. Ogień would make short work of one of the palisades. The breach was not manned now the Wojewoda had lost more men than he would have liked; it led to open country, with hills, no strategic road or river. Beyond were mountains, blued by distance, but with rough land around the deeply-cut valley of the laughing and boisterous rill which joined the river just downstream of the walls, which time it had become a little more sedate and more a stream, shrouded in willow and alder. The terrain beyond the breach, however, made the approach of any external enemy unlikely. Wojciech had managed to leave the town unobserved just by climbing over the palisade on the rough rocks of the wall, and had been sabotaging the palisade there bit by bit. The stream was not suited to any kind of boat, being shallow and rocky, with much white water and rapids, but the water was cold and delicious, and Wojciech knew that he and Jan at least could remain on the run in such country almost indefinitely. Rescuing the next group of hostages would be more risky, and an escape plan had to be in place. Everyone knew what to do if there was a need to flee, and the ability to pass through the brewery was a part of that plan.

The execution was to be a trap for the winged hussar. Władimir was very proud of his preparations. In front of the scaffold was a cart, much decorated with striped canvas and bunting. It had a platform on top, covered with an awning and with the town's flag flying, from which Wójt Krzak would make a speech about leniency if the winged hussar was given up, and retribution if he was not. The Wojewoda was certain that the arrogant szlachcic bastard would almost have to make his attack run the same as before, to show off to the crowd. And then the cannon concealed in the cart, which was under the platform on which Krzak stood, would fire, and blow the man and his unnatural horse to kingdom come. His followers would be so shocked it would be easy to pick them off. And in case horse or rider survived, the side streets would all be blocked by carts, with musketeers waiting behind them to fire on any horse attempting to jump the barrier. It was a simple but very effective trap.

"Are you sure you don't want to be my spokesmen, not Krzak, Stanisław?" Władimir asked his brother.

"No, why would I? I am fond of living," said Stanisław Trąbka. "And anyway, why would I help you out? What have you done to find my daughter?"

"I've said before, she can't get far; she's a woman, not even a woman, a chit of a girl. She's sobbing hysterically somewhere and hoping that someone will turn her in for the reward I posted. I didn't specify that I wanted her still a virgin, because it doesn't matter if she is to be the king's mistress. But if anyone has taken her, I'll have him flayed as well as rewarded, does that satisfy you?"

"Not really," said Stanisław. "I know she and I quarrel but she's still my daughter. And I don't really want her to be the king's mistress, I'd rather she made a good marriage which would cement a good alliance. I had been hoping to attract the attention of the Skrzydło Baron Płodnadolina but the idiot took to drink. A shame; handsome, rich, well-connected. Eminently suitable in every way."

"Except in one; dead," said Władimir. "I don't trust that family anyway. Normal knights are too full of nobility to have any room for brains, but the Płodziewicz family are said to be meddlers."

Irene sat on the cart horse, the unaccustomed feeling of wings on her back making her want to fidget. They were fashioned out of light wood with paper feather shapes cut out to give an impression at a distance. She was nervous, and afraid of letting Wojciech down by doing something stupid, or being late, or not managing to get off properly. She checked the position of her feet. It was something she had practised over and over, and the old horse was full of oats and ready to do his best, actually tossing his head and snorting as if he thought he really was a war horse, just for being decked out with light armour and a bright rug over him.

She heard the whistle, and nudged a heel into her mount's flank.

The old fool was *prancing*.

Well, if he was enjoying himself it would make life easier.

A trot; now a canter; then his lumbering run down the main street. And then she was swinging off the saddle, legs down, one, two, three, four bouncing strides as she felt her feet, running, letting go, running and slowing; stopping, as the horse carried on.

Then the world exploded in flame and smoke and noise.

Wojciech sat astride Ogień feeling impatient and worried. Worried mostly for Irenka, so beautiful and so brave, and so definitely not the sort of girl his parents would think suitable. She was a women one could be friends with, and admire, and could trust to do her bit ... He worried about what would happen if her father's assessment of the cannon was inaccurate. If it really was that old and was in poor condition all well and good, even if it managed one shot. Her manoeuvre to get off the horse should save her even if it killed the horse. And the horse was old; one made sacrifices. He was well-aware that in the heyday of the winged hussars, the casualties amongst horses was around one in three, even if only one in around eighteen of the riders died. Better the horse than Irenka ...

Wojciech gritted his teeth. She would do her part and he must do his, not act like a boy in his first battle. Irenka had the right to feel like that, not him. He smiled at the thought of her eager face, tasting freedom for the first time, her hair now a nondescript brown, and as a boy looking nothing like the crude copy on posters of what she told him was a portrait of her. If he was her uncle, he would be questioning those who worked at the docks and on the river, on the principle that the easiest way to travel was downriver with the barges carrying logs from the heavy forest up in the hills. Apparently, however, the idea had not occurred to the Wojewoda, who had merely given orders for all young women to be scrutinised closely, a task his soldiery were happy to undertake with a zeal which did not always concentrate on the facial features.

Wojciech tore his mind off thoughts of Irenka and composed himself.

His signal was to be the firing of the cannon.

The detonation when it came was enough to rattle the stable; and the noise of the explosion was enough to make Ogień shy in surprise. It was not a cannon shot; it was a bomb. A bigger bomb than Wojciech could ever have imagined.

"Mother of God!" muttered Wojciech, as he kicked open the stable door. "Protect the innocents this day, Queen of Poland." He crossed himself and set forth to do his bit. Ogień thundered out, for all the world as though he was pretending that he had never been startled at all.

The screaming in the square unnerved Wojciech; a huge cloud of smoke lay ahead as he set lance to charge the mounted soldiers behind the scaffold. The horses were panicking; it did not take much to panic them further, and spitting two of the hapless riders on his lance and continuing forward was enough to persuade all the horses that where they wanted to be was home in their stables where thunder and lightning stayed in the sky where it was supposed to be.

Over the scaffold, the way he had done before from the other direction, Wojciech was able to assess the situation. Władimir Trąbka was curled up in his carriage, as was his brother, agonised expressions on their faces, blood leaking between fingers over ears. Most people in the immediate vicinity, thought Wojciech, would be in like case. The cannon had exploded; the direction of the blast would determine whether any of the innocent population, including the hostages, were dead or wounded. Or Jan, Feliks and Lynx. His face was grim as he looked around, peering through the smoke. He had worried so much about Irenka he had not considered the potential danger to a man who stood in place of a father, a little boy he had accepted into his protection, and a subordinate whom he also liked. That was a bad mistake. Nobody remained on the platform; his own approach was to have covered their removal but Jan was no fool and had plainly improvised, using the diversion of the exploding cannon to make their getaway.

It seemed therefore unlikely that the hostages had been hurt. People were milling about, and some were fleeing. It looked as though the screaming was more in terror than pain, and he said a quick prayer of thanks as he urged Ogień down past the shattered remains of the cart in which the cannon had been housed. Where the cart had been remained only a pile of splinters and what looked like raw liver, with the odd, incongruous body part of the hapless gunners. The cannon barrel had been blown down the street and lay where it had rolled, the breech split and peeled back like the skin of an orange. The ball was a foot or so further down the street. It looked as though the barrel had been slung along with the ball, which had just had enough extra power to trickle out of the end of it.

The blast, mercifully, had been downwards; doubtless the flaws exacerbated by rust, from letting water sit in the barrel. In the enclosed space it had still shattered the cart, sending splinters in all directions; and the metal shards had gone down, hit the cobbles, and ricocheted back up with the force of their passage, passing twice through the soldiers in and beside the cart. Wojciech spent no time pitying them; had they lived, they would have died by his sword. Some of the onlookers might have been wounded by flying splinters of wood, but the crowd had been cordoned off at some distance, and it looked as though most of those lying on the ground bleeding were the soldiers detailed to hold them back, who had protected the crowd with their own bodies. It was fitting, thought Wojciech; a soldier is supposed to protect civilians with his life if need be.

As Wojciech started to urge Ogień to a gallop, he noticed something in his path. It was a small child, literally blown off its feet! He shoved his sword across his saddle, held with his left thumb as he put his weight on the pommel with his left hand. A slight swerve and a roll from the saddle, and the child was in his right arm, cradled carefully as he looked for a woman who seemed to have lost a child. He saw her, mouth open in silent scream, terror in her eyes and her arms held out imploringly, tears streaking her face, and blood on her neck from her own ruptured ears. Not as badly hurt as the Wojewoda, he judged, for having been further away. And then he was lowering the toddler into her arms, taking up his sword to give her a rapid salute and was away.

Irene picked herself up, and shook her head.

Wojciech had said the cannon might explode, but the words had hardly suited the extreme violence of that action. Her horse had come to a stop, and was gazing down the street in apparent astonishment, shaking his head.

Irene sought the arched doorway where a small bundle awaited her, left by Feliks shortly before the tumbrels arrived. She undid it, pulling on the skirt and shawl, as the fleeing crowd reached her. She joined them in their headlong flight, making herself one with them.

Behind her the incarnadine figure of the blood angel thundered down the road, past the fleeing townsfolk, who quickly got out of his way as he cantered down the centre of the road, giving them room on each side. He was unchallenged by the soldiers at the barricaded side roads, who had orders to shoot if he tried to pass them.

They lost any chance they might have had to fire by hesitating as he ignored the apparently easier way of escape. Irene thought he looked magnificent as he made straight to the gate, slashing a soldier out of the way as he went, and through it, out into the countryside.

As she went with the crowd she heard people marvelling over how the blood angel was blessed by Heaven so that cannons would not fire, but destroyed themselves and those ungodly enough to use them.

"And he stopped to pick up my baby!" said a woman, awed. "Right in his way she was, I was expecting him to ride over her but he picked her up without even pausing!"

Irene smiled.

It sounded exactly the sort of thing Wojciech would do.

"He's the last winged hussar," she said to the woman. "The last knight in Poland, here when he is needed."

Chapter 9

"Well done for using your initiative, Jan," said Wojciech, when they were all safely back home.

"It was Lynx who said we should take advantage of the confusion," said Jan.

"Well done, then, Lynx," said Wojciech. "It took all of you to act on it though. Were any of the hostages hurt?"

"Miraculously, no, well not exactly," said Jan. "We hustled them down the ladder and straight into the carpenter's cellar, and there was so much confusion we weren't even followed. We heaved the priest down too, and sat him down out of the way to recover."

"As well to keep our own mine hidden in case they ask questions, and any of the townsfolk saw and are intimidated into speaking about it," said Wojciech. "And the bolt-hole to the well won't hurt having, if they don't find it. And if they don't, it means we can use it again. I'm glad we decided that it didn't matter to leave the rest of the earth in bags in the cellar, or someone would have had to risk staying to brush out the footprints and the signs of the false wall moving from the dirt."

"I'd be half inclined to have a concealed rope ladder and mine away from the well, lower down," said Lynx. "If there's a ladder up, nobody would look down."

"Maybe a one or two-person niche, but with hand holds cut, not a ladder," said Wojciech. "The risk of flooding in springtime when the river is high is too great. I wonder how the soldiers are faring? I wager the Wojewoda is hopping mad. What about the Wójt?"

Jan gave a brief, mirthless laugh.

"Wójt Krzak, whose name means 'Bush' is doing a fine impression of being nothing but a pile of prunings," he said. "It was ... well, pretty horrible. He was literally cut into pieces before our eyes. And we were glad you insisted we put lambs-wool in our ears and cover them with heavy flannel scarves. We were close enough to the explosion to have been deafened for weeks. It's a good job we were behind stone pillars of the town hall, too. And then Lynx said 'go now!' and went as arranged to open the trapdoor. The poor devils from the scaffold are deaf and shocked and we brought the old man, but his heart failed, I'm afraid. His granddaughter was with him, and we will sneak him into the church for a Christian burial later. Tekla has been feeding the rest żurek, heavily laced with willow bark and wódka to help the pain."

"It should wear off," said Lynx. "I've had a misfire by my ear once, which took all afternoon to clear, and my ear ached for a few days, but it's not a problem. What is a problem is that around about now it's going to dawn on someone that I deserted. I said I had a place to stay in the town whilst my injuries healed, but I am substantially better now, and have not reported for duty."

"I wonder whether you'll be the only one," said Jan. "It can't be easy on the men having their numbers whittled down essentially by one man – even if the gun was their leader's fault."

"I heard someone say that the Winged Hussar is blessed by Heaven, and that the gun would not harm him and blew up those who dared attack him," said Irene.

"Well, who knows but that the Queen of Poland had a hand in it," said Wojciech, crossing himself. His companions followed suit. "Certainly I prayed for Her protection of innocents, and the direction in which the gun failed could not have been more fortuitous. I think we should all give thanks."

They knelt at his suggestion, and prayed.

"I am also thankful my faithful mount survived," said Irene, softly. "Thank you for stabling him at the brewery, where he will doubtless be assumed to be a dray horse. He seemed to know how to be martial."

"Yes, he trampled a couple of soldiers from the barricades," said Lynx. "It's my belief that he used to be a drum horse."

"That would explain much," said Wojciech. "I won't object to him covering my mare; her foal is almost old enough for you to ride and train beside. We need to push hard enough to mean that Władimir Trąbka has to send for aid, and to frighten his own soldiers into deserting."

"I doubt it will take much," said Lynx. "He does not inspire loyalty, and his troops are all of poor quality."

Władimir was furious. His ears had stopped bleeding, and he had some of his hearing back, but the high pitched whine of tinnitus was aggravating him beyond even his usual bad temper. He was berating the captain of the guards.

"The gun was sabotaged!" he declared, wincing at the screech in his own voice.

"I told you it was likely to be faulty," said Stanisław.

"That was more than being faulty! It was rigged to blow up! Find out anyone who was anywhere near it, and have them flogged until someone confesses!" Władimir demanded.

"It was a very old gun, my lord ..." said the captain.

"It was not the gun, it was sabotage! And if you protest, I will have you put to the question! Find out who did it and have him and his family put to death! Messily!" Władimir was beside himself.

"Yes, my lord," said the captain and withdrew.

"You'll only make them desert, and you've lost too many to do that," said Stanisław.

"Nonsense! They're only peasants, they don't

understand numbers, and they need discipline, like dogs," said Władimir.

Stanisław rolled his eyes. He was about to retire to his country house, and hoped his daughter had also decided to return there. He could see no reason why she should not do so; it was her home, after all. He had a sneaking suspicion that when the Ulans arrived, he wanted to be somewhere else.

He made a detour to the captain of the guard's office, where he interrupted the man briefing two furious lieutenants.

"Captain," said Stanisław, "I was going to leave for my dworek wiejski, my country house. Half a dozen steady men to escort me would be appreciated; I assume you are going to ride for Warszawa yourself to explain the situation here. I give you my blessing. If you happen on my daughter, if she has not got back home to my dworek wiejski by now, then pray send her back to me. Good day."

The captain looked at his lieutenants.

"Well, you heard him," he said. "I think this even beats the order 'the floggings will continue until morale improves'[4] which the Little Horn[5] issued when there was dissatisfaction over hanging townsfolk to make this winged lunatic give himself up. It isn't going to happen and I don't much care if he has God on his side or Satan, I don't fancy staying here any longer. I suggest you tell the men what the Wojewoda's last idiocy is, and let them take their families and disperse. We already drew in people from the rest of the province to cover his

---

[4] I would like to say I made this one up, but alas, it's a genuine order issued by the Imperial Japanese Navy... I just thought it suited Władimir's style of governance

[5] Trąbka means little trumpet

mistakes. And I'll ask for a real leader and men."

One of the lieutenants sniffed.

"It's what you get when the local noble is the one to pay for his troops; sometimes you get a cheapskate, who does not have the honour to provide the best possible. Our men are hired ruffians for the most part."

"My lord, my lord, the soldiers are deserting!" Mrs. Ślusarzowa almost ran into the house after having been out shopping. "Several of them swaggered into town to ask if the girls they've been seeing would go with them; they were quite open about it. And the Wojewoda's brother is leaving town too!"

"I suppose it would be insanity to waylay my father and let him know that I have played the part of the blood angel once?" said Irene.

"It would be total insanity," said Wojciech. His eyes sparkled. "Fun, but insane. We will eschew that pleasure. Well, it would appear that we have no more need to stay here, and the good people we have rescued can make their way quietly home. It will not take long for word to be taken to Warszawa, and then someone will be sent to investigate."

"You are not going to send me back to my father's country house, are you?" asked Irene.

"Did I not say that when we had finished here, you should train with the red colt?" said Wojciech. "And you shall name him too. When you are trained, we will ride together."

"Who else will come with us?"

"Jan is my man; Lynx, do you have ties here, or do you come too?"

"Pass up more excitement than I've ever had in my life? I swore I would be the Szlachcianka's bodyguard, and so I shall," said Lynx.

Wojciech nodded.

"I doubt that Tekla and Janek will want to leave home, now they can get married. Even if Tekla does not like her father. And Marianna, I will not ask it of you, but I will pay you to keep house here, as a safe house should I need to send any others here. If Feliks wishes, when he is grown, he may join me. But now he is to look after you. Janek and Tekla may reside here also."

"My lord, I would come with you if you asked it," said Marianna Ślusarzowa, tears in her eyes.

"I know," said Wojciech. "But the life I have chosen is one of wandering, and it is cruelly hard on a woman to ask her to put up with such. Walenty, you are laughing at me."

"You do not hesitate to ask me," said Irene.

"I forget you are any but my companion," said Wojciech. "Moreover, you are szlachcianka and a warrior. But you do not wish to remain, do you?"

"Not in the least; I am ready for adventure with you," said Irene. "I am glad to be Walenty, your companion, though it will be nice at times to be Irenka as well."

"Ah, well, that I cannot permit myself to think about until you are of age, or we have found your English relatives," said Wojciech.

Irene gasped.

He was not indifferent to her as a woman! But a stickler for what was proper.

She smiled tremulously at him, and never knew how close Wojciech came to losing his iron control to sweep her into his arms.

Irene opted to ride her old drum horse, and named him firmly in English, 'Jester' for his sense of humour. A decent horse must be procured for Lynx, who claimed to ride indifferently. Four sumpter ponies carried armour, clothing, tents, blankets and so on.

They were on their way out of town when a cloud of

dust ahead made Wojciech stiffen. Hastily they got off the road as a contingent of Ulans galloped along the road, some thirty or more of them.

"The banner of Biały-Kruk, the white raven," said Wojciech. "They have sent Seweryn Krasiński, who used also to be a winged hussar."

"Is that bad?" asked Irene.

"Bad! Not for the town and province, but he knows me," said Wojciech. "He's my God-brother; he and I were born two days apart, and our fathers were mutual God-fathers. They rode together in their own younger days as husaria."

"Then shall I do any talking? He has held up a hand to halt the band," said Irene.

"No, I will get it over and done with," said Wojciech. "We've fought knee to knee; there is no way he is going to fail to recognise me. It broke my heart not to tell him, but it was for his own protection."

The officer rode forward of his men and approached the travellers. He had a magnificent set of pale blond moustaches, and eyes as blue as the sky. They held reproach and glittered with anger and other, mixed emotions; and his mouth was tight.

"I would know Ogień anywhere, you know," he said, conversationally. "And the way you sit on him."

"Seweryn," said Wojciech. He sounded strained, and his voice was suspiciously thick with unshed tears.

"You recovered from death remarkably well," said Seweryn. "You had a magnificent funeral, you know. Wojciech. I grieved for you most deeply, even though drinking yourself to death did not seem to be in keeping with your character." He was angry, and tears stood in his eyes.

Wojciech shrugged.

"I never asked for one," he said. "I am sorry; perhaps I should have told you, but a secret shared is no secret. And you cannot act to save your own life. My brother, I did not want you to be in trouble for my actions."

"Granted that I cannot act. However, I could just have withdrawn as though in grief for a while. I am angry, Wojciech, but I love you, so I suppose I will forgive you, you cool, self-assured bastard. So, are you the insane hell-spawned red rider that people are babbling about?" asked Seweryn.

"Someone had to do something. And reports get sat on," Wojciech made a gesture of frustration.

"Truth; sometimes it's hard being loyal to the king and parliament, when they seem determined to lead the country to destruction. But like you said once, revolt is the quickest way to invite in trouble. Neither Russia, Austria, nor Prussia will stand for it."

"And I will not join the rebels for that reason; but nor will I be a follower when I cannot believe in what I follow any more. Losing the winged hussars made me take stock and see more clearly," said Wojciech.

"I am not cut out to stand alone. I will not speak of what I know; but I will expect you to begone from this region"

"I am leaving; I knew they were sending someone, and seeing who it is eases my mind. I'll send back those who were displaced, snatched from the gallows because nobody in the town knew enough to give me up."

"Oh, I see," said Seweryn. "And who is your young companion?"

"Oh, this is Walenty," said Wojciech, easily.

"Not your son; you were not so precocious," said Seweryn. "The boy has to be at least fifteen."

"Walenty is gently born," said Wojciech, "But not my son."

"What are you up to, you insane red maverick?" asked Seweryn.

Wojciech smiled, a happy, sweet smile.

"Probably better that you do not know," he said.

"And what heraldry does ... Walenty ... have?" asked Seweryn, looking at Irene.

"I accept my lord's heraldry of the red wing," said Irene. "Walenty Skrzydło at your service."

"He's very young, Wojciech," said Seweryn.

"Jakub Sobieski went into battle at fifteen with Jan III Sobieski," said Wojciech. "I wouldn't let anyone under my command do anything they are not ready to tackle. Walenty is a prodigy on a horse."

"I just hope it's not going to come back and bite me because you are stealing local youths," said Seweryn, gloomily."

"Somehow, I doubt it," said Wojciech, his lips twitching. "Seweryn, can I rely on you not to let anyone know I am alive?"

"I suppose so; but stay in touch. Where can I reach you?"

"You can find me as Wojciech Skrzydło in a place called Szuwary. I hope I'm doing the right thing letting you know."

"We are brothers and have been friends since you knocked me down for laughing at your red horse when we were both six or seven; Ogień's sire, as I recall. When our sires decided their Godsons should actually meet."

Wojciech smiled.

"Yes, and the horse was retired from the field of battle to start my training. I miss Czerwony Pegaz."

"I think I made fun of the idea of a Red Pegasus as well."

"And I gave you a good drubbing for having no respect for my sire's choice of name," said Wojciech.

"Good days," sighed Seweryn. "I bought your lands from the crown. What else could I do?"

"Good; my people will be looked after."

"I felt I owed it to you, my friend. Be well, Wojciech; it's no good asking you not to get into trouble but do try not to be caught."

They clasped wrists in a gesture older than time and more profound than any words; and more was said in that gesture than in an embrace.

Then Seweryn lifted his hand to his waiting men, and pointed forward.

The small group of travellers was subjected to a few curious looks as the mounted men thundered by; and were then able to resume their way unmolested.

Wojciech shook his head.

"May God go with you, Seweryn, and may you keep the realm safe and your honour intact," he muttered. "You do as the king directs, and whatever I feel he is the king. But I ... I cannot betray him, but nor can I obey mindlessly."

"You will do what honour dictates, Wojciech," said Irene. "Did I answer correctly?"

"Oh beautifully! It was quick witted, my Walenty," said Wojciech. "And now, the leaves turn colour; I will be glad to reach Szuwary. Jaromar tells me the house he has secured is outside the village and higher in the mountains, though not as high as the summer pastures. The river is stopped by a moraine, a crescent-shaped hillock across the vale. There is something of a lake, or better described as a mere behind the moraine, where the village is situated. The river finds its way through a weak point, and around one end. Our lands are above the lake, in a hanging valley and waterfalls tumble down to the river from above and to the river below. In the winter they will freeze into crystal columns like strange natural palaces of ice."

"It sounds beautiful."

"And more to the point it is sheltered enough that we shall be able to train without needing a riding house save in the worst weather; and Jaromar has had a large barn erected for that purpose, as we will not have the riding house of my former lands."

"Do you regret giving it up?"

"Never; I have no ties to the land now, and all are my people when they need me. My former people will do very well with Seweryn. And had I not left ... why, we should not have met, would we?"

"All very well, my lord, but if we do not move along, we will stand here until we are icicles for the winter," said Jan.

"You are right, Jan; forward!" said Wojciech.

Chapter 10

Jester seemed to enjoy riding with other war horses, and Wojciech started teaching Irene how to take up formation.

"Part of the success of the winged hussars lies in the approach run being loose, and not in formation, which means individuals can deal with obstacles," he told her. "It's at the point we drop our lances that we close up. And then we close up tighter than most, with less than the width of a horse between us, almost knee to knee. Our lances are outrageously long, and hollow for lightness, so we might use such lengthy weapons. Jan came up with transporting them as half lances, and joining them with a core, which makes them less strong, but better than nothing. And the ball hand-guard over the join too. We try to save the ends where we can to re-use, but it isn't always possible, or practical. And sometimes leaving them leaves a point in other ways as you might say."

Irene nodded.

"Terror," she said. "I understand. It may be a weapon of one use, but you use it to advantage."

"Yes, and there's little point of it without the speed of the attack run anyway," said Wojciech. "Though I thought one thing we might practise is a Cossack trick, wherein you throw a shorter lance to me from behind if I need to clear well-held lines."

"And it keeps me back out of the way until you deem me steady?"

"That too," agreed Wojciech, equably. "Your horse is dancing again."

"He enjoys trotting to the dance," said Irene. "I think Lynx is right about him being a drum horse."

"Poor old boy is too old to use as a general thing, but I swear he's enjoying being martial."

"And why not! He can help us train the colt." Wojciech smiled.

"Are there other people as bad as my uncle?"

"I don't know, Walenty, but I know there is much disaffection and banditry. When a country is in the throes of civil war, deserters from both sides decide that their political allegiance lies with enriching themselves, taking advantage of the confusion. They will tell you that it is not civil war, just some rebellious Szlachta; but it might as well be civil war. The saddest thing of all is that those who joined the Bar Confederation are honourable men, just as Seweryn who remains loyal to the king is an honourable man. They hate the influence Russia has over Poland; as any patriot must hate it. And they hate any change. I can see that change must happen. Deep down I even know that the winged hussars are obsolete in these days of better firearms. And yet ... and yet the charge of the winged hussars is a fearsome thing, and I still feel it could give something. Perhaps if we carried muskets rather than lances on our charge, adapting to the modern world. And it is something I will think about in my mission to protect the peasantry who try to live their lives without being involved in politics." He gave a wry smile. "Something tells me, though, that we have not heard the last of your uncle. Seweryn will kick him out, but I doubt he will string him up from his own gallows. And he is a man who will want revenge."

Irene nodded soberly.

She could quite imagine her uncle dedicating himself to what would be, ultimately, a pointless revenge.

It was somehow comforting to perform lance drills on the better roads, and Jester certainly seemed to enjoy himself. Wojciech insisted on calling him 'Błazen' and sticking to Polish, but he answered best to 'old boy'. Irene suspected it had been a term of endearment used before he was discarded and sold as a cart horse; the indignity making him contrary. Irene was learning sword drills too, the big cavalry sabre a different weapon to the rapier she had learned with. It had a satisfying weight as it descended.

Irene was glad of the practise as they passed across a heath, lonely and with intermittent fog banks.

"Someone is shadowing us," said Wojciech, softly.

"Is that why I feel that there are eyes on my back? I thought I was just being foolish, with this uncanny atmosphere."

"No, I have heard movement off to the side from time to time which was not from us; as though slithering down banks in that rolling heathland, and I caught sight of a shadow on the fog."

"I've seen at least two," said Jan.

"Me too," said Lynx. "I think there are four of them; two conferred and other shadows were on the other side of the road. They are using the terrain they know to stay ahead of us even though we are mounted and they are not."

"Lynx-eyes earns his nickname again," said Wojciech. "Loosen your sword, Walenty; Jan, Lynx, pistols will, I think be needed more than muskets."

"I've two loaded," grunted Jan. "I've heard of this damned heath."

Lynx nodded.

"I don't doubt that our hussars would make short work of them, but no point not being ready," he said. "My lord, make that six."

"A veritable band of bandits," said Wojciech. "Well, a little exercise and practical experience will do Walenty no harm, and a bit of exercise will not come amiss for the rest of us."

"Has anyone ever told him the meaning of the word 'fear?' muttered Lynx to Jan.

"Not with any noticeable success," said Jan.

They rode on, alert to the expectation of trouble.

The bandits leaped out from behind bushes three or four horse lengths in front of them.

"Hold! Hand over your valuables!" cried one of them. They had muskets, and Lynx had been correct; there were six of them. They were also on foot and did not seem to have horses as he surmised. They were a ragged looking band, with wild eyes.

They were, even so, used to their victims pulling on the reins and bringing their horses to a terrified halt. They did not expect a trained hussar, two old soldiers and a would-be hussar; and instead of shying, stopping and acting afraid, their intended victims did not behave the way prey was supposed to behave.

The horses changed gait; but from a distance-eating post-speed trot to canter, their riders low in the saddle, and those in the front pulling swords! The bandits hardly had time to wonder what was going on, for within a few strides the horses had stretched to the charge. Jester whinnied amusement. The brigands did not have a chance to change their aim or leap out of the way, so shocked were they, before the riders were on them. The brigands just had time to realise their plight to scream in terror as thundering hoofs bore down inexorably upon them.

Ogień and Jester both rode those in the centre down, quite deliberately. Wojciech, on Irene's left, as the more experienced swordsman, swung back-handed, taking the head clean off the first, the sword carrying on and cutting the second across the forehead. Irene slashed at one who cried out, and put a hand up to his slashed face, but then she was past. Jester took a little longer to turn than Ogień; he was older, and not trained for the front rank of battle. Irene turned him as fast as she might, and was round in time to see Lynx lift his musket, and fire on the one that was left unhurt. He rapidly re-loaded, looking around in case there were more. Jan took guard with a musket, his pistol also to hand. Irene rode back, sword ready, and as the man she had wounded put up his musket in blind desperation, she swung off the saddle so that his shot went harmlessly over Jester's back, and then carried on under Jester's belly, dropping to the ground and rolling out from under the big horse's hoofs, coming up in one movement to cut across the man's body. He fell with a single scream, and lay still.

Wojciech swung off Ogień in a single, fluid move, to finish off the wounded. This was his second man and those who had been trampled. Irene's eyes were big with horror, gazing at the terrible injuries inflicted on those ridden down. Wojciech touched her shoulder when he had put them out of their agony.

"They were likely to die in any case," he said, gently. "The ones on the ground have crushed organs; nothing could cure them. We will pray for their souls."

Irene clung to him.

"I ... I am going to be sick," she said.

"Of course you are. There is a convenient ditch," said Wojciech. Irene went and heaved, the stench of blood and intestinal fluids making her empty her insides. Wojciech silently handed her a canteen of water and a handkerchief to wash and wipe her mouth.

Jan and Lynx had already dragged the bodies to the side of the verge, out of the way of travellers, and Wojciech had kicked dust over the terrible stains in the road, so Irene would not have to look at them. He knelt to pray and his companions joined him.

"Ought we to bury them?" said Irene.

"There will be a village; we can send people out to bury them if they wish to do so," said Lynx. "I know one; the one milady killed. He was a nasty piece of work, even for one of Trąbka's men, he deserted before you arrived, my lord." He hesitated and added, "If milady had been in skirts, she would have been begging for death for as long as he decided to keep her. You need not feel bad about killing the likes of him, Lady."

"A piece of filth," said Wojciech. "But still I pray for his soul, that he may learn the truths of our Lord and His Blessed Mother."

"Why did they attack a band of well-armed travellers?" asked Irene. She had fought herself under control, and had managed to blink back threatened tears.

"Because we are dressed as merchants, my ... uh, Walenty," said Wojciech. "Merchants would readily give up to such; we have but two what they would see as guards. We look to be easy pickings."

"Perhaps we would have fewer interruptions if we dressed as szlachta, so they will know we are dangerous," said Irene.

"If we were in a hurry, yes," said Wojciech. "But if they had avoided us, who might they have attacked behind us? We did not ask them to waylay us, but if they do so, they must take the consequences."

The village was another four miles along the road, and the tale that there were dead bandits was met with polite approval. The suggestion that they be collected for Christian burial was met with equally polite apathy.

"We did not despoil the bodies," said Wojciech. "Some of them had good boots. They had weapons. We did not look to see whether they had money. I suspect their goods will pay for a rudimentary service."

This garnered a little more interest, and by the time the group had finished a bowl of *barszcz*, beetroot soup, served with stuffed dumplings in it, several villagers were pushing a handcart towards the church, its load covered but the covering rather stained.

Irene made a face and put down her spoon.

"The aftermath of war is never pleasant," said Wojciech. "One is never hardened to it, unless one is a cold creature, but one learns to set the feelings to one side. You are put off your meal; but you must eat."

"It will do me no good if it comes up again," said Irene.

"No; but you must look at it that being alive to eat is a gift from God even as the food is by His benefice," said Wojciech. "You are the one alive sitting to eat; they are not eating, laughing round their camp fire, over the stupid merchants they killed for their money. Nor are you sobbing at the back of their camp, tied and helpless, having been made the plaything of each of them in turn. It is fitting that he met his end at the hands of a woman."

Irene nodded. She could appreciate that. Cautiously she took another spoonful; her belly was empty, Wojciech was right.

"You must think me hopeless and too womanly," she said. "I am sorry for my weakness."

"Do not be sorry; I think you a raw recruit who still gets involved and worries about every death. It is natural; you came through your first battle well, when we were in town and you faced the cannon, but did not have to kill anyone yourself. But now you have used your sword in combat and have had to kill. You are aware that you can take away the gift of life. I know, I sobbed like a child over my first kill. But we do not kill casually like your uncle, we kill to save others. And you must hold on to that." He hesitated. "If you do not wish to pursue training, I will understand," he added.

"I think I am not so feeble to give up for something which you tell me is a natural feeling," said Irene, lifting her chin. "I will learn to cope with it."

"There's my brave one," said Wojciech. "And I suppose we should try to track them back to their camp, lest there are more."

"Almost impossible, even for me," said Lynx. "They followed on the heath; on short, rabbit-cropped turf between the furze it will be hard to find any sign, especially in fog; and even if we might, then finding which is their trail following us and which leads to their lair is nigh on impossible."

"These sorts of people don't have concepts of reserves," said Jan. "They will all have come. Not one of them will trust the others to make an even division of spoils if they don't."

Wojciech reflected briefly that a reason for not bringing all their band would be if one was wounded, and then considered that any such would not cause a problem. They might of course have prisoners.

He motioned to the tavern keeper.

"Somewhere, no doubt, those villains had a lair; there's likely the greater part of their wealth there, but we don't know this region like a local does, to guess at where it might be."

The look of sudden avarice said that the lair would be found; and as Wojciech had spoken loudly enough for other villagers to hear, there would likely be someone prepared to rescue any prisoners. His conscience salved, he left it to the villagers.

Chapter 11

The weather was definitely turning, and after leaving the village, they paused before resuming their journey to get out fur-lined garments. Wojciech handed his fur-lined czamara to Lynx, who had no fur to his garments. Wojciech had made sure he was well-dressed to be in his service, but he had nothing as yet suitable for the winter.

"We'll see you well accoutred at the next town," promised Wojciech. His own kontusz was warm, as was Irene's long winter kontusik, which was made with enough frogging to pass as male; and both had warm fur hats and fur-lined gloves and boots. Arrayed as szlachta they would pass quicker, especially when Wojciech mounted a streamer of red silk on a lance. Two warriors would be given a wide berth, and Wojciech decided that pressing on would be better than turning aside for bandits.

He was glad to have done so when they awoke the morning after next to frost on the ground and covering the tents, and a few flakes of snow settling silently and softly from a sullen sky.

The snow had stopped by the time they had reheated a rabbit stew Irene had made with rabbits Lynx had caught, to eat for breakfast.

"We should get there today, even with a stop in town to buy clothes," said Wojciech. "The town is about nine miles from the village, and we should reach it by lunch. I suggest we eat, shop, and then push on at best pace to reach our new home before dark. I don't really want to be riding up a mountain in the dark."

Their clothing saw most people happy to give way to them, and Wojciech had a brief and spirited exchange with a guard at the town gate who was suspicious of szlachta travelling with so few servants. Wojciech overawed him with beautiful and courtly Latin. He was also speaking to Irene in Latin much of the time to improve her knowledge of the language; any of the szlachta would have some knowledge of the official language.

Irene had to confess to herself that she was exhausted by the time they turned into the broad, U-shaped valley, riding past the tiny village clinging to its walls on the shores of a silvery lake. Wojciech had pushed them all relentlessly over the last few days.

"And now we dismount to lead the horses," said Wojciech. "We are going up there." He pointed up towards where a waterfall spouted down into the valley.

Irene did not sigh.

Wojciech looked at her, and saw the intense fatigue.

"Thy weight on thy comedic beast is of no moment to him; stay in the saddle and I will lead thee."

She nodded weary acceptance, smiling at the endearment implicit in using the diminutive in Latin, hidden from Jan and Lynx. Jan had some Latin; Lynx only his own rough dialect.

The path was precipitate but Irene was too tired to worry about it. Her trust resided in Wojciech.

Irene awoke as Wojciech lifted her off Jester and carried her as effortlessly as if she was a baby. She came to, aware of the warmth from the house they entered as it poured over her. She raised her head.

"Thank God," said Wojciech. "I feared you were succumbing to the cold, and had the sleep of the frozen, but all I could think of to do was to hurry you in."

"I think the cold did not help," said Irene, shaking her head. "But it is mostly fatigue."

Wojciech lowered her to her feet, keeping a hold of her arms until he was certain she could stand. Irene nodded, smiling, resisting the urge to cling to him.

"Wojciech, my lord! Who is this youth? Is he hurt?"

A young man about Wojciech's age had hurried up, his straw-coloured thatch and firm features reminding Irene of a younger edition of Jan. That he wore the kontusz of a szlachcic, albeit plain, explained much about the apparent ambiguity of Jan's position in the household.

Wojciech embraced the young man warmly.

"Jaromar! I am glad to see you; I've missed you. This is ... dear me, it's a long story. Officially this is Walenty, our little brother. Actually, meet the Lady Irenka Trąbkówna, and do not be fooled into thinking her a weakling, she has not had the opportunity to build up the stamina for a long ride that a boy her age would manage. I've been pushing fifty miles a day for three days."

"Wojciech! Over this terrain, my lord? You mad creature, I wouldn't last it out, never mind a lady!" cried Jaromar.

"Walenty is hardy," said Wojciech, turning to her to smile.

The compliment made up for all the discomfort.

Jaromar shook his head.

"Only you, my brother-by-choice, could drag a girl up hill and down dale at this time of year, and be proud of how hardy she is, instead of praising her beauty, grace and so on."

"Why, you can see she is beautiful; I do not have to mention it," said Wojciech. "Aye, she is graceful though, you should have seen her roll under the belly of her horse and come up in one movement to take down the fellow who was firing at her!"

Jaromar looked doubtfully at Irene.

"Wojciech is remembering seeing me clean," said Irene. "When I look less of a disreputable object. My sword arm is not strong enough yet, though."

"That we will remedy," said Wojciech. "I want to be assured that you can protect yourself properly, my ... Walenty."

"The only thing I wish to protect is a hot bath. If that is possible," said Irene.

"Of course, my lady," said Jaromar. "But there are no women here to help you to bathe! Or to dress!

"Jaromar, if I may call my new brother thus, I am capable of bathing myself. But to have hot water brought to a chamber would be pleasant."

"Of course; it will take half an hour," said Jaromar. "I will see to that ... you do not know the house, my lord, I must show you ..."

"Order the water and have it placed in a chamber downstairs which might be private, and when Walenty has soaked, I will make use of the water with an added kettle to reheat it," said Wojciech. "And when you have ordered the water, you can show us which chambers will be ours. Lynx is my lady's man, so place him near her."

"I cannot get used to you mixing genders like that," grumbled Jaromar. "Is not my lady to be my lady here in private?"

"No, my friend, she will remain as my little brother Walenty; there are reasons," said Wojciech.

Jaromar regarded him for a long moment.

"I see," he said, nodding. "Then if Walenty understands that, and is happy, *he* should always be addressed in the masculine, lest you make a mistake with the wrong declension in front of others."

"I knew you'd understand," said Wojciech, warmly.

"I understand that you have an excess of nobility, you idiot," said Jaromar.

Irene did not soak as long as she might have hoped, as she wanted Wojciech to have some warm water. She pulled on a night gown and a kontusz they had bought in town, and thick fur slippers. She had washed out the last of the dye from her hair, and was back to her normal shade of strawberry blonde, glad to have short enough hair that it would dry.

Jaromar raised an eyebrow when she hesitated in the big hall.

"Well, Walenty is a handsome youth," he said. "I have mulled wine; will you tell me what my lord has been up to? He's an indifferent letter writer save for detailed demands of what he needs."

Irene gladly sat by the roaring fire to tell Jaromar all of their adventures, and how she had come looking for the big bohatyr, and had been helped by Lynx.

"And I am glad that he took in good part the precautions I set up to catch any man who wished to molest me," she said. "Lynx is a good man."

"Any decent man would," said Jaromar. "You are not the sort of idiot who has thrown herself at Wojciech's head before, and no, I was not implying you were throwing yourself at him. You know he will be hard on you in training, as he is hard on all of those for whom he has affection? It is his way of showing love to make those about him as good as they can be."

"I see why he loves you so dearly, Jaromar; you understand him as well as your father does," said Irene.

A good night's sleep made all the difference, and Irene breakfasted happily on bread and butter, cheese, sausage, eggs and pancakes, washed down with coffee.

"Walenty's a healthy young animal," said Wojciech, ruffling her hair as he sat down to join her.

"I have been too tired to eat properly," said Irene.

"Well, you will need to eat well to build some muscle and to cope with exercise," said Wojciech.

"Aren't you going to give the poor ... lad ... a day or two off?" asked Jaromar.

"Certainly not; sh – he'll stiffen up," said Wojciech. "I will go easy though, and I need to sort her out some armour. And wings."

"Him some armour," said Irene. "Not her."

"Sorry," said Wojciech.

"It's official; you have been bitten by a rabid dog and are run mad," said Jaromar. "Why, you never even considered teaching me to be a winged hussar!"

"You couldn't handle it," said Wojciech. "It would make you ill with worry over having to kill, and I love and respect you too well to force that on my gentle brother. You serve in other ways, and I do not disparage a man for being unwilling to fight. I, however, have had a first-hand account of Walenty on a broken down old horse, and fake wings making a diversionary attack run, admittedly the glimpse your father got was through smoke, but he told me he could believe it was an angel of death swooping down for the kill, and he doesn't pass out compliments readily. He did used to ride with my father before he was wounded, so he knows what he is looking for."

"My goodness!" said Jaromar, mildly. "Walenty, you are full of surprises."

Irene blushed.

"When Jester and I set off it just felt so right," she said. "I don't know how to use a lance, but for a mad moment I wished I had one, rather than rolling off Jester to make them fire the cannon."

"You set that child up as bait?" yelled Jaromar.

"I was almost certain the cannon would blow up," said Wojciech. "And I knew she could get out of the way. I was prepared to sacrifice a horse for the lives of a dozen innocents."

"I was never in any danger," said Irene. "I would like armour, though."

"You shall have it; and you can practice tilting at a ring. When you have a bit more practise we will go after wild boar."

"That will make a nice change for the table," said Jaromar, who had cooled down. "There is bear around here too; bear bacon would be nice."

"We will see what we find," said Wojciech.

"Walenty, you can always sweet-talk Jaromar by appealing to his stomach."

They all laughed.

In the armoury, Wojciech nodded to Irene.

"Strip," he said.

"I ... did you say 'strip'?" said Irene.

"Of course; how else can we find a padded undershirt that will fit you without rubbing?" said Wojciech. "Only to your shift, of course."

"Yes, my lord," said Irene. She wanted armour; it was easier to just pretend she really was a boy.

Wojciech frowned at her corset.

"I'm surprised how agile you were in that thing," he said.

"I haven't been wearing it to ride, but it flattens ... things," said Irene, flushing.

"Come up with a garment which is only round your ... uh, chest," said Wojciech. "And we will postpone fitting you with armour until you have something which is suitable and comfortable. You must be able to be in the saddle in your armour for days, and I don't want to worry about you having sores which become infected from the dyes you sweat into them."

"There's a lot more to this than meets the eye," said Irene, hastily pulling clothes back on, as she noticed the dull red flush on the back of his neck as he politely turned away from her. The thought of him losing his iron control was something which made her feel nice all over; but he would hate it. "I am decent, Wojciech," she said.

He nodded and cleared his throat.

"Why don't we go and look at the colt?" he said. "Obviously he has had some basic training but now he is two we can put a saddle to him. You won't be able to ride him seriously for another year, but you and he should be used to each other. And you are light enough to do some saddle drills earlier than is otherwise recommended."

Chapter 12

"He's beautiful," said Irene. "You said I could name him?"

"Yes; he will be yours."

"Then ... Jesień, Autumn. Because you told me about him in autumn, and because he is a lovely russet autumnal colour."

"Jesień he shall be, then," said Wojciech.

"If he's used to the lunge rein, I could run round with him and leap onto and off his back without a saddle until he's used to the idea," said Irene.

"It could work," said Wojciech. "It's a lot of running."

"We'll have a lot of being cooped up."

"Good point. And he might as well get used to the idea of acrobatics from the word go. You may come off a few times."

Irene shrugged.

"I came off a few times when I was learning with a broken horse. My own horse was sired by a Lipizzaner horse; she had had some training though it took me a while to get her to perform anything like the airs above the ground of the Austrian school. And I know it wasn't anything like what they do."

"I'm impressed you managed at all," said Wojciech. "Maybe we will go and see your father after all; it seems a waste to leave her with someone as dull as tripe in oil."

"I do miss her," said Irene. "She'd make pretty foals with Ogień. Captain Zieliński encouraged us both to enjoy working together. He has been more of a father to me."

"Perhaps he will like to come with us," said Wojciech, blushing. "My own sire was a ... distant... parent. I think he closed in on himself when my mother died. Birthing Walenty ... Jan has always been the adult I ran to. And his son the same age as me, I am glad father permitted Jaromar to do lessons with me, it might have been a lonely childhood otherwise." His eyes twinkled. "And Jaromar the sensible one, to stop my crazier ideas," he added. "Mind you, the only time my father thrashed me seriously, rather than just put a slipper across my backside, was the time I persuaded Jaromar to come with me to scale the outside of the laundry chimney to get down a crow's nest. I was thrashed for unnecessarily risking the life of a dependent," he added.

"I see," said Irene. "And you might have got off easier if you had gone on your own?"

"Possibly; I appreciated by the time I had endured the thoroughgoing verbal excoriation which followed the thrashing – and I was made to sit through it to drive the message home – that I had terrified him out of ten years of his life. But you know what? I was glad I had done it, because he then gave me one of the few embraces I ever remember him giving, and that made the thrashing as nothing." He gave a wry smile. "And then I cried all over him, having managed to take my punishment stoically. He tried to be closer after that, but it was hard for him. His next embrace was a farewell to me when I went off as an ensign to Seweryn's father, my Godfather. It was the first time Seweryn and I had spent much time together, having visited each other regularly, but not for long periods."

Irene slid her hand into his.

He squeezed it, and looked down at her, his eyes soft, more like mist on the mountains than the grey steel they could be. Irene's heart hammered in her chest and she found herself moving towards him.

The colt, feeling neglected, pushed his head between them with a demanding nicker.

Wojciech laughed.

"Well that's an effective chaperone," he said, ruefully. "We will definitely visit your father."

"I don't know what he might say," said Irene. "His idea for me was to marry some baron; Płodziewicz was the name, I believe."

Wojciech stared and then he threw back his head and laughed. Then he said,

"Oh, Irenka, that is so funny."

"Why?" asked Irene, confused.

"Because that's me; or it was before I faked my own death."

"No! Really?" Irene had to laugh too.

"I'd have avoided meeting you, you know; I hated being one of the year's most eligible bachelors, and I would have been prejudiced."

"It's as well, then, that we met so unconventionally," said Irene. "I ... would probably have gone along with his plans, and tried to look more conventional than I am, consequently boring you and confirming your prejudices, because it was better than my uncle's plans for me."

"Which were?"

"Making me mistress to the king and getting a better position through it."

Wojciech's expression hardened.

"No wonder you ran. I am going to kill him if I ever see him again."

"You say the nicest things," said Irene, with a satisfied sigh.

"And you won't like me saying that I am going to move firmly back to talking to Walenty," said Wojciech.

"No; but I accept it, and understand," said Irene.

Irene spent some time sewing a quilted garment to contain, flatten and support her bosom; it was harder than it looked, but she finally managed something which was comfortable all day over her shift. She got round the problem of keeping it short, so she could easily bend at the waist, by using wide straps. On a supporting band with fabric gathered into it, she could control the degree of flattening with lacing.

It was a lot more comfortable than her stays, and if scarfs over low-necked gowns remained in fashion, she might even be able to wear it with female clothes, as her waist was already slender. Now she had one which worked, Irene set about copying it, and murmured to Wojciech, with a blush,

"I believe I am ready for armour now."

Wojciech was very professional and impersonal about fitting Irene with armour. It was easier once she had her padded jacket, which would go over a żupan, but needed to be fitted to her figure first. Irene needed to make one or two alterations before she could start adding other armour, but that was no problem. Irene was an adequate needlewoman if not an enthusiastic embroideress.

It was exciting to put on the well-jointed armour and helmet, the wings attached to her back.

"You need to get used to wearing it, and moving in it; and Jesień needs to get used to you wearing it around him," said Wojciech. "You will put it on every morning to feed him, and wear it for some of his exercise."

Irene nodded; it made sense. If Jesień could get used to her wearing strange armour and clattering wings at the same time he was getting used to her weight touching his back, he would just accept all the strangeness as one.

Snow had fallen a few times; the land was not gripped by the depths of winter but it was certainly cold. Exercising was a way to keep warm, and Irene was enthusiastic. Jaromir's man, Jerzy Fiszer was easily able to go down to the village at need, though the house was well-stocked for the winter. And Wojciech declared that it was time to take Irene out to take down some wild boar.

"They are a nuisance in winter in any case, and not easy to kill without a boar spear – or a hussar's lance," said Wojciech. "Wild boar are too stupid to know when they are dead, and it's only the angle of being on horseback and the likelihood of the lance breaking off anyway which stops them from walking up a spear through their body to take the human wielding it with them. A boar-spear has a cross-piece to stop that, when hunting them traditionally on foot. But we will combine hunting for game, doing our duty to the village by culling dangerous beasts with using your lance in a real situation."

Irene nodded, a little scared, a little excited. She made sure the leather, cup-shaped *tok* or lance-shoe was firmly attached to her pommel, to rest the butt of her lance in. It made handling the outrageously long lance much easier, both in the upright position, and set to charge. The exercise was to practise moving from at rest to charge as well as using the lance, and Irene felt wonderful as she trotted on Jester behind Wojciech on Ogień down the steep path to the main valley. The whole village had turned out to watch, and a ragged cheer went up to see their own winged hussars.

"They will tell their grandchildren of this, that they witnessed some of the last winged hussars in action," said Wojciech. "They have welcomed us here, we shall give them a good display; and share our kill with them too. Jerzy found out that there is a large group of wild pigs in the forest upstream, which have already started coming as far as the village at night to forage. Wild pigs will not scruple to take a child to eat if they are hungry. The boars tend to live a solitary life save in autumn and winter, when they join up with the females and piglings to mate and, I suppose, for mutual protection in a time of short food. There are two particularly dangerous boars, but culling any boar must help. I hoped we might take out the big ones, and Jaromar can deal with smaller ones as peasants may not hunt boar. We will head for where the females and youngsters have been seen most; the boars will protect them."

Irene nodded. She took a firm grip on her lance with her fur-lined glove.

Frosty bracken crackled under the hoofs of the two horses, and the horses' hot breath made clouds of steam. Their own breath came out behind their face guards and visors, condensation forming and dripping, occasionally missing the scarves Wojciech insisted they both wore. Irene was glad he had insisted on it; when the cold drip hit her face or neck it was most unpleasant, and she resolved to tuck her scarf higher next time. It would, however, have been worse dripping down inside her żupan.

"Knee to knee, now; sabre on sword knot," said Wojciech quietly. Irene copied his actions of drawing her sword to let it hang on the knot, standard practise to make it easier to grab the sabre once the lance was shattered. They closed up so their knees almost touched. For a ride out for pleasure, it would have been a heady business to be so close; but this was for safety and a drill both at the same time.

A rustle ahead in the undergrowth, and Wojciech gave the order,

"Drop lances!"

Irene's lance swung down in her hand, the iron tip helping to bring it down, the tok acting as a secondary fulcrum to assist the hand in keeping the unwieldy lance under control. It seemed a natural and easy action now, and Irene marvelled at how it had become so, how one day she had gone from being more of a danger to herself and Wojciech in flailing wildly with it to the smooth professional change of position. Wojciech had all but jumped up and down for glee and Irene had half wondered and hoped that he might kiss her; but he had got himself under control.

Now that smooth precision might save her life. Jester began to prance.

She swallowed hard as the rustle in the bushes burst out in the ugly form of a wild boar. Crouching low, she dug a heel into the big roan's flank and he responded with enthusiasm.

The low, dangerous grunting of a second boar heralded the arrival of another; but that was Wojciech's responsibility. Irene left him to deal with the left hand side as she dealt with the right, all her concentration on the tip of her lance, levelled at the infuriated boar, starting its own charge. Everything seemed to be happening in slow motion, and Irene had time to consider how much the boar reminded her of her Uncle Władimir, and to reflect that the Polish idiom, 'you have flies in your nose' to denote someone always angry suited him very well. And then the tip of the lance impacted with the boar's open and snarling mouth, and it squealed once, horribly. The force of the impact drove the lance tip right through the angry brain, the whole animal knocked back, breaking the lance at the iron tip as it tumbled end over end.

And then Jester was slowing, stopped, waiting for further instruction; and Irene's ears were ringing and she felt giddy. Another boar was squealing. And then the pain hit her.

"Ooowww," she groaned, dropping the lance and cradling her arm to her chest.

"My love! Are you hurt?" Wojciech was waiting for his own boar to finish thrashing.

"No," said Irene, tempted to say 'yes' and submit to an embrace and tender ministrations. "Jarred my arm. All is working."

"Pain is where?" asked Wojciech, not taking his eyes off his pig.

"Upper arm. Not collar bone," said Irene. She had endured a scolding in training for holding her lance in such a way that it was likely that impact would break her collarbone.

"You know what to do."

"Yes, my lord," she said, shaking her arm to loosen where the protesting muscles had tightened.

It hurt.

It would go off.

And then Wojciech was off his horse to inspect the carcases.

"You aimed for the head?"

"No, my lord; I aimed for the chest," said Irene.

He laughed.

"Better than going too high and missing in going for the head," he said. "I fancy that's almost made salceson of it already."

Irene managed a smile at the idea of her blow turning the boar's head into head cheese, also known as brawn.

"Yours took a while to die," she said.

"Yes, the nasty creature decided at the last minute to turn aside and go to assist his friend," said Wojciech. "By which time I had committed, and the spear went through him transversely. I am sorry not to get a clean kill, and he was still running about when I tried to finish him with my sword. But even those used to the hunt make poor kills at times! And here are the villagers come to take the carcases back."

Irene did not know what bargain Wojciech had made over what part of the boars the villagers should have, but it did not matter; she would be glad to return home.

They had ridden into the village with their kills when a horseman coming up the valley might also be seen.

"Why, I believe ... yes, it is Seweryn!" said Wojciech. "I wonder what he wants,"

Chapter 13

The two winged hussars waited for the Ulan commander and his personal servant to ride up.

"Boar hunt, Wojciech?" said Seweryn.

"It's as good a way as any to concentrate the boy's mind on how to use his lance," said Wojciech.

"It may have escaped your notice, but the lad can't joint a poczet as there are no more winged hussars," said Seweryn.

"Well, only two," said Wojciech. "You could make it three if you wanted. I've a spare set or two of wings and armour."

"No, thanks; I've left military endeavour behind," said Seweryn. "Or rather, I found I could not stand the paperwork and politicking of running a province. I've put the place substantially to rights, at least working towards it, and appointed a Wójt to do the paperwork and sent in my resignation. Give me a few hundred enemies and a company to lead and I am happy. Put paperwork in front of me and I become a snivelling coward."

"The offer stands; fight against the unrighteous," said Wojciech.

"I don't want to be officially dead and I don't want a price on my head for standing on the wrong toes," said Seweryn. "I came to spend winter with you and then I am back to my own lands to settle down. I might even get married."

"You'll be bored in a year, unless you find an exceptional woman," said Wojciech.

"Well, I'm not a cold fish like you; I like women," said Seweryn. "What, lad, hadn't you noticed that Wojciech is a perfect gentleman with women but never falls in love even a little bit?" he added as Irene looked astonished.

"I think, my lord, you mistake his air of reserve and iron will," said Irene, with some asperity.

Seweryn laughed.

"Maybe; and if you have seen him show passion, it's a relief that he's as human as the rest of us. You did mean it when you invited me to stay, Wojan old fellow?"

"Most certainly, my passionate friend," said Wojciech. "You can help me train the boy; another warrior's skills won't come amiss. You can come on hunts against anything which menaces my new villagers or not as you choose. I'm expecting both wolves and bandits as the year turns."

"Oh, that I'll join gladly. But not haring about the countryside with tents. I like my comforts."

"You've gone soft," said Wojciech.

"Well, I wonder how much the boy likes being dragged half way round the world at your usual insane pace?" said Seweryn, lifting an interrogative eyebrow at Irene.

"I am happy to follow my lord wherever he goes and at whatever pace he sets," said Irene. "But I don't know enough minecraft yet to go with him to lay siege to the king of Hell."

Seweryn laughed.

"I like you, boy; and you are realistic enough to recognise that Wojciech is quite likely to take it into his head to do something like that."

"We're on first name terms in my house," said Wojciech. "You can call the boy 'Walenty' and accept being 'Seweryn' from him as much as you do from Jan and Jaromar, or you can do the other thing."

"Jan's slippered my backside as well as yours; it does give him some right to look on me as part of the extended family," said Seweryn. "And you always were close to his son. Very well, the pipsqueak shall have use of my name. By the way, Wojciech, through the mouth of the boar? Showing off were you?"

"Oh, mine is the one that turned and had a poor kill," said Wojciech. "Walenty spitted his through the mouth."

"By accident," Irene admitted.

Seweryn laughed.

"Well, Walenty, I think more of you for admitting it was an accident than claiming you deliberately went for a risky aim.". He slapped Irene on the shoulder.

"So, why didn't you ask for something more active?" asked Wojciech, plying his guest with mead.

"Because I was a winged hussar and I am a szlachcic," said Seweryn.

"Run that by me again?" said Wojciech.

"The Ulans look down on those who transferred, because our tactics are different, though to be honest, having served under you for a while, your tactics are as crazy as theirs," said Seweryn. "But they make waves. And being essentially a Rotmistrz on active duty like a Porucznik unnerves people; they expect me to have the honour and glory of paying for my company but leaving the administration and fighting to someone else while I ponce about at court, using my position to get sinecures, gain entry to the opera after all the seats are sold, work my way through the dubious pulchritude of the wives of men who can be useful to me, and, worst of all, enter politics."

"I thought you liked women?" said Irene, innocently.

"I do; but I like women who like me, not those who will sleep with me to make sure of a good alliance for their husbands," said Seweryn.

"Picky, then," said Irene.

"Is your brat teasing me?" asked Seweryn.

Wojciech smiled.

"My brat dislikes having me criticised. I think that

was revenge."

"Oh, ho, I apologise for criticising my old friend to his new puppy," said Seweryn.

"You can, perhaps, insult him, as Jaromar does, from love," said Irene. "But I think it was a wrongful assessment of his character to call him cold. He is good, I think, at hiding his emotions."

"Perhaps you are right; he is very good at hiding them," said Seweryn.

Irene kept her smile hidden.

Had he not called her his love, when he feared she was hurt?

"How is the cramp?" asked Wojciech, plainly remembering that moment as clearly as she did.

"Much better, my lord," said Irene. "I do apologise for crying out; I was taken by surprise."

"Cramps take one that way," said Wojciech. "It will teach you to relax at the moment of impact another time."

"Yes," said Irene. "Pain is a good teacher when the pupil is able to absorb the lesson."

"Wojciech's a hard taskmaster," said Seweryn, "But you will learn more from him than any other if you can handle his regimen."

"I can handle it," said Irene, serenely.

Seweryn joined Irene and Wojciech to watch the training in the morning; they were using wooden swords heavier than the sabre, so that by comparison it was light to use. Seweryn plainly knew how Wojciech ran drills, as he turned up in armour with a practise sword taken from the armoury. He watched for a while.

"Let me fight Walenty," he said. "You can see more clearly what needs training and it won't do him any harm to fight another's style. He's gaining your style."

"The lad had only been taught foil," said Wojciech. "It would help to look from outside."

"Poor old man, do you need a rest?" said Irene.

"Less of your cheek, whelp," said Wojciech, cheerfully, ruffling her tousled hair where she had taken off her helmet. "No holds barred, Seweryn; if we are fighting bandits they will fight dirty."

"Why do I have a feeling this might end up with me regretting it?" said Seweryn.

"You might; you might not. The lad doesn't have the upper body strength yet to grab a kicking foot to make a throw, but we're working on it," said Wojciech. "And you learned a few tricks, as well, didn't you, Walenty?"

"A few," said Irene. "I learned not to be afraid to shove a thumb in the eye of someone trying to do me harm if I had no other weapon, and teeth count as cutlery."

"Good grief!" said Seweryn. "Very well, child, *en guarde!*"

He pressed her with the sword first; Irene was already somewhat tired from Wojciech's drills, despite teasing him, but had had a chance to catch her breath a little. The lack of strength in her arms was still her undoing, and as her arm dropped, Seweryn, as Wojciech did, punished that drop by hitting her lightly armoured arm.

Aiming to hook her foot out from underneath her was something Irene could deal with better, and she jumped lightly out of the way.

"Not bad; still got some beans in you," said Seweryn. He feinted with the sword and as she tried to get her own sword up to parry he aimed a kick towards her groin. Irene leaped high to avoid it, and kicked out, kicking him hard in his right hand, making it fly open so he dropped the sword.

"There aren't many boys who can avoid that attack without panicking," said Seweryn, rubbing his hand. "Deliberately aimed kick?"

"Yes, my lord," said Irene, blushing. "If I only had toes to curl about the hilt, I swear I could fight better with my feet. My arms need strengthening."

"Hmm," said Seweryn.

"Wojciech has me throwing lances for him to catch," said Irene. "It strengthens me, and is a tactic to use at need if a line needs breaking. Because we can't really take artillery, and Jan doesn't count."

"Your whelp really is cheeky," said Seweryn, equably.

"I prefer Walenty that way," said Wojciech.

"It shows spirit," said Seweryn. "What, not another session? The boy is all in," he added as Wojciech picked up his sword again.

"And that will get him killed if he cannot find reserves. Walenty! *En guarde!*"

Irene got tired arms up, and swung first, and kicked out at Wojciech's shin.

"And now we are finished for the day," said Wojciech. "Well done. You could not have done that when we started."

"I will not let you down, I am determined," said Irene. "*Jestem determinowana.*"

Seweryn turned suddenly and stared at her. Irene was too tired to notice.

Irene made her way to what had been designated the bath room, to wash off the sweat, and dress in ordinary clothes.

"Wojan," said Seweryn, levelly, "What do you know about this Walenty, who shares your dead brother's name?"

"I know enough," said Wojciech, tranquilly. "Yes, it's a pseudonym. And as I have adopted the whelp I volunteered Walenty's name. My brother Walenty would be almost twenty if he had lived, a few years older than my ensign Walenty, who is seventeen. I know it's a little old to be starting, but Walenty has more riding skills than I had at seventeen."

"Hasn't it occurred to you that a lad of seventeen should have something of a moustache? And not look so smooth-faced and rounded? I thought ... Walenty... was a lad of fourteen or fifteen when I was first introduced."

"You can think?" said Wojciech with cheerful rudeness. "That's news to me. I always thought that Ulan horses had more brains than their riders, since you switched to them."

"Unfortunately I fear with some you'd be correct, and it's another reason I am dissatisfied," said Seweryn. "Wojan, you are changing the subject."

"Yes; I don't want to discuss Walenty. It's none of my business to do so," said Wojciech. "So go stuff yourself with hay."

When they went to dinner, Seweryn held a chair for Irene, who looked startled.

"What, Seweryn, did you think me so feeble?" she asked.

"Anything but; but you were exhausted," said Seweryn. "I thought you did extraordinarily well."

"Wojciech says I am doing adequately," said Irene.

"Only adequately?" Seweryn raised an eyebrow.

Irene chuckled.

"And I thought you had known him since you were children?" she said. "He praises his underlings for success more than he berates them for failure; and treats social equals under his command with very sparing praise. Anything more effusive than a grunt and a nod is high praise."

"I suppose so," said Seweryn. "Do you not feel you deserve more?"

"I feel I deserve to be made as good as I can be," said Irene. "Wojciech will see that happen. Wojan?"

"It's what his father used to call him, and I picked it up," said Seweryn. "A family tradition to pick that pet name over others I believe."

"Indeed," agreed Wojciech. "I told Seweryn he was not allowed to use it until he had known me ten years, and he asked how long my father had known me before he used it. I had to capitulate."

Irene chuckled.

Seweryn had by now sat down.

"Can I help you to any of this wild boar?" he asked Irene.

Irene regarded him thoughtfully.

"I think I am not an invalid," she said.

"What's got into you, Sewek?" asked Wojciech.

"I am noted for my beautiful manners," said Seweryn.

"Really? Someone neglected to tell me," said Wojciech. "Leave the lad alone; you're embarrassing him."

Seweryn gave Wojciech a long, hard look, but addressed himself to the meal.

Seweryn remained seated for Irene to rise first, but Wojciech got up immediately, and as they exited the hall he pulled her into the room he had designated his study and latched the door.

Irene looked up at him questioningly but trustingly.

"You were tired and said '*determinowana*' not '*determinowany*'," he said. "Most people would hear what they expected to hear; unfortunately, Seweryn is not most people. He probably won't let go."

"It's none of his business," said Irene.

"No, I know." The imp of mischief danced in his eyes. "He has not yet decided whether I know and am being stubborn over telling him, whether I know but am being stubborn over admitting it to myself, or whether I am stubbornly unaware of your sex. I see no reason to enlighten him."

"I note that 'stubborn' enters each of those possibilities," said Irene. "May I call you Wojan at times?"

"Only when I call you Irenka," said Wojciech.

"Oh, when you forget that I am Walenty, Wojan."

He growled deep in his throat, and Irene's heart raced at the look in his eyes. He gritted his teeth.

"Walenty..."

There was a knock at the door.

"Put me out of the window; if you lower me, it is not a long drop and I will go in the side, I will not be out long enough to be cold."

He hesitated a moment, then nodded. It was not cold enough that she would cool down immediately; she had fur lined boots on. He unlatched the window and lowered her by the wrists, pulling the window to after him.

The knock came again.

"I said, enter!" said Wojciech, sounding impatient, clearing his throat to cover the sound of undoing the latch.

Seweryn came in.

"Oh, I thought Walenty was here with you. I wanted to talk to the child."

"If you wish to apologise, I expect he went to the stables to talk to Jesień, his colt," said Wojciech.

Seweryn hesitated.

"Wojciech, what do you know about Walenty? And why do you think a pseudonym is needed?"

Wojciech regarded his friend levelly.

"Walenty ran away. I should have said that being related to Wojewoda Władimir Trąbka was as good a reason to want a pseudonym as any, wouldn't you?"

"Oh! Yes, I can see why you would be ready to accept such a runaway. And does that mean you do not know ..."

"Do not know what?" Wojciech's face was full of innocent ignorance.

"Oh, devil take it!" said Seweryn, and slammed out.

"One should not enjoy his discomfort," murmured Wojciech to himself. "But just sometimes, Seweryn can be too sure of himself to be comfortable to live with."

Chapter 14

Seweryn ran Irene to earth in the stables, where Wojciech surmised she might go. She was scratching behind Jesień's ears, and then going to Jester to do the same to him.

"The colt; is he Ogień's get, do you know?" asked Seweryn.

"Yes, and Wojciech wants Jester – Błazen – to cover Pochodnia, the mare," she said. "We think he was once a drum horse, sold as a cart horse, which is too cruel."

"Poor old boy," said Seweryn. "I wager he doesn't mind, though, with a little thing like you on his back, eh?"

"He's an old fool, and he cavorts and prances as though dancing to music," said Irene, patting the old fool. "As soon as he thinks he's going into action he acts as though it is a high treat."

"Being properly appreciated is always good," said Seweryn.

"Indeed," agreed Irene, softly. "And he's thriving on it."

"Don't you like to feel appreciated?" said Seweryn.

"Why, yes; doesn't everyone?" said Irene.

"What's your real name?"

Irene regarded him thoughtfully.

"Are you making this an issue of trust?" she asked. "Wojciech knows my real name, my parentage, pedigree and background. I hope you trust him?"

"Of course I do. So ... he knows you are a girl?"

"Of course he does. Wojciech told me I made a gender slip when I was tired and that you noticed."

Seweryn stared.

"So ... all the time he has known ... and he has let me flounder on trying to drop hints to him?"

Irene laughed.

"If you had come out and said what you thought right away, we should not have played games," she said. "My father abducted my English mother in Russia; and he is the brother of the former Wojewoda. You now smite your brow and say 'Oh *that* Trąbka' like everyone else, and I wait for the same tedious questions about whether I am legitimate; yes, he married her."

"I see, my lady, why you would wish to keep your identity quiet; but why should you feel a need to dress as a boy? Especially now, if Wojciech knows who you are. And to let him subject you to the sort of training he would put a boy of your background through, who would be used to training for war?"

"Has it never occurred to you that I enjoy it? Well, of course there is discomfort, but that is true for the learning of any activity. And I learn a lot, so I get a lot out of the discomfort, which is more than I ever did out of sore fingers and a stiff neck learning to embroider. Wojciech wants to make sure that I am able enough to fight by his side without being the sort of liability an untrained girl would be."

"If you were a lad, I would understand that, but why would you want to fight by his side?"

"Why would I not want to do so?" countered Irene. "I want to stand with my lord."

"But you are a lovely woman; you could be feted, appreciated, courted by men who would want to give you anything you could want."

"Wojciech gives me everything I want," said Irene.

"But he does not know how to be warm, or to treat a woman as she should be treated," said Seweryn. "He ... I do not even know if he knows what 'tender' means."

"He understands it very well," said Irene. "You have seen the side of his love which protects by enabling me to be good enough to protect myself."

"But he is harsh, and he insists on calling you by a

boy's name!" Seweryn was confused.

"You don't have any idea how very passionate he is, do you?" said Irene. "A passion so strong he must keep it on a choke-chain and muzzled lest it burst forth howling and snarling to chew on his honour and his belief that he must treat me with respect. Do I care if he beds me unwed? No. But I respect that he does care, and I will not trample on his beliefs nor unchain the howling wolf of passion."

"I ... I would marry you right away," said Seweryn. "I offer you my name."

"Your name is not Wojciech," said Irene, simply. "And you could not marry me right away any more than he can; for he needs my father's permission or to wait until I am of age. You could probably get my father's permission, which is harder for someone who is officially dead, but then I should have to run away from you, which would be tedious."

"You wouldn't want to marry me?" Seweryn was taken aback. "I am wealthy, and have lands, and you would be clad in velvets and sable, silks and lynx fur and jewels; emeralds to match your eyes and diamonds. You would have servants and ... and anything you wanted."

"I want to ride beside Wojciech helping him right wrongs; to share his discomforts; to share his aspirations, his dreams, his eccentric sense of humour, his crazy quixotic urges; and when I might, to lie with him as well. I have a velvet kontusz lined with beaver, which is warmer than sable. In the summer I prefer linen for its lightness. What need have I for jewellery? I have my mother's jewellery to sell at need, and enough jewelled pins to fulfil the position as a szlachcic. What is the sparkle of a diamond next to the mischievous twinkle in Wojciech's eyes when he is teasing, what fur is as warm as the look in his eyes when I have pleased him? You cannot compete, my lord Seweryn. You would give me everything that a man expects a woman to want. Wojciech gives me everything I do want."

"You ... you are most unusual," said Seweryn. "A most unwomanly woman."

Irene laughed.

"You say so; and I have hurt your pride, but how often do you offer marriage?"

"I have never asked a woman to marry me before."

"Then part of you, deep down, understands why Wojciech loves me for being me, and not for being some overbred clothes-horse," said Irene.

"Bravo, Irenka," said Wojciech, coming in.

"How long have you been listening, my Godbrother?" asked Seweryn.

"Since you arrived; I wanted to be on hand in case Irenka got upset, but she is a match for you," he went over to Irene. "A howling wolf, chained; you put it very well. And thank you for understanding.". He took her hands and moved back the top of her gloves to press a kiss on each wrist.

"Do not try my resolve to behave, my lord," said Irene. "Walenty must come to the fore."

"Aye, you are right,", said Wojciech.

Seweryn blinked.

The air fairly crackled with the tension and passion between them.

"My apologies," he said. "I rather think I have missed seeing the passionate side of my friend. I feel very foolish now."

"I keep myself in check," said Wojciech. "And I confess, this is the first time I have felt like this."

"Why not just find a priest and lie about her age?" said Seweryn.

"I couldn't lie to a priest, it would be like lying to God!" said Wojciech.

Seweryn gave up.

"One thing, my lady," he said. "If anything happens,

God forbid, to Wojciech, will you place yourself under my protection?"

Irene regarded him.

"An easy enough thing to promise," she said. "For if Wojciech died, I would likely be dead too, or would die carrying out whatever mission he had started which killed him. But I would that you would accept Lynx, Jan and Jaromar into your protection."

"Willingly," said Seweryn.

Jan ran into the stable.

"Trouble, my lord," he said. "A group of a dozen ruffians have turned up in the village and are demanding food, clothes, blankets, beer and girls."

"Get Seweryn the armour we know fits him and some extra wings, as well as ours," said Wojciech. "If you will join us in a ride down the mountainside, Sewek?"

"Willingly – for old times' sake," said Seweryn.

Irene was already saddling Jester, and it was in short order that all three were arrayed for battle.

"Walenty between us?" asked Seweryn.

"Yes, but concentrate on your own side and do not underestimate her," said Wojciech. "She's good. Don't show her disrespect."

Seweryn nodded.

For Wojciech to describe someone as good meant they were good. He was not a man to let partiality stand in the way of his judgement.

The winged hussars made their way down the mountain side. The ruffians had seen them coming, but had failed to make out the wings at a distance and in mist and had drawn themselves up to deal with whatever pitiful mounted defence this isolated village might put up. The country house had been empty for many years, and the bandits expected nothing more than a few mounted herdsmen making a show of trying to drive them off, or perhaps some upstart who barely counted as szlachta and a couple of his men.

It was something of a shock to them once the horses of the winged hussars picked their way out of the mist to a gentler slope and began the first loping canter. Those with firearms loosed off their weapons, too ill-disciplined to wait until their adversaries were close enough to make it worth their while. And then, as they were beginning to realise just what their adversaries were, there would be no time to reload. The winged hussars were within charging distance!

"Close up knee to knee ... sabre on sword knots..." Wojciech took command and issued the orders. "Drop lances!"

Fifty strides to go, the lances dropped, and the horses moved smoothly into a gallop. Irene knew she was grinning like a loon; it was exhilarating, especially in formation with companions. It felt good to be part of Wojciech's poczet!

Winged hussars, even only three of them, unnerved the brigands somewhat; The motley horses of the brigands shied in terror at the sight of the wings, hissing in the wind and it was unnerving too to the superstitious brigands, who had never seen winged hussars in their lives, and had only ever heard stories.

They were about to become unwilling victims of the stories of the village.

It was the machine-like lowering of the lances as if done by a single hand which really made them falter. Wojciech had made Irene practice it; and Seweryn was an old hand used to working with Wojciech.

At the sound of the hussars singing 'Bogurodzica', 'Mother of Poland', some of the brigands tried to break and run, but it was too late, and there was no more room to manoeuvre. The peasants had dragged a cart behind them while they were watching the winged hussars arriving.

The lances of the three crashed into the front rank of the brigands. Bunched up as they were, it was almost inevitable that the lances carried on to at least wound one of the men behind. Irene's lance went through the centre of the chest of the one at whom she had aimed, and his eyes widened and blood came from his mouth like some terrible vomit. He was already falling from his horse as the man behind him screamed, and was pulled off his own horse, joined to his former comrade by the spear point now embedded in his arm. Irene swallowed. She regretted the necessity to kill, but was angry enough that these villains had threatened the people of her new home. She dropped the now-useless lance, glad that the village carpenter was making more. She felt for the hilt of her sabre, and found it immediately with the ease of practice. The hours of drill paid off, bloodless battle like the Romans, the end result a fighting style which was little more than a bloody drill. And the steel sabre was light by comparison to the wooden practice sword. Irene swung her sword with efficiency and grim determination. She scarcely registered that she was beside one of the brigands who was wounded, but not dead; and that he was swinging a sword at her back. Wojciech stood in his stirrups with a bellow of rage, and brought his sword down on the brigand's head, before turning immediately back to the fellow he had been about to decapitate, who had tried to use the hussar's preoccupation to make good something of an escape. Wojciech merely stepped up onto Ogień's saddle and leaped on the fellow, who was trying to fight his way through the hasty barricade the villagers had erected behind the brigands. It was a short, ugly fight, and perhaps not fair to take out his fears for Irene on this one, but snapping the fellow's neck relieved Wojciech's feelings somewhat.

He got up and looked for more enemies, and was surprised to find that all the brigands were dead.

"I thank you, my son," said the priest, who looked a little shaken; the brigand had been attacking him.

"Father? He would harm a priest?"

The priest gave a shaky smile.

"In truth, I was helping to stop them crossing the barricade; this band has descended like wolves on the fold many times, and have made our village suffer as a result, leaving our girls bearing bastards, killing such of their menfolk who would protest, and stealing food sorely needed."

"If you have shortages, you will apply to me," said Wojciech. "As to the girls; I cannot ease their distress, but I can make sure that no others suffer the same from now on."

That some of the villagers were harrying the brigands from behind in support of their new lord, using bills and pitchforks meant that the battle had lasted sheer minutes.

Irene and Seweryn joined Wojciech in dismounting when all brigands were dead, and took off their helmets, kneeling, as he did.

"Let us all offer prayers for the souls of these sinners," said Wojciech. "For who knows by what straits they came to be brigands. Let us pray that their fate is not ours one day. Father, will you lead us in prayer?" he addressed the village priest, who hastily put down the mason's hammer he had been using to hit brigands over the head.

The priest prayed for the souls of the dead and for those who had needed to take life in the protection of all they held dear.

The hussars tended the wounds of the peasant defenders, offering praise for their stoic support.

"We are glad to have a lord who will fight for us,"

said the sołtys, the village mayor, who was the blacksmith, Jósek Kowalski.

He had accounted for two of the brigands and might have been heard to mutter that he felt his soul in no need for having done so, any more than he did when he poured away nightsoil.

It was apparently an on-going discussion between him and the priest.

Chapter 15

Winter's onset rolled on in earnest. Snow blanketed sound and became eventually deep enough to insulate, though frost forming on the top of the counterpanes overnight was common enough, and the windows were thickly rimed with frost flowers. Training helped to keep warm, but the three ember days in the run-up to Christmas were hard. They spent time praying rather than training and Wojciech observed the fasts, and Irene was not about to admit to how hard she found it. After a hard day of training on the Thursday, when she had been too tired to eat much, she was swaying on her feet by the middle of Friday.

Wojciech took one look at her and picked her up to lie her down on a chaise longue.

"Oh, I am so sorry, Wojan," said Irene.

"You're an idiot, Wojciech," said Seweryn. "You're letting the child fast when she is not only not of age but is busy developing muscle."

Wojciech paled and then reddened.

"I forgot how very young she is," he said. "Irenka! Why did you not say anything?"

"I did not want to let you down," said Irene.

"And I have let you down; I have failed one in my care, and that is a serious sin," said Wojciech.

"No; it's a culpable oversight," said Seweryn, sharply. "A sin would be if you did it deliberately. Now stop mentally flogging yourself and go find something for the child to eat."

"Yes, you are right," said Wojciech, hurrying off.

"Thank you; you are a good friend," said Irene.

"Wojciech has too tender a conscience at times," said Seweryn. "He needs to be reminded at times that people make mistakes, and the Good Lord forgives them for it. It's moping around indoors; it always takes him like this when there's very little action. What we need is to go on a wolf hunt or something, and persuade him that the village needs protection. I'll talk to Jan about it."

"Thank you," said Irene.

Being brought up essentially in the manner of the Church of England, despite having a Catholic chaplain in her father's house, she had never observed a fast before, nor the strict observance of fish days. Fish had been served on Fridays by the cook, but often enough her mother had ordered meat.

One had to be honest that her father did not observe the Church of Rome's culinary strictures very closely either; but that was less due to a difference in religious belief and more to do with his total impiety. At least he was not as inclined as her Uncle Władimir to use the name of the Lord only to swear.

"My lord, Jósek the mayor would like to talk to you about the problem with wolves," said Jan, later.

"Well, I shall be at his disposal of course," said Wojciech. "I will ride down tomorrow."

"I would like to come," said Irene.

"If you are sure you will be well enough recovered ..." said Wojciech, concerned.

"I feel much better already," said Irene. "Honestly, I do ... and it was not entirely because of fasting, for ... for a female manifestation has also made itself known."

"You mean the monthly courses?" said Seweryn.

"The what?" said Wojciech.

"Are you telling me, you idiot, that you are not aware that women bleed for several days once a month?" asked Seweryn. Irene was blushing.

"Bleed? Why? Where? What is wrong? Why did you not tell me?" Wojciech was panicking.

"It is normal, my lord," said Irene, cheeks glowing.

"Go away, Walenty, and I will explain the birds and the bees to my friend," said Seweryn.

Irene hastily left the room. Seweryn was inclined to be earthy enough when he forgot she was a girl, and she really did not want to listen to an explanation about the differences between men and women of the kind he usually probably gave to young officers under him.

Fifteen minutes into Seweryn's blunt explanation, Wojciech was blushing. Five minutes more and he was spluttering in horror.

"I ... why, it explains why there have been days she has been less able ... and a little irritable ... and ... why did she not say?"

"Because she adores the ground you walk on, you idiot, and doesn't want you to think her weak!" said Seweryn, exasperated.

"Well how am I to know if nobody tells me?" said Wojciech. "My father never warned me beyond pointing out that when a horse covers a mare, there will be a foal, and if I did not want foals or to sit opposite a mare for the rest of my life at breakfast I should be careful."

"Yes, well, I've heard better explanations," said Seweryn.

"Mares don't bleed from ... there ... once a month," said Wojciech, defensively.

"Well, no, but being animals they are without sin, and it's all part of the woes Eve put onto women, I think," said Seweryn. "You can't make a direct comparison; human women don't have hoofs either, and I wager if you put a bridle on your Irenka, she'd carve out your tripes."

"She'd have every right to do so. I ... good grief!"

"For goodness sake! Anyone would think you were still a virgin!" said Seweryn.

Wojciech went very red.

His friend sighed.

"I'm going to have to give you lessons in how to please a woman, aren't I?" he said.

"Perhaps that would be wise," said Wojciech, meekly.

When Irene returned, Wojciech took one look at her, and promptly burned red.

"Oh dear," said Irene. "What has Sewek been telling you which is that awful?"

"He ... I ... he gave me some advice for when we are married," said Wojciech.

"I was going to make it up as I went along," said Irene. "Please tell me he has not been telling you how to turn it into a drill and to advance lance and charge?"

"Er ... not quite," said Wojciech.

Irene knelt beside him and leaned against his knees.

"Nobody had to explain it to Ogień the first time, but he got there," she said. "I am sure we will manage to do so too. My mother explained the process to me, you know."

"You are so practical," said Wojciech.

"So is Seweryn, but he tends to overthink things," said Irene. "And you worry too much about things outside of military matters."

"Well, when we have your father's permission, I shall let you take the lead," said Wojciech.

"Of course, my lord," said Irene, smiling to herself. Wojciech was too masterful for that idea to last long, but if it made him feel better, she would agree with him.

The three hussars prepared to ride down to the village the next morning, Irene feeling much better, and moreover wanting to get out into the air. They did not armour themselves just to discuss a problem, and Irene tied a light veil over her face to combat the cold.

"Ah, woman enough to be vain and not want chapped cheeks," said Seweryn.

"Certainly, Seweryn; I can't grow a moustache to do the same job," said Irene. Wojciech laughed.

"Walenty has you there, and I could tell a story or two about how long you take over waxing it to its proper degree of aggressive glory."

Seweryn posed dramatically, with an outflung finger pointed at Wojciech.

"Insult a man's mistress, or his horse, or his tailor, but never insult his moustache!" he declared.

Wojciech laughed, entirely back to normal today.

"Well, I am at an unfair advantage, being clean-shaven."

"And very odd it looks with a kontusz, not the French garb of those surrounding the king," said Seweryn.

"It would look odder with the excuse for a moustache my family manages," said Wojciech. "I don't like whiskers; they are uncomfortable."

"How often do you have this argument?" asked Irene.

"Oh, every few months when we are reminded of it," laughed Seweryn.

They took a gentler, longer route down to the village, and consequently had ridden in amongst the buildings before realising that there was something of an altercation in progress in the market square. Two rough looking men were there, one of them holding a young girl with a sword to her throat, while the other harangued the fearful villagers. The szlachta dismounted quickly. They were to the side of the ruffians, having come in on the street which led up to the church, and the priest was hurrying along to join them, and to get to the crossing of streets which made the market square.

"And you can send for your precious szlachta and we'll take my brother's life out of their hides," the ruffian was saying.

"I am here, fellow, and you can let the girl go right now," said Wojciech, striding forward. The man turned, looked at all three, and gave a nasty smirk.

"Well now! I'm going to take away your little brother as payment for mine," said the brigand, bringing into view a lit candle and a grenade. He lit the fuse and hurled the grenade at Irene.

Wojciech picked her up bodily and threw her into the shallow ditch at the side of the road, throwing himself over her. Seweryn dived sideways, collecting the priest in one arm and dragging him with him.

There was an explosion, which Wojciech was surprised to consider was considerably less than that from the exploding cannon. He looked down into Irene's shocked face, and for a moment the world stood still.

"Danger, still," said Irene, certain that he planned to kiss her and terrified that he would be killed by the crazed ruffian if he did so. Wojciech nodded and rolled off her, drawing his sword as he did so.

Apparently Seweryn had been less pre-occupied by having saved the priest from the blast than Wojciech had been and had drawn a pistol and shot the man holding the girl, taking him in the head, before moving forward to dispatch the grenadier with his sword.

"Wojan, we are going to have to release some of this which is between us or we will start making mistakes," said Irene.

He ran his hand through his auburn curls, realised he had lost his cap and jammed it back on his head.

"We will talk about it at home," he said.

"My lord! Are you and your little brother unharmed?" asked the blacksmith.

"Aye; but that house is on fire from the blast," said Wojciech, suddenly noticing it. "A bucket gang, man!"

The blacksmith leaped into action, shouting for a bucket gang in a stentorian voice. Villagers ran to do his bidding, most people owning buckets, and the river being convenient. The three szlachta positioned themselves by the building without thinking, to take the most dangerous part of the fire-fighting, going into the building with buckets of water to dowse the dry wood.

A woman shrieked. "My baby! My baby is upstairs!

Wojciech did not hesitate; he dashed back into the burning house and ran upstairs.

Irene continued taking buckets, taking turns with Seweryn to dodge into the acrid smoke of the burning building to fight the flames. She tried not to think of how the hungry flames licked out of the window already, and were consuming the stairway up which Wojciech had run, sucked up into the trapdoor to the upper floor like a chimney.

"I don't understand; the blast was not great and passed right over us," she said to Seweryn as they waited for more water.

"It won't be the explosion as such," said Seweryn. "I've seen this before, when a candle or lamp has been blown over. The woman was careless."

"But it's not her baby's fault," said Irene, relieved to see Wojciech kick out an upstairs window. "Keep the chain going," she added, darting out of line for Wojciech to drop the infant to her. He climbed over the sill, dangled and dropped beside her.

"My baby!" the woman squealed, running over to snatch the child from Irene's arms.

"In future, woman, do not leave a burning candle to be blown or knocked over," said Irene, sternly. The woman covered her mouth with her hand, in horror. Irene added, "You should seek shelter with your child in the house of some relative or friend; the house will not be habitable." She returned to the bucket chain, not bothering to check if the woman went or not.

"As curt with foolish women as Wojciech, I see," chuckled Seweryn.

"I have no time for idiots," said Irene, shortly.

With the whole village mobilised, the flames were brought under control, and they might rest, the fire substantially out. It was getting dark by this time, but it was safe for the other buildings.

And then a wolf howled.

Chapter 16

"We do not have our lances," said Seweryn.

"Pitchforks," said Irene. "We don't have a tok to balance them either, but they won't be so long. We can use them as well as short spears."

"Pitchforks – bring us pitchforks!" called Seweryn to the villagers, as the three hurried back to their horses, waiting patiently in a shelter next to the church. They trotted out to their riders.

Irene leaped onto Jester, without even bothering with the stirrup to get up, Wojciech doing the same to Ogień. They settled their feet as they were already on the move, Irene holding out a hand and deftly catching a tossed pitchfork without even looking at it. Wojciech did the same, and the villagers cheered them. They loosed their swords, letting them swing on the knot.

"What is it Jan always says about flashy buggers?" muttered Seweryn, mounting more conventionally, and accepting the offered pitchfork.

Armed with weapons of reach, the trio of mounted warriors headed in the direction of the howls, Seweryn accepting a burning torch of pitch from blacksmith Jósek for extra light in the dark forest. The snow was less thick under the sharply-scented pine trees, and the horses' hoofs made a hollow drumming on the thick pine-needle carpet, sending word ahead of their approach.

The wolves were hungry, and they could smell fear in the air as well as the more frightening scent of fire. However, the thundering hoofs of enemies who smelled like prey and behaved like predators was not something they wanted to face. The wolves started to slink away into the shadows of the forest, yellow eyes reflecting malevolently in the torchlight, as they glanced backwards.

"It's not enough to just drive them off," called Wojciech. "They need to know not to come back. Pick your target, act singly. One kill each should be enough."

Irene hefted her pitchfork, weighing it in her hand, feeling how its weight was distributed; and then she hurled it, the way she had practised tossing lances to Wojciech. It spun in the air, and clumsy thing that it might be, the spinning gave it some stability, and it pinned a wolf to the ground, where the creature thrashed. Irene carried on at speed, seizing her sword and slashing open the wolf's throat as she passed by. Wojciech had copied her, and Seweryn had used his pitchfork more like a lance than a javelin to pin down a wolf and then finish it off with his sword.

"And as I'm supposed to be the Ulan, lighter and on a more manoeuvrable horse, that makes a mockery of the argument," he said.

"It's not entirely about the horse and the armour, it's also about the attitude you take to war with you, and the training you do to suit the attitude," said Wojciech. "I practised horse tricks; you did not keep up the practice. Walenty puts my efforts in the shade, but then she's eight years younger and a good number of pounds lighter."

"And in theory her horse the slowest and least manoeuvrable of all," said Seweryn.

"He enjoys himself," said Irene.

"He certainly does," said Seweryn. "And you make a good team."

"And, my love, you have earned a wolf-skin to wear over your armour," said Wojciech, proudly. "We will take them back to the village to be skinned and tanned; and they will hang the bodies on sticks near the forest to frighten the rest away."

The horses were made much of when they were back in their stables; horses do not like wolves at any time. Rubbed down and fed, the horses were happy, and the tired hussars might also go in.

"About that talk...." said Wojciech, nervously.

"When we have both washed the stink of fire and wolf off our skin and hair, in your study, my lord," said Irene.

"Why is it when thou call'st me lord, it is an endearment, as if thou hadst used my pet name, and yet even more so?" Wojciech lapsed into Latin.

Because I love thee, my lord, and to be thine is all I could wish," she replied.

Irene was waiting in the study, having dressed carefully in one of her gowns, choosing a dark red velvet, and a feminine kontusik over it of silvery silk lined with sable. She walked into Wojciech's arms and lifted her mouth to his.

He kissed her.

Irene melted against him, her heart hammering, her whole body an explosion of wonderful feelings. She reached up with one hand to bury her fingers in the collar-length curls at the back of his neck. The other arm she wrapped around his waist above the decorative kontusz sash, pulling him closer.

Wojciech felt Irene's mouth open under his, her lips surrendering to his. Tentatively, as he held her close with one arm, he touched her face, and let his fingers drift down the side of her body, careful not to touch anywhere too private. He almost leaped away as a shiver ran through her; but it was not a shudder of revulsion as he half feared, for she was arching her body to press closer to him. Oh, now that was embarrassing, his kontusz swept away from the sash at the waist and she must surely feel how she affected him ...

Miraculously to Wojciech, his beloved did not seem to mind his physical reaction, and moaned gently deep in her throat.

He lifted his mouth from hers, and growled his own feelings back. Lord, no wonder she called him a chained wolf. He pressed kisses on the pulse at her throat, and down to... she had a décolletage? He had scarce registered that she was dressed as a woman, seeing only her beloved face. Irene pressed against him, and Wojciech gave up the unequal struggle, and buried his face in her hair as his body betrayed him with its release.

He was going to have to change his clothes again.

"Irenka!" he gasped.

"Wojan ..."

"I ... my darling! You ... you are wonderful!"

"Oh, Wojciech! You make me feel so nice!"

He picked her up and sat himself down on the wide window seat, perching her on his lap.

"Rules; we must have rules," he said. "We must remain clad. I ... I want to touch you more …"

"I want to touch you more," said Irene. "Perhaps ... perhaps we might set aside half an hour in the evenings ... something to look forward to ... but no more ... Jan asked to interrupt?"

He nodded.

"Yes," he said. "I ... you were right. Not acknowledging it properly was driving me insane."

She dropped her head onto his chest, content to be in his arms. He tightened his hold about her, not wanting to ever let her go.

When Wojciech took himself later to the great hall where Seweryn was enjoying some mead, the blond hussar considered making a jocular comment in asking how his friend had enjoyed the girl; but he decided instead to hold his tongue.

If Wojciech had lost control to that extent he would be remorseful and would want to talk about it without being teased.

And it was not respectful to Irenka, either, Seweryn decided.

Wojciech smiled serenely on Seweryn and Jaromar, who was also in there.

"Do we have a well-tamed wolf then?" asked Seweryn.

"The howls are at least muzzled," said Wojciech. "You heard our conversation in the village?"

"So did the priest," said Seweryn. "I had to talk very fast and explain that you had rescued her from an evil uncle and intended to marry her and that she was dressed as a boy for her own protection. He blinked a few times as he assimilated that she rode into battle with us, murmured that at least she would not lose her beautiful soprano when singing 'Bogurodzica', and said that so far as he was concerned he would count you her guardian to give yourself permission to wed her. I said you were stiff necked to a fault and would feel it improper as her father lives and so do her English relations. But I said I would pass it on."

"He's an unusual priest, and a man of the people," said Wojciech.

"I like him," said Seweryn. "He asked if our, er, lady ward needed a maid, and I said that the chit probably wouldn't be able to find a maid enough to do."

"You're probably right at that," said Wojciech.

"Where is Walenty?" asked Seweryn.

"She went to bed," said Wojciech. "She was very tired, and I think she was embarrassed to face you after we had a serious talk."

"Good grief, Wojan, I hope you did more than talk," said Seweryn.

A dark flush spread up Wojciech's neck and face.

"We ... uh, did not just talk," he said.

"Thank goodness for that," said Seweryn. "You aren't such a hopeless case as I feared. I take it that all was amicable? You haven't fallen out or anything?" he added anxiously.

Wojciech's blush deepened, but he smiled.

"Perfectly amicable," he said.

Irene felt shy at breakfast, but Seweryn asked her how well the pitchfork had handled, being thrown, and she explained how she had twisted her wrist to throw it, imparting spin, which seemed to carry missiles straighter. It broke the ice, and Seweryn was keen to watch the throwing of lances as a tactic to provide more for a front runner who was good with a lance.

Wojciech too was pleased, being able to join in the conversation and work with Irene with no loss of the camaraderie between them, something he had feared losing.

The days went back to normal; with the addition of time alone in the evenings.

After that first, frenetic exchange of kisses, they could contain their feelings, and it could be enough just to half sit, half lie on the window-seat together, content with the physical contact. It made the nights they kissed sweeter and more poignant.

And then Christmas Eve was upon them, with the traditional carp for this vigil served with other traditional foods like barszcz with *uszka,* stuffed dumplings served at this holy time without meat.

"Where on earth did the carp come from?" asked Wojciech.

"There's an artificial fish pond," said Jaromar. "But the ones we're eating have been in the bath tub for the last couple of days, so just as well you haven't had any more adventures of a smelly nature, with fires or wolves."

"I wondered why we had a bowl and ewer to wash after training," said Irene. "I thought something had happened to the bath."

"It'll be there again from tomorrow," said Jaromar.

"Season's greetings, all; may God bless us all."

They exchanged greetings, solemnly, thoughts of the Holy Family prompted by the straw under the table, and the extra place set lest any were in need. There were twelve dishes to a Christmas feast, and eating them was taken seriously and in an unhurried way, sampling each.

Then they rode down to the village for midnight mass, and were greeted warmly by the villagers.

Seweryn smiled to himself on the way home to see that Wojciech and Irene rode knee to knee but not as soldiers, and holding hands. He had almost succumbed to the come-hither look of a buxom young widow, but had decided that even frustration brought on by promoting his friend's romance was not enough.

He had been spoiled for his normal choice of women by Irene.

Christmas passed, and the new year was upon them; and with it something of a brief thaw.

"I think I should be moving on," said Seweryn. "I have enjoyed myself prodigiously; and I have learned a lot about the hidden depths of my friend."

"We will both miss you," said Wojciech, "But you do have your own family and lands to see to."

"I could happily do without most of the family," said Seweryn.

"Really?" asked Irene.

"I love my mother dearly," said Seweryn. "I am very fond of my father. I could, however, be happy without eight younger sisters."

"Teach them to be younger brothers then," said Irene.

"Mother of God! I'd be crucified by my older sister if I tried!" said Seweryn.

"If you have eight younger and one older sister, I am not surprised you have a slightly jaundiced attitude towards women," said Irene. "But somewhere the right woman is waiting for you."

"Well, if you had had a sister..." laughed Seweryn. "Wojciech, may I share with my father that you are alive?"

Wojciech froze, considered, and then nodded.

"I have always respected your father," he said. "And he is my Godfather."

They watched Seweryn ride away.

"I hope he doesn't get caught in a snowstorm," said Irene.

"He moans about not being hardy but he's perfectly capable," said Wojciech. "And if he was caught out anywhere, he has a mattock and would dig in with his tent. And not scruple about sharing body heat with his manservant; he may be a more traditional szlachcic than I am with regards to proper behaviour with underlings, but he's not an idiot."

"Good," said Irene. "I did not think at first that I liked him; but I have learned to like him very much, like a brother."

"You almost made me jealous there," said Wojciech.

"And you have no need, not now or ever," said Irene.

"When spring comes we will seek out your father," said Wojciech.

Chapter 17

"I need to get you a betrothal token," said Wojciech. Irene smiled at him.

"You gave me that a long time ago," she said, pulling the chain around her neck out from under her clothes. "I had to tuck it inside my shift when you had me strip to fit me for armour, but I knew the moment I saw you that I was going to be yours. And then you left this." She displayed the half-feather which had fallen into the open carriage on the occasion of the first attempted hanging. She had pierced it to hang from a chain.

Wojciech gaped.

"I found out when I took my wings off that your uncle's shot cut one in half after you disrupted his aim," he said. "I had no idea what had happened to it, and ... you mean you have kept it all this time?"

"It was an omen," said Irene, simply. "A token that I had a hero to look up to, a man to cleave to. When I saw you in that tree, I looked into your eyes and was lost, tongue-tied as you were. I was much relieved you spoke in cultured tones, though," she added candidly. "I would have found it hard had you been a stable hand."

"I fell in love with you the first time we met too," said Wojciech. "It was one reason I was so tongue-tied; you took my breath away." He took her hand with the feather in it, marvelling that she had kept it. "I ... my love, let me have this made into jewellery after the fashion of hair jewellery for mourning, bent into a circle, the vanes intertwined to signify our lives intertwined. Held on a gold plate and protected with glass and a jewelled surround it will last forever. It will not last long as a feather, for it will become bedraggled."

"It is getting a little sad," said Irene. "Yes; and then

I can display it, and wear it in my cap or on my bosom."

Wojciech blushed at the word 'bosom' and went a trifle boss-eyed in efforts not to have his eyes drawn to that intoxicating place.

Irene flushed too.

"I am sorry," said Wojciech, hastily.

"Do not be sorry; I do not mind you looking on me in ... in such a way, as you have love in your eyes too," said Irene, going darker red.

"Who else has looked on you in such a way?" growled Wojciech.

She looked down.

"My uncle," she said.

"I'm going to carve out his tripes!"

"You say the nicest things!" said Irene. "My father at least remonstrated with him."

"So I should hope," said Wojciech.

Irene sighed in happiness that he could be so protective and yet still respect her ability to fight at his side and do her bit. The winter might feel long and cold and dark, but their love was like sunshine.

Wojciech also spent time teaching Irene how to play cards, playing Mariasz for tricks and points, and the gambling game Scherwentzel with Jaromar and Jan as extra players, for promissory notes of favours.

"I lose again; more mending to do for you, Jaromar!" said Irene cheerfully. "You know I'd do mending for you all anyway?"

"Yes, Walenty, as I'll happily clean your mother's jewels for you and my father will fix your leather. I think it adds a bit of fun to it though," said Jaromar.

"I was not happy with betting, but this is a good way round it," said Irene.

"They say the English will bet on anything," said Wojciech.

"They will," said Jaromar. "I've dealt with a few

Englishmen doing a grand tour searching places most of their countrymen do not go. They are all worse than infantrymen, and I swear, Wojciech, most of them are as crazy as you are."

"Seriously?" said Wojciech.

"Seriously," said Jaromar. "I have no doubt that the children you rear between you will either combine the natural English craziness with your own, or else they will be as dull as ditchwater and conventional."

"Here's to the crazy streak," said Irene, raising her glass. "I wouldn't know what to do with conventional children. Er ... does everyone know our business?"

Jaromar snorted.

"The pair of you are quite blatantly besotted with each other," he said.

"You are," said Jan. "I was only surprised it took Seweryn as long as it did for him to get it."

"Well! We will have to be more formal out of here," said Wojciech.

"And it will be still a little while before spring, when we leave," said Irene.

"Don't you want spring to come quickly so we can get married?" said Wojciech.

"Yes, but I am afraid of my father saying no," said Irene. "I know it's an irrational fear, so don't tell me what I already know, I ... it is just a foolish worry."

"You are concerned that since I no longer exist officially, and he cannot use me to forge contacts, that his former choice as your husband will not count?" said Wojciech.

"Something like that," said Irene.

"Wait, what?" spluttered Jaromar. "Your father wanted you to marry Wojciech and you still ran away – right into his arms?"

"Well, it wasn't that simple," said Irene. "For one thing, I had no idea that my magnificent bohatyr was the man my father meant, and for another, my uncle preferred to sell me to the king as his new mistress. And I knew, for all his protests, that my father would capitulate; because essentially my father is lazy. And I was afraid that he might capitulate too if my uncle decided to ... to break me in for the King, so I was more knowledgeable."

"I will cut his tripes out one snip at a time with your embroidery scissors," snarled Wojciech. "And then plait them into a rope to strangle him."

Irene leaned against him happily.

"I had no idea your uncle was so evil, Walenty," said Jaromar. "Little brother-sister, if you need it, I will help Wojciech to do it."

"That means a lot from a gentle soul like you," said Irene. "I was thinking of impaling him on my lance."

"As in battle, or after the Wallachian fashion?" asked Wojciech.

"Why, how do they do it there?" asked Irene.

"Lengthwise," said Wojciech.

Irene shuddered.

"I don't think I could," she said, candidly. "Even Uncle Władimir."

Spring came faster than Irene might have liked, for having to worry about her father; and they bade a warm farewell to Jaromir, and set off on the long ride east. The Trąbka estate lay in the easternmost part of the kingdom, the nearest town being Minsk.

"We will go through Lublin; we should find it easy enough find a jeweller to do the job there," said Wojciech. "We couldn't really be a lot further from your old home if we had chosen to be at the other end of the kingdom, but it doesn't matter."

"This is what you get for telling Jaromar to find somewhere out of the way where nobody is likely to visit," laughed Jan.

"It hurts that we cannot be Polish in those parts of

Poland taken by Austria; even as the Trąbka home is perilously close to what has been stolen by Russia," said Wojciech, bitterly. "Maybe I should have joined the rebellion; the great betrayal will give our country a piece at a time to our enemies."

"You said yourself that those who rebelled only hastened Russia's intervention," said Irene. "We cannot do anything about it; are you going to let the Russian Woman and her catamite, King Stanisław, ruin our happiness?"

Wojciech blinked.

"Did you just imply that she is more a man than our king?"

"Yes," said Irene.

"I don't say you're wrong," said Wojciech. "And yes, I know I am bitter over losing the winged hussars; and at having my country only permitted to make laws which Russia agrees, taking our autonomy; what's going to be disbanded next, the szlachta?"

"Hush, my love; nothing will ever stop you from being the last winged hussar," said Irene. "And nobody surely would ever consider doing without the nobility!"

It was a fine morning; birds were singing and the sun shone. Larks sang their liquid song from too high above to be seen, whilst wood pigeons crooned their preference for the Rococo style. The harsh call of a pheasant contrasted with the song of the warblers in the margins of the mere, and Irene's eyes were drawn to the intense flash of blue of a kingfisher, and in doing so saw a majestic crested grebe in the margins of the waterlands.

She sighed in delight.

"It is beautiful, isn't it?" said Wojciech.

"Good game in this mere," grunted Jan in satisfaction. "We've had plenty of duck, boar and deer."

"And Jaromir is quite capable of taking down deer

or boars, and all szlachta have equal rights so there will be no problem about that," said Wojciech. "God gave man dominion over animals and did not specify their rank. Gifting venison to the villagers in the worst times helped, I think, but they should be able to take such beasts themselves, protecting themselves from the depredations of deer to their crops, and protecting themselves from wild boar. Especially when they have no lord to do it for them."

"You won't find me disagreeing," said Jan.

"Nor me, my lord," said Lynx. "It's been a pleasure to serve you, I must say."

"You weren't leaving, were you?" asked Irene.

"My lady, I swore to your service, and I do not change my mind. Oh, you are thinking of how I put it? I meant it was a pleasant surprise, and I look forward to many more years."

Irene smiled at him; she owed much to the one-time sergeant. He worked well with Jan, and had only been a trifle put out to find that the older man was of noble birth, albeit a dependent of Wojciech.

"Step carefully once we get to roads which are more travelled," warned Wojciech, mostly for Irene's benefit. "There are places where the passage of heavy wheels start ruts which are washed away in melt water and spring floods, until an innocuous looking puddle turns out to be deep enough to swallow a mounted man, and no room in it for a horse to clamber out before both drown."

Irene shuddered.

"Travel is a dangerous business for the unwary," she said. "Poor roads, brigands, the chances of coaches falling over or horses being lamed in places a long way from succour."

"Travel is not something to undertake lightly," said Wojciech. "One reason we do not wear armour is to be lighter, in case of accidents. Also armour gets perishing cold worn for long periods, when the weather is still chillsome, and bakes you in the summer. Two pistols each and our swords and my axe should be enough to deal with most chance-met brigands, and Jan and Lynx have muskets."

"And you have a pistol of many chambers, a wondrous thing," said Irene.

"It's not hugely accurate but it does constitute a bit of a surprise," said Wojciech, with a grim smile.

The party rode on, having reached a road slightly more travelled, leading as it did towards the main road which ran all the way from Kraków to Wilnius. They would join the main road to go into Lublin at some point. The equinoctial sun was dropping fast.

"Looking for a spot to camp, soon, people," grunted Jan.

"I was looking out for somewhere suitable," said Wojciech mildly. "There's a bridge ahead, and where there's a bridge there's water. The land to the left rises; we could set up a defensible campsite there amongst the rocks."

"There are people sat at the side of the road," said Lynx, shading his eyes. "Three of them."

"Sabres on knots," said Wojciech automatically. Irene hid a smile that it was only her to whom he could order as his companion. Jan and Lynx readied their muskets, and added bayonets to them.

They upped the pace to a canter, crouching low in the saddle.

One of those at the side of the road leaped up with a scream, pointing at them. The scream was piercing.

"They're women!" said Irene, as the other figures scrambled up.

"At the trot ... raise lance... er, I mean stand down arms," said Wojciech.

"With respect, my lord, let us stay vigilant, lest they

are a trap," said Jan.

"They are dressed - one of them is dressed – in finery," said Lynx.

"Doesn't mean three bandits haven't killed women and taken their clothes," grunted Jan.

"They move like women," said Irene. "And two of them have the manner and attitudes of gentlewomen. Brigands could not learn that."

"No, love, you had enough trouble," smirked Wojciech.

"Yes, but learn it I did," said Irene. "There are ways of standing which betray a woman used to the panniers the westerners are so fond of, which I believe many noblewomen adopt."

Wojciech nodded and they dropped to a non-threatening walk. The women were plainly a young girl clad in brocade, with her soberly-clad companion, and a maid. The women might plainly see the rich caparisons and fine clothing of the pair of szlachta, and there were looks of relief on their faces.

"Oh, I pray you, can you help us?" asked the girl. She was a pretty girl, petite, with a cloud of dark curly hair.

She spoke in English.

Chapter 18

"Well aren't you lucky I speak English, having an English mother," said Irene. "My Lord hasn't a word of English ... well, maybe a word or two, but unless you speak Latin, you will have to go through me."

"Oh, that is good, we can use Latin," said the older woman. "We came from Vienna; Lady Phyllis is travelling to Warsaw, where her parents have gone on ahead. Her father was with the embassy in Austria."

Irene frowned.

"Lady Phyllis ... so your father is a nobleman."

The girl nodded, and continued in Latin not quite as smooth as her companion.

"Yes, he is the Earl of Wicksawlchester," she said.

"Were you not in a carriage? Several carriages?" asked Wojciech.

"Yes Lord ... I am sorry, can we effect introductions?"asked the girl.

"Certainly; I am Wojciech Skrzydło; my relative, Walenty, my master of horses, Jan and our batman, Lynx. We travel light."

"I am Phyllis Sawlchester; my governess is Miss Devon. Our maid, Jadzia, is Polish and is teaching me some Polish."

"I will undertake to teach you more, while we get you to safety," said Irene. She did not like to disparage the maid's efforts, but there was a big difference to the Polish spoken by an ambassador to that spoken by a maid. "Latin will do you well at court in any case; it is the official language, but knowing the local language will stand you in good stead. Tell us what happened."

The governess took over the narrative.

"Somehow we got separated from the other carriages," she said. "I think we are off the main road, but we did not realise that for a while. And then there was the thunder of hoofs and we were surrounded. Our coachman, poor man was killed. He fired off his blunderbuss," – this word had to be in English - "and fought with his whip, but it was not enough."

The Poles automatically crossed themselves, the maid joining in, assuming the situation warranted it.

"We will bury him, and arrange for a priest to say prayers," said Wojciech.

"Thank you," said Miss Devon. "And then we were being pulled out of the coach, and they ... they looked on us most hatefully."

"They were going to despoil us," said Phyllis.

"And then Phyllis started throwing herself about, and drooling at the mouth and screaming nonsense," said Miss Devon. "And Jadzia, whom I will allow is a quick girl, managed to scream something at them which made them back off, and she signalled to me and I, er, twitched and pulled faces."

"I told the pizdy that we had all been bitten by a mad dog and were hurrying to find a doctor," said Jadzia, who followed that her part in it had been mentioned, hearing her name.

"Good girl," said Irene, managing not to blink at the vulgarity. "And what happened to the coach?"

"They took everything out of it, and set fire to it," said Jadzia. "I managed to persuade them that killing us would be bad luck, and that our spirits would haunt them."

"How many were there?" asked Irene.

"A matter of a dozen," said Jadzia. "Better armed than some; they were ex-soldiers I think. They were Poles from the part stolen by Austria, and would not fight for the Austrians."

"One can see why," said Irene, dryly. "But it does not give them the right to terrorise travellers, even if they took you for Austrian. Which way did they go?"

"Up into the hills," Jadzia pointed.

"My lord?" said Irene.

"We have to seek them out and neutralise so large and dangerous a band," said Wojciech, and then repeated this to the women in Latin. "*We plan to camp here in any case; tomorrow we will seek them out and kill them. Then we shall have horses for you as well, and we will escort you to Warszawa. Sorry to delay,*" he said, turning to Irene.

"It is a matter of duty," said Irene, simply. "I would be a poor ... companion if I wished to push on with our private business when there is duty to be done."

Wojciech's smile was her reward, and she basked in it. She did not notice the sharp look Jadzia gave her.

"I have never camped," said Phyllis. "We do not have anything with which to camp."

"We have three tents," said Irene. "Jan and Lynx will share one, we will share one, and you must be a little cramped with three of you in the third. It will keep you warmer in any case. We will build a shelter for the horses, and set the tents by it, so their heat also helps. Now, as you are not injured, we will pick a camp site, and see first to our horses, who are our first charge; if you wish to help you shall gather stones to make a fireplace and wood, and kindle a fire."

"I have never kindled a fire in my life," said Phyllis.

"Why, what sort of noblewoman are you?" said Irene, in scorn. "Any lady knows all the jobs of the servants, so she can show them how to do them better."

Phyllis flushed.

"We have spent so much of my life travelling or in diplomatic quarters," she said. "You are a rude and abrupt boy; have you no respect for my position or our plight?"

"I concede you have excuse not to have learned," said Irene. "Your position at the moment is someone who eats our bread and salt, and your plight would be made easier if you learn how to handle the exigencies in which you find yourself. A girl your age must have some skills."

"Of course; I sing and play the harpsichord and harp, and I paint with water-colours, and I can make conversation in French, sew a fine seam and I ride of course."

Irene smiled a little mirthlessly.

"Have you ever ridden a Lipizanner horse?"

"No, of course not; Papa and Mama would not think it suitable."

"You and your governess will have to ride astride to Warszawa; the brigands will have no side-saddles," warned Irene. "Unless you plan to run along beside us."

"But ... can you not get side-saddles?" asked Miss Devon, horrified.

Irene looked around with her hand shading her eyes.

"I think the saddlery has become invisible," she said.

"You are a rude little boy!" scolded Miss Devon.

"I'm a warrior, not a little boy, and I am turning aside from my wedding arrangements on thy account, woman," said Irene, irritated.

It was very easy to slip into the arrogance of a szlachcic.

"Share a tent with me? Are you insane?" spluttered Wojciech as they set up camp. Lynx had found the coachman's body and laid him out ready to bury.

"Am I supposed to share with one of the women while you squeeze yourself in with Jan and Lynx? You are all large men, and for me to rattle around in a tent on my own would be suspicious and silly," said Irene. "We will be tired enough not to manage to get carried away, and a night in your arms would be welcome if we are to go to war tomorrow."

He nodded.

"I concede the point," he said. "I was taken aback.

Goodness, Irenka, they know nothing; it will be sheer torture taking them to Warszawa."

"Oh, the girl Phyllis is clever, and she resented not having the skills. I will teach her a few things I wager before we get to Warszawa. If we can get her thinking for herself, she might even survive to escape from Poland when That Russian Woman decides to eject English diplomats from Poland as too independent, and likely to infect Poles with Englishness."

Wojciech laughed.

"Little cynic."

"I learned to be one, growing up. Tell me I'm wrong, then."

He sighed.

"I cannot do that, I fear," he said.

They buried the coachman, and Jan fashioned a rough cross. The English women stared as the Poles knelt in the damp grass at the graveside, heedless of their clothes, to pray.

Phyllis asked Irene,

"Why would you pray so devoutly? He is nobody you knew; and he was not of our class."

"Not of our class? Why, today, for defending you as well as he could, he sits beside the Queen of Poland in Heaven for his efforts on thine account. Thou owest him respect for that, little girl. What more can a man give but his life in the defence of the weak?"

"I ... I had not thought of that; I am sorry," said Phyllis. "I did not know the king was recently widowed."

"He isn't, what ... Oh! I suppose you would not know; The Queen of Poland is our honorary title for the Mother of God."

"Oh! I did not know. How ... very interesting."

"It is something you will do well to remember; you will hear it often."

"The English have more religions than soups, and have no more deep attachment to religion than to their cuisine," said Irene to Wojciech after they had eaten and crawled into their tent.

"Says the English woman," said Wojciech.

"I think I will not like it as well in England as I thought when I was young," said Irene. "But it will be better than becoming Russian or Austrian."

"And we can observe our Faith as we choose in private now they have stopped burning Catholics at the stake," said Wojciech. "Lay close to me, my love, wrapped in thy blankets so we do not misbehave, and we will be fresh tomorrow for the fray."

They had set trip-wires with bells about the camp so that they could all sleep, to the consternation of the English women. Jan had pointed out, in his rather basic Latin, that if they relished being killed in their sleep by brigands, he did not, and that the latrine was within the trip-wires.

It was a basic structure; a blanket as a screen, a rough hole and a straining bar, which was, as Irene had told the women bluntly, a lot more sophisticated than their usual practice of digging a hole in the ground.

Irene snuggled up to her beloved, and was soon blissfully asleep in his arms. She awoke before dawn and went to relieve herself and wash.

"I was right," said Jadzia, appearing beside Irene, washing in the stream.

"Oh?" said Irene, ignoring the girl to continue washing.

"You are a woman," said Jadzia.

"I am also a warrior," said Irene. "Today you will see me accoutred for war, and it is not for show."

"The Lady Phyllis would probably like to be like you; she is very young, but she is not as silly as she looks when her governess is with her," said Jadzia. "What, did you think I have not picked up enough Latin to follow conversations? I was with the Polish embassy in Vienna and leaped at the chance to go back to Poland for a while even though I am not strictly speaking a lady's maid. When you have seen her to Warszawa I will be happy to stay with you when you marry your lord. He is a bohatyr, I think."

"He is; and your cheek talked you into a job," said Irene. "If you had tried to blackmail me, I should have driven you away at the first village."

"I am not a blackmailer. But I do like knowing things, my lady," said Jadzia.

"Get used to that being 'my lord'," said Irene.

"Of course, my lord," said Jadzia. "Do you want it kept secret?"

Irene considered.

Having the patronage of an Earl's daughter when they went to England might not come amiss.

"You may indicate your suspicions to Lady Phyllis, if you wish," she said.

Jadzia giggled.

"It would be as well; I fancy she is half-way to wondering if you are old enough to court her, and if the marriage arrangements you spoke of are nothing but preliminaries yet."

"Saints preserve us!" Irene almost yelped. Jadzia ran away giggling.

The ladies were not up when the hussars breakfasted. Jadzia ate with them, and promised to feed them when they emerged. The sounds of getting the horses arrayed for battle awoke Phyllis first, and she crawled stiffly out of the tent. She gasped to see two winged hussars armed and armoured.

"You do not look such a little boy now," she said to Irene.

Irene smiled a mirthless smile invisibly behind her face guard.

"I grew up when I killed my first man," she said.

"Have you killed many?"

"Too many, alas; but I have learned not to fear dying, nor killing to save others," said Irene. "Excuse me."

Wojciech beckoned her over and they all bared their heads as they knelt to pray for the success of their mission and the safety of the women they protected. They sang 'Bogurodzica' and mounted up. Phyllis gasped to see Irene and Wojciech leap into the saddle from a short run, and a quick vault. And then they were away.

Jan and Lynx carried bayonets, and would ride behind and flanking the szlachta. Lynx had scouted already, the night before, while the others raised the camp, and had returned with the location of the hidden brigand base.

"I keep meaning to ask, Lord Jan, why do you not ride with a lance with the other hussars?" asked Lynx.

"I can't do it any more; I broke my shoulder when I was careless with a charge, and I have some problems with the mobility of the joint," said Jan. "Wojciech's father made me master of his horse instead, so he could see me well-cared for." He hesitated. "It was partly his fault too, as he sent me to take out a cannon, and I skewered the gun captain and, uh, rammed my lance right down the cannon behind him and went catapulting off my horse. I should have let go, but I was determined to carry out orders and make sure of things. I keep telling you, lad, on campaign I don't take offence at being just 'Jan'."

The warriors rode up the hill at a steady trot, raised out of the saddle to rise and fall with the motion to make it easier on the horses. Lynx had described something of a hollow in the hills, a largely dry valley, sheltered and almost a natural fortress.

Almost.

Lynx noted that if they went past the hollow they would be able to come down on the enemy.

"Even if they are ready for us, we will have terrain on our side," he said.

"Is there any reason they should not be ready for us?" asked Wojciech.

"Considering that they were drinking and singing, I doubt they will be ready for us even if they are up and about," said Lynx, dryly. "I think they did not all come; I counted fifteen."

"Four each then, and the last one to charge only gets three," said Wojciech gaily.

"Back to crazy and no longer maudlin; praise heaven," muttered Jan.

They came over the rise Lynx indicated, and looked down. Some brigands were up and about, and a few had seized muskets and swords, and mounted up. They were looking towards the entrance of the valley, presumably having heard horses.

"Close up knee to knee. Sabres at the knot," said Wojciech. "Fix bayonets, and ready muskets. Pick your target and fire when you are close enough to pick their teeth with your bayonet. Lance... down. Forward!"

Chapter 19

The galloping hoofs alerted those brigands who were ready that they were under attack. They wheeled about but were in poor order.

"Shoot them! Shoot them!" shouted ... somebody.

These brigands were better trained than some, and were holding their fire; Wojciech was glad that they had horse armour. As they thundered towards the few who were ready, Ogień winced as a bullet winged his flank; and Irene heard a bullet strike Jester's face armour.

Apparently this was not about to deter the old drum horse, who appeared to take the maxim that getting even was better than getting mad, riding straight at his assailants. Irene's lance took the musketeer as he seized a pistol, but he was already squeezing the trigger; and Irene felt a burning pain as the ball hit in the gap between her breastplate and left pauldron.

She vomited to the side in the sudden shock of the pain, spat hard, and seized her sabre. If the opposition was this steady, Wojciech could not afford to lose a hussar to mere pain. Her left arm was numb from the shock, but her right arm still worked. She could ride with her legs. And so she fought on, through a fog of pain. Their initial onslaught had reduced the odds considerably; Wojciech managed to spit two on his lance, and Jan and Lynx each shot one and bayoneted another almost immediately. Five men had been ready; all of them were dead. The poczet turned almost as one, Jester well aware what to do, without needing guidance, to meet the ragged band of men pouring out of their tents.

"There are only four of them, boys, it'll be easy, think what those horses will fetch!" called a shaved-headed man with long moustaches.

"Easy, will it?" muttered Wojciech, picking his next attack run. "Knee to knee, my love," he called, a little chidingly to Irene, who gritted her teeth and closed up. It made them more effective to ride in formation, and she had to admit that Seweryn had made a considerable difference in being a third to their poczet. She had not been aware of drifting away from Wojciech with her concentration distracted, and made herself run through the drills in her head. Jan and Lynx kept slightly to the rear, with their bayonets and pistols. Wojciech drew his pistol and fired left handed to discourage a man with a musket, and Jester rode down another. He did not approve of firearms. Another thought Wojciech now defenceless on his left, and was to be surprised to be shot by a weapon already discharged. He was not surprised for long with a pistol ball in the throat.

"Draw your pistol, Walenty!" said Wojciech, sharply, thinking she had forgotten in the excitement.

"Can't," said Irene. "Sorry!"

Wojciech frowned, glanced over ... and saw blood.

His jaw tightened, and he paled. Well, there was nothing he might do for her until their enemies were no more of a nuisance. That shaven headed bastard would pay.

"Do what you can, love," he said, gently, Irene nodded to acknowledge that she knew the anger in his eyes was not for her, aware the gesture was unseen as he had turned his attention to those remaining brigands. The second charge was just reaching the shaven leader, having cut their way through his picked men. The leader had just come to the realisation that his men were only a trained band by comparison to other brigands, and that the stories about winged hussars being good for nothing but ceremonial was apparently seriously bad intelligence.

He started to raise his arms in surrender; but it was too late. An enraged Wojciech took off raising hand and head in one blow.

The few surviving brigands were easy to chase

down, as Jan and Lynx checked the tents for any hiding, and for any captives.

And then it was all over, and Irene could relax, putting her sabre back in its scabbard, and clinging to the pommel.

Wojciech turned to Irene in time to catch her as she fell from the saddle in a dead faint.

She awoke cradled against his chest, with water splashing on her face. She reached up for the canteen to wash her mouth, turning from him to spit out the vile taste in her mouth before taking more to drink.

"How bad?" he asked, his face a mask of fear.

"Nothing vital," said Irene. "Oh! How it hurts though; I think the ball is still in there."

"We'll get it out in the camp. You did splendidly," he said.

Irene smiled at his praise and let blissful unconsciousness take her again.

She did not hear Wojciech's orders to Jan and Lynx to set the heads of the brigands up on spikes along the road, and to bring back to the ladies such of their possessions as might be found. Neither of the men resented him riding back to the camp with his precious load, to treat the musket wound, and called their prayers and good wishes for Irene as he rode away.

Phyllis looked up at the sound of galloping hoofs, to see the big red horse alone, and its rider cradling the smaller hussar in his arms.

Wojciech came off Ogień in one fluid move, which Phyllis had to admire, especially burdened as he was.

"*You! You said you know horses; see to my steed,*" snapped Wojciech to Phyllis. "Jadwiga! Boil water!"

"Yes, my lord," said Jadzia. "Is she badly hurt?"

He gave her a startled look, but accepted that the girl somehow knew.

"No, but if we don't get the ball out, she will be," he said.

"Hold her, my lord, while I improvise a trestle," said Jadzia.

Wojciech had to admit to being impressed. The girl tossed the canvas off the warriors' two tents, took down some of the poles they had cut from trees to build the shelter for the horses, and threw a blanket over the rough wood.

"My thanks," he said. "Somewhere inside what used to be my tent is a red canvas bag, it has salves and medical equipment in it."

Jadzia gave a gamine grin and disappeared into the wreckage of the tent, emerging with the bag.

"Good; dip all the knives and tweezers into the boiling water and bring them to me on one of my tin plates," said Wojciech. "Then there's a pot of salve in there; if the chit has not managed to wash Ogień's cut, do so, please, and put salve on it."

"Yes, my lord," said Jadzia.

He had not bothered to ask if she understood or could do as asked; and that, reflected the girl, was very nice. He assumed she could do her job, and let her get on with it. This was a departure which was very welcome.

She found Phyllis inspecting the wound on Ogień's flank, smiled at her and washed it off, and put salve on it.

"What do now?" asked Phyllis, in broken Polish.

"Ask my lord," said Jadzia.

Phyllis went over.

"What can I do?" she asked.

Wojciech had been taking Irene's armour off.

"Help me undress her," he said.

"She is a female?" Phyllis was betrayed into her own tongue.

"Not female; lady" managed Wojciech, irritably.

"I say to you, she girl," said Jadzia in rudimentary Latin.

Phyllis blinked, but helped slide Irene's good arm, and then the bad out of the padded under-armour, and then out of her kontusz, and Wojciech turned to Jadzia.

"Will you unbutton her żupan?" he asked, a little helplessly.

Jadzia obliged.

"How good will you be on your wedding night, my lord, if you cannot break into your bride's clothing?"

"Oh, you figured that out as well, did you?" said Wojciech. "I'm hoping she'll help."

Jadzia smiled demurely.

"Buttons are a very good chaperone," she said.

"Yes," agreed Wojciech, a little shortly. But it was good of the girl to distract his worry, he should not snap at her.

Jadzia had to admit herself very impressed with Irene's foundation garment; and so was Phyllis. Wojciech was able to move it and her shift aside to see the wound.

"Ball is visible," he said, in relief.

"Thick fur and wadding," said Jadzia.

Miss Devon came over.

"Phyllis, what is going on? Oh my!" she said, and passed out.

Wojciech rolled his eyes, looked at Phyllis and jabbed a meaningful thumb towards the tent the women had used.

Phyllis nodded, and went for a blanket, onto which to manhandle Miss Devon, to drag her away.

"She isn't a bad girl," said Wojciech to Jadzia.

"The old besom trammels her," said Jadzia.

"Oh, well, with luck she will learn to rebel," said Wojciech. "And I never said so to you, my girl."

Jadzia beamed.

"Said what, my lord?" she said.

Irene stirred as Wojciech felt for the ball.

"*Hellfire damnation and brimstone!*" she yelped in her own language.

"Only for the brigands, my darling, you will do very well when I have the wadding as well as the ball," said Wojciech, extracting the ball. "And I can ... Jadzia, take these large forceps and hold that ruddy wound open for me."

"Yes, my lord," said Jadzia.

"What a good steady girl you are," said Wojciech, as she stretched the wound mouth for him to see inside. "How would you like a change of employer?"

"I already accepted an offer to be your lady's maid," said Jadzia. "I have never done surgery before, but I am sure I can learn; I am a country girl so I am not squeamish."

"Ooooh" said Miss Devon. She spoke in her own language to Phyllis. "Oh my dove! How can that horrid man dare to make you help him tend one of his men? That wound! Too much for any gently-bred lady to look at!"

Phyllis opened her mouth to snap something about it not being too much for a gently-bred but rather less tenderly trained lady to take for their peace of mind, but realised that it was not the revelation of the girl hussar's gender which had made her companion pass out, but the wound. She said instead,

"Don't you think it would be churlish and most improper of any well-bred lady not to aid those wounded in her service? The hussars went to deal with the brigands on our account. I am a Sawlchester of Wicksawlchester, not some diluted bloodline of the line of impoverished curates. It is a matter of noblesse oblige. I was able to help, not being as feeble as some females, and it behoved me to do so."

It was unkind, and Phyllis knew it was unkind. Miss Devon blanched. The Earl had spoken sharply to her in the past about trying to instil middle-class values into a girl of quality and had shouted that he wanted the girl to be decent, not 'naice'. He expected his daughter to be able to tend her own mare, and to ride like a mad thing across country with him, and placed the neat layout of accounting above beautiful embroidery. She could have taught Phyllis housewifely skills if only she had known it was expected, but had seen her own skills in such endeavours as shameful, for not having had enough servants when growing up to escape having to do some housework for herself.

"What about the other men?" she asked.

"They have not yet returned; I do not know if they are dead or have other duties," said Phyllis. "I did not like to ask."

"Oh!" said Miss Devon.

The sound of more horses answered the question of where Jan and Lynx were. The two men carried over an Imperial between them, and laid it down in front of the English ladies.

"Your clothes, ladies," said Jan. "Milord say, you sort out packs. He no carry big luggage to Warszawa."

"*Thank you,*" said Phyllis. "Dziękuję Ci," she managed to add.

Jan smiled and nodded.

Phyllis said to Miss Devon,

"Let us use the sheets we were advised to travel with to make up clothes bundles, to distribute them better on the pack horses."

"Yes, I suppose we had better do so," sighed Miss Devon. "It seems a shame to have to leave that fine piece of luggage though."

"Better than leaving our lives," said Phyllis. "I will be glad of clean clothes."

Jadzia came over.

"Young hussar do well" she said. "Milord say young girl look after; Jadzia cook."

"Your Latin is very much better than I realised," said Phyllis. "It seems fair; I do not know how to cook."

Irene was conscious, propped up against the horse shelter on a blanket whilst Wojciech sorted out the tents again. She had been bandaged and partially re-dressed, and sported a sling. Phyllis sat down by her.

"What can I do to help?" she said, in English.

"You can learn Polish to keep my mind off the pain" said Irene.

"What is your real name? It cannot be Walenty; is that not a male name?"

"Say '*Jakie jest twoje prawdziwe imię*?'" said Irene.

In broken English and Polish, Irene told Phyllis her story. Phyllis was much impressed.

"I wish I had learned how to fight," said Phyllis.

"If two trained hussars, an ex-hussar and a trained soldier took a casualty in fighting them, you would have died," said Irene. "You were quick-witted, and saved yourself and your dependents. It was well done."

"It was a risk that they would just kill us, but that would have been better than being ... used," said Phyllis. Irene grunted.

She had a horror, as any girl might, of being violated, but felt that if she had been sold to the king, she might yet have escaped to build a life for herself. Death before dishonour was a proud sounding phrase but Irene considered that the dishonour fell to the violator, not the violated.

There was a squeal from Miss Devon, who passed out again.

"You had better see what has set her off," said Irene.

"I think it is that your men are setting the heads of the brigands on stakes," said Phyllis, dryly.

"And I know enough French to know that the phrase

for that is 'pour encourager les autres', said Irene. "Ah, what an excellent idea; Lynx has found a portion of red feather to tack onto the pole of the leader's head with a notice, to mark our claim. I dare say he will find some smaller feathers now he has thought of the idea, to strike terror into the hearts of brigands."

"What do you suppose the notice says?"

"Something like 'so perish all brigands, the blood angel does not sleep' or something equally melodramatic," said Irene.

Chapter 20

Irene was a little feverish by the time of the evening meal.

Miss Devon was thin lipped.

"My lord, I do not like it that you make my lady dance attendance on that boy. I am also concerned when you will be on the road for Warsaw," she said.

Phyllis winced.

"Since I was not originally going to Warszawa and turned aside to give you and your charge succour and aid, and since my young relative was wounded in the pursuance of our duty regarding the safety of travellers such as yourself, I do not think that you are in the position to like or dislike the dispositions of those I have taken into my protection," said Wojciech, coldly.

"Surely you would place the care of a well-born girl over some boy?" she said

"I find it appalling that you have the gall to question the care of *Lord* Walenty; would you expect me to question you over asking for a few days going at a slower pace to take into account, say, the exigencies of your charge's monthly manifestations of womanhood? Or would you expect me to hurry you on, should Lady Phyllis trip, and knock herself out, or occasion some other accident? No, you would doubtless demand that she be given consideration and time to recover. Strange as it may seem to you, but Lady Phyllis is not the highest of my priorities. My concerns are in my duty to Poland and the furtherance of my House as represented by Lord Walenty. We will be on the road when the lad can ride without becoming ill. You are safe. You have protection and you have food. I ordered my men to find such of your luggage as they may. I have gone out of my way to show courtesies to a pair of foreigners who have caused me considerable trouble. Without you we should have been half way to our destination by now, so if you are going to make demands couched as dislikes and concerns, you may pick one of the horses we took from the brigands and get on the road. The girl is a lady; you are not."

He turned away from her, leaving Miss Devon's mouth hanging foolishly open.

"***But*** ..."she lapsed into English.

"Which in Polish means a shoe, and most appropriate, since like a shoe you have a lot of tongue," said Wojciech. "I tolerate you for Lady Phyllis, who is a nice child."

"I'm afraid you asked for that, Devvie," said Phyllis.

"But ... it is appalling that he leaves you caring for a young man, and he has no feelings whatsoever! He does not care about the privations we are undergoing!" cried Miss Devon.

"You realise if he was at war he would not even question his wife's abilities to handle these conditions, in accompanying him?" said Phyllis.

Miss Devon shuddered.

"I pity his poor wife," she said.

"As I understand it, a ... a szlachcianka would consider herself above complaining," said Phyllis, who had picked up some of Irene's views on life in general. "They did not have to stop and help us; it was the courtesy any szlachta would expect to give to women in distress, especially szlachcianka like me. Lord Wojciech resents the way you try to order him about. He takes it from an old retainer like Jan Nowak, but then, Jan is someone he considers your social superior because he is someone he owes duty to. I believe he is a szlachta of sorts but I don't quite understand how it works and he is also a retainer or something. Lynx is not a noble, I think, but he has made himself useful enough to be given respect and his care is under noblesse oblige."

"But ... but I am of the gentry! My great grandfather was a knight!" said Miss Devon.

"But he was knighted for improving some process in manufacturing, wasn't he? I don't think they count that. And this is one thing I am learning from Walenty – who is, incidentally, eager to go and get married to his sweetheart," said Phyllis, reflecting that this was not that large a bending of the truth. "There are no gentry. There are the szlachta and the peasantry. In England, more people are likely to own land but ... I ... I think it is as if the upper ten thousand were all who counted as part of the *ton* and the rest ... not. Lord Wojciech thinks you encroaching. And if you do not learn how the Polish nobility think, you will always be treated as an uppity upper servant by them. Jan Nowak tells Lord Wojciech what he should do, but he and his family have been in service to the family for time immemorial. Jan's ancestor rode with his lordship's ancestor at the siege of Vienna, as a ... pacholik. Lord Walenty told me that he and Lord Wojciech look upon Jan as a ... oh dear, this language is awful to get my tongue around ... a towarsysz. That's wrong but it's as close as I can get. It means companion, anyway. He is in charge of his lord's horses but that does not make him a glorified groom. There is a greater social divide than there is in England, and the nobility are more exclusive. The other man treats him respectfully and calls him *Waćpan Jan*, which I think is Lord Jan."

She did not mention that Jan despised Miss Devon in a way he had never despised anyone like Lynx, or Jadzia, who behaved, according to Jan's description, properly.

"It is the lot of the governess to be between family and servants, but I am only asserting myself for your comfort, my love," said Miss Devon.

"And this I plan to explain to Lord Wojciech," said Phyllis. "Indeed, I will do so now, and beg him to consider only that your concern for me makes you press him in a way he finds rude. Walenty means more to his Lordship than anyone else in the world."

"I definitely pity his wife," said Miss Devon, with a sniff.

"Oh dear, I will have to tell you," said Phyllis. "I think it must be the worst-kept secret in Poland anyway, that Walenty is in fact the Lady Irenka, and she and Lord Wojciech were on the way to arrange their own wedding, and we have forced them into the impropriety of having to share a tent before they are married."

"But ... but she is in breeches! And wore armour! And ... and ..."

"And has undergone the same training any winged hussar would have, because her lord loves her enough to do his utmost to make sure she survives," said Phyllis. "I think it mightily romantic myself, if more uncomfortable than I would like to experience. And she fought for our sakes and is wounded, and at no point have she or Lord Wojciech countered your complaints by pointing out that an earl's granddaughter much my own age is injured quite seriously. I ... I cannot but respect her."

Miss Devon was staring in shock.

"But ... but it is scandalous! How can her mother permit this?"

"Her mother is dead. She did not like the way her uncle looked at her, the way those brigands looked at us until I play-acted. So she ran away and was lucky to be rescued by a ... I think the word 'bohatyr' means hero, but I am not precisely sure."

"Poor child! Perhaps your father would take her in so she does not have to marry this wild man with his crazy ideas of making women act like men," said Miss Devon, who had rather strange and vague ideas that Wojciech had alternative preferences, and needing to marry found a girl cowed enough and desperate enough to pretend to be a boy for him.

"She adores him and loves the lifestyle," said Phyllis. "I did ask if she would not prefer to be at court, wearing beautiful gowns and meeting all the world, and she shuddered and said she would rather take a cup of wild boar urine with Epsom salts."

"What a very odd girl to be sure!"

"And a very happy one," said Phyllis.

She did speak to Wojciech about her companion.

"And it is only that she worries about me," she said, "And perhaps about losing her position as my governess and having nowhere to go."

"I appreciate her concerns," said Wojciech. "But her manner sets my teeth on edge. I am not normally intolerant, but something about her just rubs me up the wrong way."

"Since Irene has told me about how you have worked alongside artisans and others, I am aware of this," said Phyllis. "I cannot say I find her convivial, but she is a kindly creature. I ... I found I had to reveal Irene's secret to stop her, and I was upset that she then decided that you were in some wise exploiting Irene," she added.

"*Exploit ... oh...*" said Wojciech.

"I have missed something," said Phyllis.

"Yes, but I'm not about to explain it," said Wojciech. "It would serve the old biddy right if you asked her to explain but I doubt she'd manage to do so without confusing you further."

"She isn't always noted for her clarity," said Phyllis.

Irene was delirious when Wojciech joined her in the tent. He bathed her hot head with cold water, and when she shivered in fever he held her against him, her bandaged arm uppermost, and tucking his hand to cup her elbow.

That engendered a little grunt of relief, and

Wojciech determined to hold her thus as long as he could. Even if he had to put up with the indignity of asking Jan to hold a utensil so he need not to move. He fell asleep holding her against him, and woke in some horror to the sound of the birds to find that his other hand was on one breast.

"What time is it?" said Irene.

"Coming up dawn," said Wojciech. "I ... I am sorry ... I seem to have ..."

"...Moved into a very nice position from my point of view," said Irene. "But I am desperate to leave the tent!"

"My arm has gone to sleep!" said Wojciech, in horror. "I ... I will need to get the blood flowing before I can carry you."

"Surely I can walk," said Irene. "It is my shoulder, not my legs."

"The blood loss may be a problem," said Wojciech, helping her out of the tent. "Put a cloak on; you are saturated from the fever breaking."

"Be nice and bring me some clean clothes; I would wash," said Irene.

"You carry her, my lord; I will bring clean clothes," said Jadzia, appearing from the other tent.

"Invaluable girl," said Wojciech.

Irene did indeed need help to get to the latrine, but managed to walk.

Her most pressing need satisfied, and too glad of Wojciech's support to be embarrassed by being held by him, Irene was keen to wash.

Jadzia, having got clothing, came to help out. She shooed Wojciech away.

"I will call you to carry her back, my lord," she said.

"I hear and obey, oh mistress of the lamp," said Wojciech.

"That sounds as though it is from a story," said Jadzia to Irene.

"I think it is some fairy tale," said Irene. "Perhaps we can talk him into telling it around the camp fire."

"That would be right pleasant. And speaking of talking people into things, Lady Phyllis would love to wear your clothes, I think," she said.

"Poor child, I am sure she would," said Irene. "You think we should order her to do so, for her own safety, and give her a reason to do so?"

Jadzia grinned.

"She won't ask," she said. "Mind you, I do not think she is cut out to be a warrior."

"No; but if she learns a few things she'll do very nicely," said Irene.

"Do very nicely for what, my lady?"

"Oh, I was thinking of introducing her to someone," said Irene, with a small, hidden smile. "Will you help me change the dressing on my wound? I might as well deal with it while I am undressed."

"Certainly, my lady. My lord praised me for holding it open whilst he extracted the wad; he says it should not fester."

"He ought to know," said Irene. "Thank you for helping; it must have been unpleasant."

"I think it was more unpleasant from your point of view, lady," said Jadzia, dryly.

"It hurts and I feel as though my legs are without bones, but I am alive to complain about it, which is cause for rejoicing and to give thanks," said Irene.

Jadzia giggled.

"Some ladies I have worked for have hysterics over a splinter in their finger," she said. "I know which I prefer. But try not to get shot too often."

"It wasn't actually my idea," said Irene. "But when I feel a little better, I shall find the head on the spike of the one who shot me; and wave to him, like this." She gave a silly little wave. "And I shall revel in how childish it is," she added.

Jadzia went for more gauze to replace the dressing, and helped Irene to dress.

"You should let me do it, lady," she said.

"Am I making it harder for you?" Irene was apologetic.

"No, lady; but it is harder on you and I am here as a maid."

"I am used to fettling my own tack," said Irene. "I hope you will not be bored as my maid."

"I will find something to occupy myself," said Jadzia. "And if he is not taken, I find the man called Lynx rather interesting."

"Not as far as I know; but you would have to ask him," said Irene. "He told me he had no ties, but that can mean many things. I ask no confidences which are not willingly offered."

Jadzia gave her a blinding smile.

"And you don't say 'no followers'," she said.

"Well, that is because I trust Lynx," said Irene. "And to be honest, if you had other followers, I'd set him to investigate them, for your protection as much as mine."

"I ... that is fair, lady," said Jadzia. "I will call my lord now?"

"Thank you," said Irene. "Then we shall choose such of my clothes for you to take to Phyllis to put on."

"Your .... undergarment is most interesting," said Jadzia.

"I have several with me; if you wish to use one to copy for yourself and for Phyllis, you certainly may."

"I will be ready to ride tomorrow," said Irene. "I would like to say I could ride today, but I would rather not as there is no emergency. I am sorry for Phyllis' father, but I am afraid that is just too bad."

"I want you wearing that sling at all times and to stop sneaking your arm out of it," said Wojciech. "Do you think it a sartorial statement?"

Irene smiled at him.

"No, my lord; how very masterful you are," she said.

"I'll show you masterful when you are healed and we've seen your parent," growled Wojciech.

Irene sighed in contentment.

Phyllis emerged from her tent in one of Irene's sets of clothes. Miss Devon was twittering disapprovingly behind her.

"Do we ride today?" Phyllis asked. "Are you better? I am sure I could not manage it if I had been shot."

"Not today, but I thought you should get used to the feeling of the clothes," said Irene. "You will also want to choose a horse to ride, and practise riding astride. Also mounting without aid."

"I have ridden astride, but don't tell Miss Devon," whispered Phyllis. "I would like to be able to use a sword too, but I do not think I would like to be a hussar. Don't you ever wonder what it would have been like if you had been ... well, more ordinary?"

"If things had gone the way my father wanted, and the winged hussars had not been disbanded, I should still have likely married my lord, and I suspect I should have found a way into his poczet," said Irene. "Who can know? I have more freedom and joy than in a conventional life."

"So you don't think you will ever settle down at court?"

"No; for one thing Wojciech faked his own death, and for another, once you're hardened in battle there's no coming back. Dying of old age with the sum total of my achievements being three hundred pairs of embroidered slippers and seven thousand footstool covers is not my ambition."

"Why I quite see your point! Irene, I see dust on the road."

"Wojciech! We're going to have company!" called Irene.

Chapter 21

"I can look intimidating ..."

"You will have my multi-barrelled pistol to sell your life dearly," said Wojciech. "Jan and Lynx will be out of sight, off the road to get you and the others to safety and Jadwiga, my girl, tell the old goat that if she doesn't stop screeching you have my permission to slap her and gag her."

"With pleasure, my lord," said Jadzia.

Wojciech's armour was truncated, just a breastplate and helmet, but with a lance and pennant flying, defiant in the middle of the road filling the width of the bridge on Ogień he looked very imposing.

Wojciech's thoughts were that if this was another band of brigands coming to join the first, he would sell his life dearly for the women, including his own beloved. If she were beside him to die together, he would even be happy. However, if she were beside him, he did not think there was a bandit force in the land who would survive.

The dust was not as bad as might be found in summer; but over the rise beyond the bridge it was hard to make anything out.

"There are pennants!" said Lynx. "Those are no bandits!"

Round the corner swept the horsemen.

"The white raven! The white raven of Krasiński!" called Lynx. "It's Lord Seweryn!"

"Queen of Poland! The man is ubiquitous!" said Irene, a smile across her face even as she dashed away tears of relief. "*A friend*" she told Phyllis and ran out onto the road. Wojciech had seen the pennant too, and Ogień stepped backwards carefully to clear the bridge.

"There's an English pennant too," said Irene. "The red, white and blue."

"Maybe our guest's father," grunted Jan. "Good."

The leader of the riders held up a hand. He passed his green pennant with its white raven off to someone else and rode forward over the bridge.

A wrist clasp, and then an embrace as Seweryn and Wojciech greeted each other.

"Where's Walenty?" asked Seweryn sharply.

"Here, my friend," said Irene, running up. "Oh, it is good to see you, and not brigands."

"What, you are wounded? Wojciech! Have you permitted some brigand to wound the only woman I ever proposed to?"

"They paid," said Wojciech, indicating the heads.

"The two of you and Jan and Lynx took down ... I make that fifteen?"

"Yes, of course," said Wojciech. "But some of them were better trained. Ogień got a small wound, and Jester a bruise."

"Hah! Now my friend, we are looking for some women."

"And that's different to normal how?" asked Wojciech. "However, if, as I collect, you are looking for Lady Phyllis ... bah, I cannot recall the barbaric word ... and her maid and the goat-dragon set to guard her, we have them safe in camp."

"Goat-dragon?" asked Seweryn.

"You'll meet her and see what I mean," said Wojciech, sourly. "A female who would depress Irenka's spirit were she in her charge."

Seweryn shuddered.

"I don't look forward to that meeting," he said, swinging off his horse, and gesturing to the rest of those with him. "And, by your jocular manner, unharmed?"

"Frightened but unhurt. The girl Phyllis pretended hydrophobic fits and the brigands left them untouched."

"Walenty, my friend, I am learning English, but come and use your language skills to explain to Lord

Wicksawlchester," said Seweryn.

Phyllis had also come onto the bridge.

"Papa! Papa!" she cried, running towards the horsemen. Muskets were raised.

"Stand down your weapons!" bellowed Seweryn.

The older man dressed in the English fashion was dismounting, holding out his arms as his daughter ran to him.

One of the Polish contingent pointed at Wojciech.

"That is a dead man!" he cried.

"He got better," said Seweryn.

"You had better come and water your horses and set up camp to eat," said Wojciech. "Apparently Walenty and I are being made out to be bohatyry by the girl." Phyllis was gesticulating wildly and pointing back to Wojciech and Irene.

"You are *my* bohatyr," said Irene.

"And you won't shift her on that," said Seweryn, draping an arm around his friend's shoulder as Wojciech dismounted.

"And what are you doing here, looking for stray Englishwomen?" asked Wojciech.

"Like an idiot, I went to court, and was talked into being a liaison to the new ambassador," said Seweryn. "'It's a sinecure', they said. And then two coaches arrived with servants and luggage, but no Lady Phyllis. So ..." he shrugged.

"We could have done with you a couple of days ago," said Irene, severely. "It was glorious, but three winged hussars really make the whole charge better."

"You're as insane as your man," said Seweryn without rancour.

"Just as well," said Irene.

The ambassador was coming over.

"My daughter is effusive and a little confusing," he said in English, bowing. "Am I correct in believing that you are a lady who rides with her husband to fight brigands?" he addressed Irene.

"We had to share a tent to cede one to your daughter and the ...er, her duenna," said Irene. "We do not live as husband and wife until we can be lawfully married. We were on our way to get that sorted out when we happened on three women at the side of the road. And your daughter is a perfect lady, may I say, and a credit to her escutcheon ... or whatever they have in England. I am sorry, my mother was English, but I am not wholly conversant with the customs."

"I understand one of the Ulans riding with Lord Seweryn to say that your betrothed husband was dead," said the earl.

"He faked his own death; it's not illegal," said Irene. "The crown got his barony from it, so who are they to complain?"

"It will get out," said the earl. "The matter of damage limitations, however, regarding how it got out ..."

Irene rapidly translated to Wojciech. His shoulders slumped.

"I will not be paraded through Warszawa to further anyone's political agenda," he said.

The earl switched smoothly to Latin.

"My dear fellow! No reason that you should. Just that if I drop the right word at the right time about you seeking out enemies of the kingdom ..."

Wojciech sighed.

"I am a loyal Pole," he said. "But I will not be a party to the Russian influence. I just want to be left alone to pursue my personal vendetta against brigands, and to marry my Irenka."

"I quite understand," said the earl. "And I will do what I can to let the whole matter die down. Nothing is too much for those who have rescued my only daughter. I have been beside myself, and my wife is prostrated."

"Your daughter is spirited," said Irene lapsing back

into English. "I would advise that in case of political tension and trouble during your tenure here, you should let her learn to look after herself. To pose as a boy as need be, as my mother made me learn. Have her taught swordplay and dirty fighting."

"Good grief!" said the earl. "You really think it would be a good idea?"

"I think it could save her life," said Irene, simply.

"I ... I do not know who I would trust to teach her," said the earl. "I do not have time, myself."

"Why, send her to Lord Seweryn as his page," said Irene.

The earl looked speculatively at Seweryn.

"What is the whelp talking me into?" demanded Seweryn. "I shall make a note to myself; never permit Wojan's whelp of a bride negotiate in a language I do not know well."

The earl smiled brightly.

"Lady Irene suggested that you should take my daughter as your page and teach her sword-play, dirty fighting, and how to pass as a boy," he said.

Seweryn looked horrified. Wojciech choked.

"I know nothing about little girls!" Seweryn said.

"Nonsense, my friend, she is much the same age as I am," said Irene. "Perhaps in your parents' house, so your mother is there as chaperone, and to help out ...."

Phyllis was looking back and forth between those speaking. She clasped her hands together and gazed appealingly at the big blond one-time hussar.

"Oh, please, Lord Seweryn, I would like to learn. I do not want to go to war like Irene, but I do want to be able to take care of myself. And I would like to escape from the goat-dragon," she added.

Wojciech coughed.

"You were not supposed to hear me use that name for your duenna!" he said.

"Damned appropriate," said the earl, who had been

having his ear bent by Miss Devon, and had with difficulty shooed her away. "Lord Seweryn, will you consider it?"

"I ... yes, I suppose so," said Seweryn. "I am not sure what Walenty's devious little mind is cooking up, though."

"Why, Sewek, it would be nice to know another girl my own age who shares some of my interests and is not a complete idiot, of course," said Irene, opening her eyes wide.

"Why do I wonder if I entirely believe that?" sighed Seweryn.

"All right, what are you up to?" asked Wojciech when he had extracted Irene from the mass of newcomers.

"Isn't it obvious?" said Irene.

"You're matchmaking," said Wojciech.

"Seweryn thought himself half in love with me," said Irene. "He is attracted to an able woman, but he finds my whole-hearted embracing of being a winged hussar a trifle intimidating as anything but a friend, which is just as well. It would make life difficult if our best friend was also in love with me. He needs a capable woman who is yet ready to be all woman for him as well in letting him rescue her. Not," she added, leaning on him, "That I have any problems with you being masterful and rescuing me, because I love it. But I also love that you respect my skills, expect me to close up knee to knee and have my sabre ready to do battle, supporting your right."

"Seweryn respects your skills or he would not fight beside you."

"Yes; and he loves me too, but as a little brother. He would find it hard to switch from battle-brother to lover."

Wojciech nodded.

"I see what you mean," he said. "And you think ..."

"There is a lot more to her than the goat-dragon permits to surface," said Irene. "And she was looking quite speculatively at Seweryn, did you not think?"

Wojciech sighed.

"Let us hope she accepts him for what and who he is," he said. "Seweryn will never curl and powder his hair for anyone, nor wear English clothes, which look stiff and uncomfortable."

"Women's English clothing is, certainly," said Irene. "Ohh Wojan, my shoulder hurts, and I am so tired, do you think I might slip away and have a sleep?"

"Go, sleep; I order it," said Wojciech.

"May I strangle your whelp?" asked Seweryn.

"No; but you can always strangle your own," said Wojciech.

"It will be harder to hide this one as a boy, she is too pretty," said Seweryn.

"Not as lovely as Irenka," said Wojciech. "And if you are thinking about the curls, well, I endured much teasing in my youth."

"How that nasty bully howled when we beat him up," said Seweryn, rubbing his knuckles at a memory. "Went running to my father, who knew just what sort he was, and was glad to have him find an excuse to leave his household."

"I came across him later, with his own poczet," said Wojciech. "I beat him up again for old times' sake. I heard he was accidentally shot in the back several times."

"Wouldn't surprise me," said Seweryn.

Two lancers had been sent to go and buy, borrow, steal or requisition a carriage or cart for Miss Devon, who was having hysterics about the idea of riding astride all the way to Warszawa.

"You lads will have to dice for who is in charge of driving her and escorting her," said Seweryn.

"You mean, whoever loses," said the Ulan officer who had recognised Wojciech.

"Obviously," said Seweryn. "I expect the English Lord will keep her as a pensioner and find someone better suited to look after his daughter."

"Could hardly be worse," muttered one of the Ulans. Apparently he had been one of the escort of the three coaches who had lost the important one; and by the look of his fellows, he was going to be one of those who lost. One way or another.

"I heard from the maid that she faints at the drop of a hat," said Seweryn, cheerfully. "So if she's in your ear, just make sure she sees someone pee at the side of the road. That should send her off."

This suggestion occasioned much laughter.

Seweryn reflected that for all that he did not understand his friend's bride, Irene did not turn a hair at men answering the call of nature, even if she was more discreet about doing so herself. He was glad that his own retainers would not have to escort the woman.

The main body might at least be on their way, taking the earl and his daughter back to the city; and as Phyllis dutifully mounted up beside her father, he waved mockingly at Wojciech, who was stuck with Miss Devon until a cart was procured.

The cavalcade was barely out of sight when the Ulans returned. They had a hay cart, with slatted sides, and some hay in it.

"*Ah, Miss Devon, your conveyance awaits,*" said Wojciech, with an unholy glee in his eyes.

"But – but I cannot go in that! It is not seemly!" cried the woman.

"Woman," said Wojciech, "You would not ride; a conveyance has been procured. And you refuse that. I see there is no pleasing you. I will tell the Ulans to return the cart, and you can either begin walking now, or when we leave tomorrow, since we shall be packing the tent and blankets, and I doubt you will want to camp out without those."

"But ... surely you will let me take the tent?"

"Woman, you must be insane," said Wojciech, coldly. "You have caused nothing but trouble, and I have no intention of depriving my betrothed wife of her privacy any longer. And if you speak one word of the filthy and slanderous thoughts you are formulating, I will see you prosecuted ... if I do not hand you over to my bride to chastise you. Lady Phyllis made the best of a bad situation. You, I think, always find that people are unkind to you, and your situations intolerable. Let me tell you that if you were kindlier and you were more tolerant both to people and went half way to meet them in accepting arrangements made, you would then find that people would be kinder to you, and go further in making your situations comfortable. Do I think the Ulans went out of their way to find a humiliating and uncomfortable form of transport? Yes, actually, I do, though I'll not accuse them of it. And why would they do that for sheer spite if they did not see it as getting back at you? Now, I will leave you with some advice. Accept the cart. Accept it with good grace, thank the Ulans for their trouble, and make jokes about feeling like a turnip on the way to market. You will find they will warm to you."

"Why would I want them to warm to me? They are only soldiers."

"They are better born than you are, but they understand duty," snapped Wojciech. If the silly besom would not learn, then it would soon not be his problem.

And he made it clear that he would not send them for any better carriage, so she must accept it, or walk.

Jadzia quietly retrieved the blankets she tried to take

with her, and murmured that stealing from szlachta was not a good idea.

And Wojciech heaved a sigh of relief to see her depart.

Chapter 22

"I know I have been ungracious to that woman, but she started on at me when I was out of my mind with worry about you," said Wojciech, telling Irene all about it when she awoke. "Was I too harsh?"

"She got on my nerves too," said Irene. "Poor Phyllis! Why do you think I organised some light relief for her, training as Seweryn's page?"

Wojciech laughed.

"I suspect you'd consider training as a hussar light relief."

"By comparison? Well, actually, yes."

He considered.

"I wouldn't actually disagree," he said. "And what you didn't hear, being delirious, was that she was in that poor child's ear all the time, how she should sit, what a pity it was they did not have their embroidery silks, what was she thinking of helping to gather firewood which would roughen her hands, all in this dying whine of a voice like a mosquito on laudanum."

"Harsh, but graphic," said Irene. "And what I heard of her, accurate. I consider putting such a woman over a child to be worse than occasional judicial beating."

"Were you ever beaten?"

"Captain Zieliński put his belt across my backside once or twice when I scared him with being crazier than he intended; It was a point made, not something to leave marks. But I deserved the time when he gave me three hard strokes, and I got over it and it did not affect my affection for him because he stood in place of a father, save that not being my father, he felt more responsible for me, in a way. And to be honest, I would rather have had his harshest punishment for every infraction than have a continual complaint like that female. I don't know how Phyllis could describe her as kindly."

"She probably was ingratiating to the girl's mother, who told her daughter what a kindly woman she was," said Wojciech, cynically. "Are you still game to set off tomorrow?"

"Yes," said Irene. "But I have been quite spoiled by the opportunity to sleep in your arms, and I don't want to go back to sleeping alone."

Wojciech sighed.

"Well ..." he said, "I confess I slept better than I have ever done on campaign before."

"Then it's good for us," said Irene.

"Casuistry, but let it pass," said Wojciech. "I can't believe I just agreed to let a casuistry pass."

"Because I wore you down a little bit, my love, and it's not as if you weren't going to marry me anyway," said Irene. "We remain chaste, which is what counts in the eyes of God, and I don't really care that much about the eyes of man."

"I concede the point," said Wojciech.

It was a good night's sleep, and Irene felt much better in the morning.

"And we will diverge from Seweryn's path to resume our former plans," said Wojciech.

"Jadzia," said Irene. "We must find out if she can ride."

"She's a country girl," said Wojciech. "She's also a good judge of horseflesh, and picked herself out a decent mount from those we took from the brigands. We may as well sell the rest. The coach horses have gone off with the rescue party, Phyllis is riding one, and with Jadzia on another, that leaves thirteen, and Lynx has claimed the leader's horse as better than the one he has been riding, which might well go in with the others. Though a spare horse does not come amiss. Jadzia had only a band-box for her clothing, which will not add much to the sumpter-ponies. I'll place them in the hands of the wójt, and ask if any belong to anyone, and if the owners are not found, ask that they be put up to auction. One of the safe-houses I had Jaromar set up is in Lublin, so any monies from auctions can go there."

It was a long day's ride, and Irene sighed in relief when the distinctive Kraków Gate of the city came into view, with its cupola and clock.

"The city is enormous," she said.

"It's a royal city," said Wojciech. "Some of the buildings are fine and relatively new ones, though, after a fire caused much destruction some sixty years ago. However, the castle wasn't harmed, nor the chapel in its grounds, which has paintings all over the inside in the Byzantine manner; the Church of Rome and the Eastern Church were co-operating with each other at the time."

"I should like to see it."

"I will see if it can be arranged. There are portraits of King Władisław II Jagiełło in it, being built on his orders."

They were lucky to get into the city as the gates were closing, and were quickly in the Rynek or market square. Wojciech dismounted to go into the Crown Tribunal building which dominated the centre of the cobbled square. He returned with an official who regarded the twelve horses – they had decided to keep Lynx's former horse –with some agitation, stroking his moustache as though, murmured Irene to Jan, to calm it down, like a frightened cat.

Jan had a nasty coughing fit.

"We have a house near the Grodzka gate; the land drops away quite sharply each side of the road so the houses are on two levels. Jaromir thought that might come in handy," said Wojciech as the reluctant official led the extra horses away. "There are also interconnecting cellars." He laughed self-consciously.

"Not that we need it here; after Pomaranczowemiasto I am a little over-cautious."

"I wonder what happened to my uncle when Seweryn threw him out."

"With luck he ran back to Russia to his mother with his tail between his legs," said Wojciech. "Oh, that's the cathedral; I don't know if we will be here long enough to attend Mass there, I do really want to get on. I have some sense of urgency."

"I don't deny I'd like to hurry now, though I am too dog-tired to appreciate its splendour properly," said Irene.

"It's the first baroque building in the city, but beyond that I can't tell you a lot," said Wojciech, waving a hand in the direction of the cathedral, which dominated the town.

The house they reached was a high building, the upper storeys decorated with some kind of chequer-board pattern, which it was now too dark to see in detail. Wojciech knocked; and the door was swiftly opened.

"My lord! I thought you were dead!" gasped the man who opened it.

"You didn't guess when Jaromar Nowak gave you instructions to hold this house?" said Wojciech, recovering fast.

"No, my lord, only that it was your last instructions ... please come in, you and the other lord... we have stabling ..."

"Direct me, lad, and I'll find it," said Jan.

The obsequious caretaker did so, and shouted for his wife.

"I'll go out shopping right away and see what I can get," he said.

"If you've dried mushrooms enough for pierogi in soup, we shall do very well on that," said Wojciech. "And if there's not enough bread we'll eat it in bowls. I gave orders that there should always be plenty of dried foods and preserves in the house, in case of visits."

"Why, yes, of course, my lord, and the wife will have a baking of bread in no time, but we were not expecting ..."

"Andrzej, isn't it? My digestion and that of Lord Walenty work as well as anyone else's on good simple food," said Wojciech.

"Yes, my lord, of course, my lord," said Andrzej, who had nodded eagerness to claim the name.

It was disappointing to have to sleep alone, but at least it was in a down mattress, not a tent. And tomorrow they were going to go and find a jeweller! Irene snuggled down, unaware that many young ladies of her estate would be unable to understand why her excitement was over the making of a slightly battered feather into jewellery when she could have asked a fabulously wealthy young man for almost anything.

The jeweller looked at the feather.

"Yes, yes, I can make it into a jewelled clasp, but I can find better feathers, and dye them to any shade you wish ..."

"It is that feather which has more value than all the jewellery in your shop to me," said Irene, firmly. "The sentimental associations outweigh its rather well-travelled state."

The goldsmith did not mention that in his opinion, if the feather was well-travelled, the sea was damp, and winter was coolish. He had, however, made very rough hair samples into things of beauty, and he smoothed the feather with his finger.

"It will be better if I split it in half," he said. "I can join the ends ..."

"Would it then make a heart shape?" asked Irene. "What?" she added as Wojciech raised an eyebrow. "I can be sentimental and romantic, even if my idea of a love token is more likely to be the heads of my love's enemies than anything more traditional."

Wojciech laughed.

"Well, the opening on the cheek pieces of a hussar's helmet are heart shaped, too; I make no objection."

"And what sort of jewellery did you have in mind?" asked the jeweller.

"Oh, a jewelled pin for a hat," said Irene. "Nothing too showy, though, a plain sort of frame."

"Edged in diamonds," said Wojciech, firmly. "When you want to show a girl that you love her, you do it with diamonds."

"As you choose," said Irene.

The jeweller showed diamonds, and when Wojciech chose what he thought suitable, diffidently suggested a sum. When Wojciech just nodded, the jeweller determined to make the feather into a thing of beauty for so profitable a piece of business.

"May I watch you shape the feather?" asked Irene.

The jeweller was startled that a young chub would ask so politely.

"To be sure, my lord; you need not fear that I will discard it and get another," he added.

Irene shuffled.

"I apologise that I was so blatant," she said.

"I understand, my lord," said the jeweller. "You won a token from your sweetheart and it is a symbol. I, too, can be sentimental."

"Thank you," said Irene.

His fingers were skilled, and shaped the feather, the broken end forming the point of the heart, and the skillfully separated plumed end making the two lobes. He secured wire to the feather's shaft to shape it better, and divided up the barbs to weave in and out of each other.

"I am going to cut a piece of red flannel to lay underneath this," he said, "for there are a few barbs missing, and I think it will disguise that, and add to the depth of colour. Boy! Go and bring the mistress's rag bag," he called to his apprentice. "If you wanted flannel purchased purposely, my lord, it will take longer."

"Oh, I am happy to make use of remnants," said Irene. "If your wife does not mind."

"Bless you, my lord, it will delight her that one of her pieces furthers the course of true love."

There was some red flannel in the bag the boy brought and the jeweller deftly snipped a heart and laid the feather on top of it.

"Oh, I do see what you mean," said Irene. "It does not show through as flannel but it makes the feathers show fuller. How clever!"

"I will have a setting for it by the middle of the afternoon," said the jeweller.

"Thank you; we will return then," said Wojciech. "You loaned out some of your clothes to a distressed traveller, Walenty; we must get more."

A tailor promised several suits of clothes for the young milord to be delivered by the time the shop closed, being paid in advance, and if Wojciech found it amusing that, like him, she just agreed with what was suggested to get it over with, he did not tease her.

"And now we shall have to wait over another night," grumbled Irene.

"But we will have your promise token," said Wojciech.

"I didn't need it set with diamonds," said Irene.

"But I did," said Wojciech. "I am your lord, after all. And you like me being masterful."

Irene laughed.

"I love thee and I adore thee and I cede to thy will as I cede to you my life and my body," she said.

"And only you could make a vow which manages to combine a marriage vow with duty to your rotmistrz, which position I must take as the only one to be raising

195

a poczet."

"Who was your rotmistrz?"

"Seweryn's father. It's mostly an honorary position. Seweryn raised his own, and firmly served without another lieutenant in his place. It was more fun when we were both just companions though."

Irene had to work not to squeal with delight like a girl at her hat pin. Her pleasure was clear in her green eyes, however, and the jeweller was glad.

"I will be certain to mention who made such a beautiful piece," said Irene. "Why, you did such a beautiful job with the feather, that I can only see where it was damaged because I know."

The jeweller was happy, and sincerely wished the young lord good luck with his lady.

"We ought to get you a bridal gown," said Wojciech.

"I can wear one of Mama's beautiful gowns," said Irene. "She did love to embroider, so there are plenty to choose from. I know you are more interested whether my armour is on properly."

"Brides are supposed to enjoy dressing up," laughed Wojciech. "I think you are beautiful whatever you wear."

"And it's only for the village that I don't suggest getting married in armour," she said.

"And the bride wore feathers ... on her wings," laughed Wojciech.

Chapter 23

"It's three days at a sensible pace to Białystok or as the horses are rested we can push them to do it in two," said Wojciech.

"It's *four* days to Białystok at a sensible pace, my lord, three days at a push and two days for the insane," said Jan. "Thaws and rain. The going will be sticky to say the least."

"I like going fast," said Wojciech.

"Jester doesn't," said Irene.

"Oh well, I suppose it is one horse one vote, and any one horse may cast a veto like our idiotic parliament," said Wojciech. "Though any one of our horses is probably more sensible than most of the parliament. And I hate to admit it, but Jan is right. Three days."

"We can manage that," said Irene. "And how long then?"

"Er ... four or five days?" said Wojciech.

"It would be nicer if there were larger tents available," said Irene.

"Oh, there are, but they really need a cart, not sumpter beasts," said Wojciech.

"I see; in that case it makes sense," said Irene.

"I knew you'd understand," said Wojciech enthusiastically. "I always have to argue with Jan."

"My bones are old enough to have liked the idea of carrying a decent size of tent, such as an officer usually has," said Jan. "And in a cart, one carries hay and palliasses to stuff it into. And other provisions. But cart horses can't do more'n thirty miles a day and rest every fourth day, and that won't do for his lordship, oh no."

"You didn't have to come, Jan," said Wojciech.

"Who would keep you out of trouble if I didn't?" grunted Jan.

"What a pair of frauds you are," said Irene. "You say contradictory things but they all sound like 'I love you' to me."

"Don't tell everyone, Walenty, I'd lose my reputation as a grumbler," said Jan.

The road to Białystok was the main road to Wilno, and was consequently well travelled and generally safe, and the travellers maintained a good speed to be there in the three days. They were also able to stay in inns, which suited the horses better too. It came on to rain as they reached Białystok and the rain was cold.

"I am not moving on until the weather clears," said Irene. "I feel a little feverish again, and I am sorry, my lord, I prefer to be safe than sorry. I can't stop shivering. I am so cold."

Wojciech, concerned, nodded.

"Of course. I hate this penetrating rain myself; I swear it has a way of mining through clothes."

"And you can hang damp clothes up in a large tent," said Jan. "And officers' tents have fireplaces."

"That must be risky," said Irene.

"Only if you don't take care ... or are unlucky," said Jan.

"Yes, but this is Wojciech," said Irene, her eyes laughing at him.

"Oh, I see, it's pick on Wojciech day," said Wojciech. He was laughing.

The two young szlachta were given adjoining rooms in the large inn, with Jan across the corridor and Lynx on a truckle in with him. Irene walked into Wojciech's arms, as soon as they had changed into dry clothes.

"I have missed being with you; an advantage of the tents," she said.

"It is," he said, kissing her tenderly. Irene pressed against him, and it may be said that they both became somewhat mussed, before Jan cleared his throat loudly.

"Thought I ought to interrupt," he said.

"Thank you, and less complimentary messages,"

said Wojciech. "Irenka, are you going to take advantage of it being a big inn to get your female garb ironed? It's a little soon to change into it."

Irene blinked.

"Why would I want to change into female garb at all?" she asked.

"Oh, I rather thought that you might want to be a woman to meet your father," said Wojciech.

"I was planning on riding up the steps and into the vestibule knee to knee with you in full armour and wings," said Irene, mildly. "It ought to get his attention."

Wojciech laughed merrily.

"Yes, I should think it would," he said.

"Mad, both of them," said Jan.

They were in the tavern, and Wojciech was paying for mead when another szlachcic strode up to him and laid a hand on the wrist which was on the bar. This young man was dressed in the Western fashion, with tightly curled wig, close-fitting brocade jacket, embroidered waistcoat and striped silk breeches.

The newcomer was staring at Wojciech's hand.

"Where did you get that ring?" he demanded.

Wojciech's ring was a distinctive piece of jewellery; a ruby, carved on the underside to show through the cabuchon-cut top in the semblance of a wing.

"I inherited it; take your hand off mine," said Wojciech.

"You are lying! It last belonged to Wojciech Płodziewicz of the Skrzydło Banner and he is dead. I am the heir!"

"Mother of God! Cousin Kacper!" said Wojciech. "I am amazed, I thought someone surely would have found a way for you to have a deliberate accident on your visit to France. You look ridiculous."

"No! You are dead! You can't be Wojciech!" howled the young man. "You are an imposter!"

"Reports of my death have been a trifle premature. You have a circular scar on your left buttock where I caught you with an un-tipped lance when you were running away," said Wojciech. "Anyway, you won't ever inherit; I'm married."

It was a small stretch of the truth.

"Accidents can happen," said Kacper.

"Certainly; probably to you," said Wojciech. "My wife wields a sword as well as any hussar. She killed her first wolf over the winter."

"I still say you are lying!" said Kacper.

"I get tired of talking to you," said Wojciech, and hit him, hard.

Kacper went down.

"Someone take out the trash," said Wojciech.

"My lord .... he is a szlachcic; I cannot throw him out," said the landlord.

"Oh? Has he luggage?"

"But yes; it has not yet been taken up."

"Then I will throw him out for you and his luggage as well," said Wojciech. "I outrank him. I am the head of the family and he is from a cadet branch."

"Very well, my lord," said the landlord, relieved.

Wojciech hoisted the unconscious Kacper over one shoulder, and nodded to Jan and Lynx, who were eating in the main room.

They went in search of Kacper Płodziewicz's luggage as Wojciech dumped his cousin out into the middle of a large puddle which was forming in the inn yard. Kacper came to.

"You'll pay for that!" he spluttered.

"Never have paid yet, in all the years you've been a nuisance," said Wojciech. "Stay in another inn. Do not come near me. Do not look for my wife. Do not ever touch me again. It will take me much washing to feel clean again."

He turned and walked away.

Kacper pulled a pistol from his pocket and aimed it. Wojciech's warrior-trained sixth-sense had him duck out of the way of the ball as he heard the pistol cock, and he turned around.

"I think that gives me a free shot," he said. Steam arose from the cold puddle in the region of Kacper's groin. Wojciech laughed, as he drew his own pistol, took careful aim, and fired.

Kacper gasped when he thought that Wojciech had missed; but suddenly realised that his wig had been shot off his head! He put his hands to his bald pate and howled in horror.

"Don't push me," said Wojciech.

He went back in.

"And just who is this cousin of yours?" asked Irene.

"A nasty little tell-tale who loved – and probably still loves – provoking people and then running away, and telling about how they hit him when he had pushed them beyond endurance," said Wojciech. "My curls were one of his targets. Jaromar was another as there was nothing Jaromar could do to a better-off child. Although in theory and in law all szlachta are equal, in practise it doesn't work like that. When Kacper got older he would interfere with maidservants. You know the type."

"Yes; just like Uncle Władimir," said Irene, dryly. "I heard shots but I did not want to make a scene; I knew Lynx would get me if needed."

"He fired at my back so I shot his wig off," said Wojciech. "I'm a better shot than he is. But be aware of him. I told him I was married and implied that I was a father."

"A matter of dates; a bagatelle," said Irene, waving an airy hand.

"Well, yes, so thought I," said Wojciech. "You are becoming too good at persuading me to accept casuistries."

"Oh good," said Irene. "Should I put on a dress so that you can be seen with your wife?"

"No!" said Wojciech. "I don't trust him not to try to shoot you in the back; and in a city it is easier to escape into a crowd."

Irene nodded.

"You had no difficulty handling him, so I did not think of that. Such a man is not worthy of my sword."

"Don't let that stop you cutting him down if he makes trouble for you, my beloved," said Wojciech, seriously.

"I won't," promised Irene. "Wojciech, what am I going to do if I have to appear in public as a woman? I will feel naked without a sword, now."

"That is a problem," admitted Wojciech. "I know! Some men have sword sticks, and it might not be a bad idea for me to have one, and we can have a sword parasol made for you."

"What a clever idea!" Irene was delighted. "We can have one made for Phyllis as well."

"Excellent idea," said Wojciech. "While we are kicking our heels here, I will see if I can find a cutler able to make one." He laughed suddenly. "You know, I wonder if Kacper is likely to be kicking his heels around the new midwifery school, founded by the king's sister, thinking me to have brought you here over some difficulty?"

"If Białystok is famous for it, then that keeps him out from under foot," said Irene. "Is that snow I see out of the window?"

"It wouldn't surprise me," said Wojciech. "Winters here on the plain are long. This is the coldest part of Poland, though surely it was as cold in your father's lands?"

"No, it's cool but not so bitter feeling," said Irene. "Only when the wind is in the east, when it does not trouble to go round you, it takes a short cut right through. Mama used to call it a 'lazy' wind, and said she wished she was home in Cambridgeshire where so-called lazy winds were gentle in comparison."

"I've only stayed here once," admitted Wojciech. "My father went to some conference or other hosted in the Branicki Palace. It's a French conceit complete with formal gardens and outsize quasi-classical statuary and it's perishing cold, being built for show and not for Polish winters. I spent the greater part of the visit in the orangery, as the plants at least got a bit more warmth. There's a statue of a rather chunky Actaeon in the gardens wearing nothing more than a strategically draped cloak and I got cuffed by one of the other guests for commenting that the cloak hid where his assets had been frozen and dropped off, and serve him right, because only an idiot would go hunting naked, even in good weather. To be fair, I was only ten at the time."

Irene chuckled.

"Whose silly idea was this palace?"

"Hetman Jan Klemens Branicki, who had aspirations to rise to the crown. He and his wife built it, and redesigned the main city square."

"Goodness, all by themselves?"

He chuckled.

"You know very well that I mean 'caused to have it built,' you whelp. He managed to die childless despite having three wives."

"That sounds greedy. Not all at once, I hope?"

"No, sequentially; he divorced the middle one. I saw a portrait of him in the palace, and his moustache looks like a declaration of war. But then, for a Hetman, a military commander, later Crown-Hetman, I suppose that's fair enough. He and the third wife were patrons of the arts."

"Art is all very well, but I'm more interested in keeping warm," said Irene.

Wojciech left Irene by the fire and went in search of someone to make sword-parasols. And at least in a large city, fewer questions were asked than might have been in a small place. Wojciech found he had to supply his own parasols, which necessitated a search to find such exotic and arcane items. He ended up getting a white lace parasol and a green silk parasol which he felt certain matched Irenka's eyes, and another white lace one for Phyllis, on the expectation she could take off the lace and dye it.

"What, one for each wife, my lord?" laughed the cutler when he presented them.

"No, one each to do several costumes, with one for dyeing," said Wojciech.

"Ah, a wise husband," said the cutler.

"I do my best," said Wojciech.

The poor weather lingered for several days, and Irene went shopping. Being Irene, she shopped largely for supplies and more fur and for down-filled quilts for all of them.

"They will be awkward to carry," said Wojciech.

"Then we can have another sumpter pony," said Irene. "I'd rather know we were all warm than have diamonds. Jadzia is alone in her tent when we are not staying in inns, and she will be freezing without something more than a few blankets. I have to say that if I had known about weather conditions in this part of the country, I would have supported Jan."

"I'll get another sumpter pony," said Wojciech, hastily. "I thought we might push on the fifty odd miles to Grodno and stay in an inn there overnight. Then we need to decide whether to stay on the road to Wilno, or the road for Mińsk or strike off between them."

"I'm for striking off between them and getting away

from people, but you are the seasoned traveller," said Irene.

"At least it's flat and we shall make good time," said Wojciech. "We shall attend mass at the cathedral tomorrow and set out the day after, unless the weather is seriously inclement."

Spiritually renewed, and with a thin, but at least visible sun they set off on Monday.

"Only two weeks to Easter," said Irene. "How time flies!"

"Well, we shall be able to get married right after Easter," said Wojciech.

The journey to Grodno was tiring but uneventful, and Irene admitted to herself that a comfortable bed was an advantage. However, she was looking forward to being back on the less well travelled routes and sleeping in a tent with Wojciech. Consequently, she was singing happily to herself when she went down to fettle the horses ready for their continued journey.

"Irenka!"

The hated voice was shocked, and Irene turned round to look directly into the eyes of her uncle, who was looking out of the window of a carriage pulled by six fine horses.

Terror froze her, as he flung open the carriage door and seized her, throwing her up into the carriage.

Chapter 24

Wojciech was finishing dressing, with Jan's help to get his kontusz sash bound properly around him. He had helped Irene with hers as they had played cards for who was to go down early to get the horses ready, and Irene had lost.

There was a shrill, female scream from outside, and Wojciech stiffened.

"Was that Irenka screaming?" said Wojciech sharply, at the window in one bound.

"Of course not, Irenka does not scream," scoffed Jan.

"Yes she does when she needs me," said Wojciech, in soft-spoken fury, recognising his beloved as she vanished involuntarily into a coach which started off briskly. "Bring the rest on at best speed: Ogień and I are going hunting. Someone has abducted Irenka!" Like a panther he leapt to grab a cloak and hat and his sword and pistol on their belt.

And then he was running downstairs, buckling on his sword as he went, angry with himself that he had not insisted that Irene wear a sword at all times, even in an inn. She was ... no, his Irenka was never helpless. But she had no sword or pistol, not even a knife. She had her wits, though something had addled them enough to enable someone to grab her. What on earth had possessed her to let herself be seized like that?

Probably her uncle, he reasoned. She was more than a match for the disgraced Wojewoda, but she was still afraid of him.

He tore into the stables, and made himself saddle Ogień carefully and calmly, and lead him out.

"On our way boy," he said, leaping into the saddle even as Ogień started to the canter from a standing start. Head down and holding his fury in check, he headed out of the city, pausing to ask if a black coach with six black horses had headed that way.

"Yes, my lord, and the man inside shouted to his coachman to take the northern road, not the Mińsk road, why, thank you, my lord!" the gate guard had rarely handled dukats, worth six zloty, and certainly not a handful of them.

"Tell my man when he follows," called Wojciech, kicking his heels to Ogień's flanks. The horse exploded into action and the gate guard reflected that such a horse would be worth enough to buy his home village; what a steed!

Wojciech took the northern road, coincidentally the one they had intended to take, narrower and less well travelled than either the main road to Mińsk or the even more northerly one to Vilnius. The damned black coach had fifteen or twenty minutes start on him, and with six horses on the flat could make ten or twelve miles an hour without difficulty for a couple of hours. The coach was limited by its stability; much faster and it might overturn. Wojciech slowed his enthusiastic horse to a canter; he might catch the coach at the gallop before he was exhausted, but it would be unlikely. If they cantered for a mile and then alternated trot and canter to allow Ogień time to recover they would do better. Wojciech calculated in his head, the coach must be four miles ahead. He could do that in around a quarter of an hour, by which time the damned coach would be another three miles further on. He wished he was good at mathematics! He needed to know if it was feasible to overtake them without dropping to a trot. Could it be done?

"Ogień, oh Ogień, bohatyr amongst horses, I place myself and my beloved in the care of your hoofs," cried Wojciech, in anguish. "Take me at the speed you can manage, beloved companion."

Ogień snorted, and continued at a smooth canter. Fit

and strong, well-exercised, and not labouring under the extra weight of armour and wings, he felt able to run all day.

Wojciech murmured his love and appreciation to his noble steed, and let himself relax as a passenger. Ogień did not need the constant pressure of his knees to maintain the canter; he was a war horse and he knew what urgency was. He would slow to a trot when he felt a need to do so, and not before.

Wojciech started considering what he would like to do to Władimir Trąbka. At least at such a prodigious pace the fellow would be unable to be able to assault her sexually; the coach would be bouncing along and swaying, and any man who attempted to ravish a maiden under such conditions was asking for trouble, even with a girl who was cowed. And his Irenka would not remain cowed for long. Her temper was too hot for that.

Irene, once landing on the floor of the coach, and banging her knee in doing so, was furious. Furious at herself for freezing and at her uncle for daring to abduct her.

She got up, slowly, regarding him with loathing.

"So you ran away dressed as a boy! Now that's something I did not expect," said Władimir. "Where on earth did you find the clothes of a szlachcic?"

Irene measured the difference between them, scowling. The hatch to the coachman's seat opened.

"Which way, my lord, through Mińsk or directly?"

"Not through Mińsk, take the northern road," called Władimir. "And get those horses running!"

"Yes, my lord," said the coachman. It was a well-paid job and he could not afford to be nice about his lord's fits and starts, and they had travelled with an extra passenger before. Always female, and of a variety of classes, though never szlachta and never male. Oh well, he was not paid enough to wonder whether the effete decadent fool wanted a change. Or maybe it was as simple as a kidnapping to exert pressure on someone. Who knew?

The coach began to sway and buck. Irene watched as Władimir took a grip on the hand hold, and leaped for him. Władimir squealed with fear. Irene plied her knee judiciously, and got her hands to Władimir's throat.

He started gurgling, terrified, slapping at her. Then he pulled a pistol.

"Let me go or I shoot!" he managed to croak.

"Like I care?" said Irene. "I'd rather be dead than go with you."

"I don't have to kill ... shoot you in elbow or knee ..." He pointed the gun towards Irene's leg.

Irene swallowed. She knew what a bullet wound felt like. Unless he was lucky and hit her knee or shattered her thigh bone, she could function.

It was at this moment that bad luck struck.

A particularly violent swerve of the coach to avoid some obstacle, whether a stone or a pothole Irene would never know, and the coach rocked violently. Both were thrown to one side and Irene hit her head on the door frame. Bright light flashed for a moment and then darkness took her.

When Irene came to, her uncle was moving away from her. Her hands were tied with his kontusz sash. It was not well done, but it would be hard to work it looser with him watching her.

"You are a little spitfire," said Władimir. "I don't know what you've been up to, but it hasn't improved your disposition."

"I wager you'd be surprised," said Irene, trying to sound amused.

"Well, I doubt you have been whoring; you're too frigid," said Władimir. "And whilst it might be amusing for a man to tame you into performing anyway, you wouldn't know what to do go get clients. You'd sneer at them and lose their money. You won't sneer at me, though, when I get you back to your father's house, and then I'll school you, with a whip. Your reputation's ruined anyway."

Irene laughed.

"I would love to see you explaining that to my husband," she said.

"Husband? I find that hard to believe. Who would you find to marry you?"

Irene laughed again.

"Really? You can't work it out?"

"What? Now don't you try to fool me by talking about the man your father had picked, the Baron of Płodnadolina is dead."

"Really, are you so dense?" sneered Irene. "I meant a far more immediate threat to you; the man you never did cow or capture. The Blood Angel."

Władimir paled.

"You ... you are insane!" he tried. "If I could not find him, how could you?"

"What, had it not occurred to you that he came for me?" said Irene. It was far from the truth but had Wojciech already been her lover, he would have come for her. "You fool. Who else do you think rode the second red horse towards the defunct cannon?"

"The cannon was sabotaged!" he yelped.

"Really?" said Irene. He stared.

"Oh! I see! You knew I would use it and sabotaged it before you left; no man would let you face a cannon if he did not know it had been damaged. You unnatural female!"

Irene smiled.

Her Wojciech took an informed risk in letting her, or rather, Jester, face the old cannon. But that was Wojciech. He accepted that there were risks and that his people would walk into them with their eyes open. That he expected to be the one to take most of the risks was also very much Wojciech. And that his bride would take the next level of risk. But if her uncle wanted to think she had sabotaged the cannon, it did no harm to let him think so.

She sat, smirking and sneering.

"It wasn't ever difficult for us to fool you," she said. "Your men were stupid little inadequates, taking after their leader. A dolt for a wojewoda leads to dolts amongst his men. Not the calibre of an adequate leader, but then, your calibre like the rest of your manhood is only birdshot."

"You little bitch!"

He leaned over to slap her, hard enough to knock her off her seat.

It hurt, but Irene continued smirking. He was infuriated. Perhaps if she angered him enough he would make a mistake. She lay on the floor, drawing up her knees.

"My blood angel will come for you," she said. "In an hour ... in a day ... in a week. He will find that you have taken me and he will pursue you for me to the ends of the earth if needs be. Did you plan on outrunning him? Six horses are hardly enough, you know, nor my father's house, which seems to be the direction we are taking. My blood angel would take Moscow if he had to in order to retrieve me, and when he catches you ... oh, I wonder what he will do? He won't crucify you, especially so close to Easter, it would be blasphemous. He might shoot you full of arrows." She paused, looking thoughtful. "It would take a while, though, because good as he is with a lance he's not that good an archer," she added.

Dispassionately considering the Blood Angel's skills and those he lacked were not to Władimir's taste.

"Be silent!" he cried.

"Or what? Of course he might break you on the wheel. Or have you thrown to wild boar. Or emasculate you and sell you as a eunuch to the Ottomans," said Irene, smiling evilly up from her position on the floor.

Władimir was terrified of the Blood Angel, and his blood ran cold. Any one of those things so terrible a fellow might consider ... if his sheltered niece had heard of such, the terrible Blood Angel must have done such things for her to be aware of them!

He leaned over her to grab her by the neck of her żupan and slap her again, and Irene rocked back onto her shoulder blades, her legs straightening with a pile-driving force straight into his chest! Władimir was hurled backwards, winded.

Wojciech thundered along, flattened against Ogień's neck, balanced to give the horse as light and easy a load as possible. They had been going for half an hour, maybe a little more, Ogień having taken a couple of brief rests trotting. They had caught up time by cutting across curves in the road, and Wojciech had felt the need to throw some coins to an irate farmer whose spring planting had been rather disrupted by Ogień's churning hoofs after having leaped a hedge onto the soft, turned soil. Wojciech had whispered a prayer of contrition and promised a number of hail Marys when one of the plots they cut across turned out to be a graveyard; and privately and with a touch of guilt at such irreverence wondered if any of those buried there who had known love would be cheering him on.

Ahead there was a tell-tale cloud of dust. The road swung to the right.

Ogień knew a dust sign when he saw it, and put himself at the ditch and hedge to the right of the road. Wojciech moved to facilitate the jump with the ease and grace of a man to whom the saddle is a second home, and let Ogień find the best line across country.

212

It cut a mile or more off the distance; and when they re-emerged onto the road, the dust cloud was closer.

Ogień gave a questioning neigh.

"Not yet, old friend," said Wojciech. "Taking position."

One more curve.

The coach was less than half a mile away. They were slowly gaining.

Trąbka had nothing to gain in killing Irene. No man could ravish her in a bucking, swaying vehicle. No point making a mess of things now for impatience.

A quarter of a mile.

He loosed the sabre and let it hang on its knot.

Two hundred yards.

"Let's get her, Ogień!" he whispered.

It was not a conventional call to charge, and whether Ogień just recognised the familiar action of loosening the sabre or whether he really did understand Wojciech so well, Wojciech never would to his dying day know. But the horse moved smoothly to a ground-eating gallop and as they drew level with the back of the coach, Wojciech was up and standing on the saddle in one fluid move, something he had never tried at this speed; and as Ogień overtook the speeding carriage, Wojciech leaped from the saddle onto the coachman's seat, knocking the man clean off it, and took the reins, bringing the sweating steeds to a smooth stop.

Chapter 25

Irene knew she had to take advantage of her uncle being winded, and let the momentum of her kick bring her back and let her roll to her feet, not easy with her hands tied. She could, and did, kick him hard in the crotch, which gave her more time to fight with the knotted sash about her wrists, biting at the silk and pulling at the knot.

The coach lurched sideways and started slowing! Irene worked faster. Perhaps there was a chance here of escape.

She managed to get the knot undone at last while her uncle groaned, and as the coach came to a stop, she freed her hands and bounded over to the door, which suddenly opened, almost causing her to fall out. She turned the fall into a leap.

Right into Wojciech's arms.

Wojciech leaped from the driver's box as soon as the team stopped, and went to wrench open the door. He was not expecting Irene to leap right into his arms.

"My darling! What has he done to you?" cried Wojciech in outrage, looking at her bruised face.

"Oh he isn't capable of doing much, but I'm cold and I've banged my knee," said Irene.

"My love! Put on my cloak; I want to speak to your uncle," said Wojciech, removing his cloak and wrapping it tenderly about her.

Władimir was cowering in the coach.

He gaped at Wojciech.

"The Baron of Płodnadolina! But you're dead!" he cried.

"I recovered remarkably quickly," said Wojciech. "Really, you recognise me? How lowering. Now, get out of there; I am going to kill you, and if you get a move on, I'll let you fight me so you can die with a sword in your hand and bring less shame on my bride by being related to her."

Władimir got out of the coach, limping slightly.

"Your bride ... my brother went behind my back, then," he said.

"Leaping to conclusions is why you were so easy to defeat," said Wojciech. "Hurry up, I don't have all day to waste with your execution."

Władimir shuddered.

"The bitch kicked me in the cods," he whined.

"Well I am glad she was accurate enough to find such a small target," said Wojciech. "You don't do much with them, so why worry?"

Władimir drew his sword with a snarl.

Wojciech parried the wild attack, and batted the sword right out of Władimir's hand.

"Pick it up," he said.

Władimir bent to pick up the sword, but as he came up straight, with a snarl on his face he brought up his pistol – and fired right into Wojciech's face!

Wojciech cried out and fell.

Irene gave a scream of rage and seized her lover's sword, dropping the cloak on his still body.

"En guarde!" she cried.

Władimir laughed.

"With you? Gladly," he said. "A good beating with the side of my blade will do you the world of good."

Like all szlachta he had been trained in sword fighting from an early age. He might not have learned as much or practiced as assiduously as some, but he should be able to make a fool of an untrained woman.

The cold, well-trained, well-drilled valkyrie of a szlachcianka countering his moves and pushing forward her own attack was not what he expected. Irene swallowed her anger, knowing that anger made mistakes, and treated it as a drill. Parry ... thrust ... parry ... slash ...recover .... parry ... slash, recover, use the mistake, thrust.

Władimir's panic meant a wild parry left him open, and Irene brought her sword up through his gut after following through the feint, sidestep and attempt at the classic Polish Quarte crosscut. Lacking strength, and with an unfamiliar sword, she failed to take the blade all the way from gut to armpit and did not kill him in one blow.

Władimir screamed and fell backwards, his hands scrabbling futilely towards his gut as though to hold the rent in them together as Irene withdrew the blade.

She went straight to Wojciech.

The coachman had managed to get up and was approaching. Irene held her sword loosely, standing over her lord.

"Get the hell out of here and I won't kill you," she said, levelly. "And unless you want to be indicted for abducting a minor, you will stay got."

The coachman nodded nervously. He did not see a distraught young girl on the defensive; he saw a dangerously competent young warrior with hellfire in his green eyes. He got. His employer was on his own; he had picked the wrong people to irritate.

Władimir was groaning in agony from the imperfect cross cut but Irene ignored him. She knelt down by Wojciech, who gave a moan of his own.

"Wojan! Beloved!" she whispered, tucking the cloak more securely about him, trying to get some of it under him to prevent cold killing him with shock.

"Irenka!" Wojciech managed. "Knocked me silly ... my ear ... hurts."

"It's running blood like the people after the cannon exploded," said Irene. "That's the least of my worries right now. Let me bathe all the black powder off your face ... there will be a canteen of water in the coach, surely ..."

She leaped up into the coach. There was a canteen of wódka, but it would have to do. She wet her kerchief with it and wiped away all the soot, Wojciech gritting his teeth as the wódka stung.

"Can you open your left eye?" asked Irene.

He tried.

"Hurts," he said.

Irenka muttered something which he hoped was not the word he thought it was and wondered where she might have learned it. He decided to blame Władimir.

Irene had actually learned it from Seweryn, but as Wojciech was blissfully unaware of this, he did not curse his friend. She went to look in the boot, and soon found some water for the coach horses.

She used that to bathe Wojciech's eye, and he sighed with the relief of the cool water.

"I think it's swollen, not damaged," he said. He managed to crack it open a little.

"No blood," said Irene, relieved. "It looks as though the ball scored along your head from the corner of your eye, it's bleeding sluggishly, and there's no ball. You may take a while for the powder burns to heal." She fixed him with a firm gaze. "It looks terrible, and if for one moment you do something stupidly noble and decide that you ought not to marry me because of having a bit of a scar, I will tie you to your bed and use all your wing feathers to tickle you until you give up."

"Fiend!" chuckled Wojciech.

"I mean it," said Irene.

"I could not give you up unless you told me you did not want me," said Wojciech simply. "I'm not stupid enough to think you would really mind. We are companions."

"Aye, and I'm going to give my captain orders to get himself up into the coach if he can," said Irene. "I had better finish off Uncle Władimir and put him out of his misery. Only seeing to you was a priority."

"Decapitate him," said Wojciech. "It's the quickest way. I ... I can try to do it for you ..."

"I suspect at the moment you are concussed and likely to wonder which of the three necks to aim at," said Irene. "I started it; I will finish it. Pray for my aim and fortitude."

"I will," he said.

Irene took the bloody sword back to where Władimir lay on the ground. She was uncertain if he was already dead; he might well be. She took a deep breath, swung it, and took his head cleanly off.

Then she turned aside to vomit.

The wódka did to rinse out her mouth, and she knelt to pray for her own soul as well as that of her uncle, as Wojciech climbed into the coach.

And then she got up to use the blanket from the boot to rub down Ogień, who had been cooling himself by walking up and down. She then turned to rub down the six carriage horses, who had sweated profusely. They might well take cold and die, but Irene could only do her best. She threw blankets from the box over each of them, and was wondering whether to unharness them or not when she saw dust on the road.

"People coming," she said to Wojciech.

"Hopefully ours," said Wojciech. "Thank you for seeing to Ogień. He got me here in time."

"He's a hero," said Irene.

The dust belonged to Lynx, who had ridden on ahead on his new horse.

"Lady! Is our lord ..." he could not frame a question, not seeing Wojciech but seeing the body of Władimir.

"Our lord was wounded foully in the head; my uncle thought that a pistol constituted a fair weapon in a sword duel," said Irene. "He will recover but his wits have been a little addled."

Lynx grinned.

"Jan would ask how you can tell," he said.

"Yes, he would and I'd ask if it took one to know one," said Irene. Lynx grinned again, unabashed.

"I am relieved he will be quite all right," he said. "I saw a man dressed as a coachman making good speed in the opposite direction."

"I might have threatened him a little bit," said Irene. "In retrospect he had just watched me cut out my uncle's tripes, so I suppose he may have believed me."

"A wise move on his part," said Lynx. "Lady, if I ride on to find a farm where we might drive this carriage, you and my lord might sleep in the carriage overnight, having rested today, and be better to go on tomorrow?"

"An excellent idea, Lynx; I am glad I met you that night," said Irene. "You are very reliable and resourceful."

Lynx looked pleased, and set off. Irene resumed her prayers, and Wojciech, feeling more himself, joined her. Jan found them thus when he arrived with the rest of the horses.

"Amen," he said, firmly, crossing himself. Wojciech was paler than he liked.

The young couple rose.

"Oh I am glad to see you, Jan," said Irene. "Lynx went to negotiate a place to take the coach and stay. My uncle shot Wojciech in the face but was fortunately a terrible shot. We need to bury him."

"I'll see about that," said Jan. "Lynx will help when he gets back. You and Wojan just get in that coach and have a good cuddle and cry about it all."

"Yes, Jan," said Irene, meekly. "How does he know that I am feeling weepy?" she asked Wojciech as they obeyed.

"Jan always knows these things," said Wojciech. "My love! Let me hold you."

Irene went to his arms, and cried. And then he

kissed her, and just held her, and it might be noted that both of them drifted off into such a deep doze in each other's arms that they did not notice the coach start moving again. Indeed, it was the jerk as it stopped which awoke them!

Lynx had found an obliging farmer, who was willing to let people use part of his land, and to let their horses run in his own paddock and share the rude shelter in there with his own horses.

"Oh good, you are awake, my lord, my lady," said Jadzia. "I will make you up a proper bed on the floor of the coach, we have bought hay."

"You could sleep on the seat," said Irene.

"Oh, no, lady, I will leave you to your privacy. With a quilt and hay I will be perfectly comfortable," said Jadzia. "Are we going to load the roof of the coach with hay and take it all the way?"

"Yes, I think so," said Irene. "I don't like the idea of jolting a head wound on horseback."

"Who's going to drive?" asked Wojciech.

"I won't object to you driving if you feel like it," said Irene. "Or you can stay lying down in the carriage whilst Lynx drives."

"I'll drive," said Wojciech. "Is this actually your uncle's coach?"

"I think it's his father's coach and so my father's coach; it was in the coach house when I was growing up," said Irene. "And whatever else you might say about my father, which is doubtless plenty, he is a good judge of horses. Jadzia, was Jan concerned about them taking cold?"

"He said they seemed to have escaped the worst of it as you rubbed them down," said Jadzia.

"I am relieved; I made Ogień my priority," said Irene.

"So I should hope; he is owed our thanks," said Wojciech. "I swear that horse understands more than most humans."

"A splendid horse for a splendid rider," said Irene.

"And as well Seweryn isn't here or he'd make some cutting comment about lovebirds," said Wojciech.

Wojciech felt a lot better for a good night's sleep; that it was in his lady's arms made it even better. Whilst he desired her, just being with her was what made their nights special. Hearing her soft breathing relaxed him.

Much as he loved being on Ogień, Wojciech had to admit that it was an easier day driving rather than riding. Ogień plainly considered that he was in charge and Jan gave up trying to lead the big red horse, and permitted Ogień to lead the cavalcade.

"Silly old fool," said Jan.

"I called him a bohatyr of a horse yesterday and he acknowledges it," said Wojciech. "Let him have his triumph!"

Jan laughed and shook his head.

"Anyone of your family is just plain awkward," he said.

"It's taken you near on forty years in our service to realise that?" laughed Wojciech.

It took nearer five days than four to come close to Stanisław Trąbka's lands, with Wojciech and Lynx taking turns to drive the carriage.

"Still of a mind to ride right into the vestibule in full armour?" asked Wojciech.

"Yes," said Irene. "I am tired of Trąbka men underestimating me."

"Then it shall be so," said Wojciech.

Chapter 26

"Captain Zieliński?"

"Who wants to know?"

"I'm a servant of the Lady Irene Trąbkówna," said Lynx. "I wanted to know how far you'd go for her."

"I wouldn't kill my lord unless he was harming her," said Zieliński.

"Oh, nothing that drastic," said Lynx, grinning. "Only she wants to get married and rather planned to make something of a ... statement ... to her father when demanding ... uh, requesting ... his permission."

Zieliński's moustache twitched as his mouth quirked in amusement.

"You know her well enough to be aware that the first is more accurate when she has her mind set on something."

"It does sound bad, though, and she is a very considerate employer," said Lynx.

"And whom does she want to marry? I want to know if I approve because she's not too big to spank."

"I wouldn't bet on that," said Lynx. "Not since she went through hussar training."

"She .... no, I didn't hear that aright," said Zieliński.

Lynx chuckled.

"She's got more notches on her sabre than most people," he said. "One of her notches is Władimir Trąbka; she duelled him and killed him."

"Dear God! He is ... moderately able with a sword."

"Not any more," said Lynx.

"So what does my favourite minx want?"

Lynx told him.

The sound of hoofs made Stanisław Trąbka look up.

"Ah, doubtless that is my brother ... he is coming quite fast," he said to his secretary. He got up and looked out of the windows. "Merciful God! The Blood Angel ... two Blood Angels!" He crossed himself.

Stanisław Trąbka was a moral coward, but not a physical coward. He swallowed hard and walked out into the vestibule, where his captain of the guard and one of his men were pulling open the big double doors, regardless of the protests of the butler. The two winged hussars coming at a canter looked enormous. They had not, however dropped their pennants to be set to charge, nor did they as they crashed up the steps to the front door, doing who knew what damage to the marble tiles. The hussars tossed off their lances to the captain and his man, and drew sabres from the knot. The horses stopped, reared, then as they came down both hussars came off their backs like one man, saluted with their sabres, and sheathed them. The horses turned and walked back down the steps where a man had appeared to take care of them.

"Who ... who are you?" asked Stanisław. "And what do you want?"

The small hussar took off his helmet. Her helmet. Stanisław gaped to see his daughter.

"I'm glad you asked that, father," said Irene. "I want to get married."

Wojciech suppressed the urge to laugh at how direct she could be at times. Still, she had certainly got her father's attention. Wojciech regarded his future father-in-law thoughtfully. Stanisław Trąbka was not a tall man, nor in any way charismatic. He had the sort of straggly moustache which afflicted Wojciech's own family, which strengthened Wojciech's belief that no moustache was far better than a half-hearted excuse of a wispy smear on the upper lip. He was a paler blond than Irena, whose red lights presumably had come from her mother. He was also giving covert and worried looks at Wojciech.

Wojciech took off his helmet.

"I think you should know my ring," he said, removing his glove to show it.

"But ... I thought you were dead?" said Stanisław.

"He did a bit better than some people have managed, didn't he?" said Irene.

"Undoubtedly," said Wojciech. "Without his brother, he might even improve with keeping."

"What do you mean, Lord Płodziewicz? Have you killed Władimir?" Stanisław would not have been able to explain exactly how he felt about this idea, but there was a distinct element of relief over the thought. There was also something distinctly unnerving about the way the big hussar smiled.

"Oh, no! I intended to do so, but I treated him like a szlachcic and he replied like a street urchin and drew gun in a sword fight," sneered Wojciech. "Irenka killed him."

Stanisław gaped.

"Irenka?" he said.

"It was not a clean kill, so I beheaded him after I spilled his guts out. He won't interfere with any more girls," said Irenka.

Stanisław saw red.

"*After all I did for him and he ignored me and touched you?*" he bellowed.

Irene looked at him anew.

"You know, if you can get that angry for me, I might even manage some respect for you," she said. "He confined himself to what he called 'avuncular affection', which is to say unnecessary holding of my hand and brushes of my arm and face. However, I know he ruined plenty of girls. And he had tried to abduct me while we travelled here. It seems to run in the family."

Stanisław went white. Wojciech was visibly simmering.

"Your mother drove me mad with desire," Stanisław whispered. "I ... I could not help myself."

"My choice of husband, however, considers that a girl should have the choice in the matter; but then he's a man," said Irene.

Even Wojciech winced slightly at that.

"I do whatever my lady wishes," said Wojciech. He fingered his sabre as he did so.

"I wanted you to marry someone who could take care of you," said Stanisław. "I ... I do love you, and I wanted you safe. It appears you can take care of yourself."

"Oh, but only in my lord's poczet, as his companion," said Irene, turning a look of total adoration on Wojciech.

"She does herself down," said Wojciech, suppressing a chuckle over the tart comments Jan or Seweryn would make over that look of fatuous adoration. "Anyone who can kill a wolf with a pitchfork is worthy of respect."

"But I had to finish it off with a sword blow," said Irene.

Stanisław paled again; the casual way she spoke of it!

"The comment stands," said Wojciech. "She's wearing her own wolf's skin," he added. "Your daughter is an exceptionally able warrior, Trąbka, as well as the most beautiful woman in the world, and I intend to marry her."

"And what would you do if I refused permission?" his voice, embarrassingly, was almost a squeak.

"Take her to her English relatives who would consider your part in the conception to be moderately irrelevant," said Wojciech. "And failing their support, wait until she is one-and-twenty. I wager she'd have a longish grudge list by that time, though."

"It was a hypothetical question," said Stanisław, hurriedly.

"I would like your permission to marry your

daughter in writing," said Wojciech.

"I ... yes, certainly," said Stanisław, and was then struck with a horrifying thought. "Irenka! Were you the second hussar when the cannon exploded? Facing down its muzzle?"

"You said it was flawed; I know you know weaponry so I knew I was in little danger," said Irene. "I had very little training then, though, only of horsemanship, courtesy of Captain Zieliński. Oh, may I take my horse? She has pretty ways."

"She's an unrideable demon; take her and welcome," said Stanisław. "You ... you will stay for a few days?" He seemed to actually mean the invitation.

Irene looked a question at Wojciech.

"It would be courteous," he said. "We could stay for Easter."

"Then yes," said Irene. "Wojciech, you will sleep in my mother's room. The one she chose, not the one connecting to the master bedroom."

"I am relieved to hear that," said Wojciech.

"Uh ... and the connecting room is ... uh ... occupied," said Stanisław.

"Well, I am glad you have not put a mistress in Mama's room at least," said Irene.

Stanisław flushed a dull red.

"I was lonely," he said, defensively.

"So long as you haven't abducted anyone else, it's none of my business," said Irene.

He looked surprised, but pleased.

"She's szlachta. Poverty stricken, but well born," said Stanisław. "She is a widow. I was considering marrying her, for an heir; it's not the passion I had for your mother but she is comfortable to be with."

"Well, then, you can marry her and provide me with half-siblings," said Irene. "What? I have no say in the matter; I only resent that you have a hand in my business and I have to ask your permission to wed. It seems strange that I need permission to create life but not to take it."

"Most girls of just turned eighteen aren't seasoned warriors," said Stanisław, dryly. "Er... do you mind appearing in a gown until I have filled in Aneczka – Anna - all about you? She is staying above stairs today since she did not want to have to see Władimir. I suspect she will warm to you when I tell her you have killed him," he added dryly.

"I like her already," said Irene.

"Irenka, this is Anna," said Slanisław, bringing her into the room when Irene had had a chance to change. He retired hastily to let the ladies get to know each other.

"Please, Irena, call me Aneczka," said Anna.

"I answer to Irenka, too," said Irenka. She was a little wary, but the young woman looked pleasant.

"I hear you beheaded Władimir Trąbka; I told your father I love you already," said Aneczka.

She was a woman in her late twenties, with reddish hair. Irene thought she looked Russian, but her Polish was accentless. Plainly her father had a taste for red-haired women, as her mother had also been ginger.

"I think we are going to get on just fine," said Irene.

Aneczka embraced Irene.

"I owe you a favour," she said. "I loathed Władimir Trąbka; he was trying to take advantage of me when your father stepped in and installed me as his mistress. I was feeling very low, my husband and both our children had died of a fever."

"If you want to leave and find someone better than my father, don't feel that I would be insulted by telling me so," said Irene. "I know he's not exactly a prize."

"He is rather suggestible," said Aneczka, "But if I make sure I am the one he heard last, I think I will be moderately happy. And it is nice not to worry where the next grosz is coming from."

"Then I wish you luck," said Irene. She would never settle for second best herself; but then, she reflected, Aneczka had already lost her first choice. Survival and comfort could not heal loss, but comfortable misery was better than desperate misery.

"You are not angry that you may have siblings and all this fine house and land goes to someone else?" the widow asked. Irene laughed.

"Not in the least! We have a perfectly good house for the winter and tents for travelling," she said. "I would live in a barn if it were with Wojciech."

"Isn't finding somewhere to eat hard when sleeping in a tent?" asked Aneczka, timidly.

"Not really; food grows free in the countryside, and one can snare rabbits or take down boar or deer, or catch fish," said Irene. "I don't have a good disposition for fishing, actually, so I rely on Jan who has the patience."

"I think you lead a more active life than I do," said Aneczka.

"Oh well, if we have not gone to England, you can always send your children to spend some time as pages with us to learn," said Irene.

Aneczka thought her a kind but rather exhausting young lady. She had heard all about the girl the servants called 'Panna Irenka' and how kind she was; and was gratified enough that they had started calling her 'Pani Aneczka' and treating her to confidences about how they had loved their former mistress, Pani Katarzyna, and her daughter.

Irene sought out Captain Zieliński as soon as she might, and embraced him warmly.

"Papa Captain," she said. "I owe you all my happiness, for being able to demonstrate to my Wojciech that I was a very able horsewoman. I wish you could have been my father."

"Ah, Irenka, I had the best part; I was able to watch you grow up into a clever and able girl, and teach you how to be a clever and able boy," said Zieliński. "I had a son and a daughter in one person, and could relieve the fears of your lovely mother."

"If you wanted to join us, we do have another set of wings," said Irene.

"I ... would certainly consider it," said Zieliński. "And I approve of your winged hussar."

"Just as well; I am not about to give him up."

Irene's winged hussar watched her fondly as she re-made the acquaintance of the horse which would not permit Stanisław or Aneczka on her back. Irene ran out into the paddock, ran three strides alongside the white horse and vaulted lightly onto the mare's bare back. Here she put her through the paces of dancing, slow trotting with high lifted hoofs, and then something sufficiently close to airs above the ground to make Wojciech break into spontaneous applause.

"Merciful Heaven, how does she stay on?" marvelled Stanisław.

"Because she's good," said Wojciech. "Not a war-horse though; I'm going to have to break it to her that the mare isn't likely to be happy to walk on the enemy."

"I don't want to know," said Stanisław, hastily.

Epilogue

By the end of April, they had returned to Szuwary, with Captain Tomasz Zieliński joining them. And there, Father Kamil married them, and the village feasted and toasted their good health. Irene was wearing a robe Anglais belonging to her mother and altered by the obliging Jadzia to fit Irene's rather trimmer figure. It was a cream silk, embroidered all over in different coloured gold threads in a floral pattern and Jadzia had threatened to tell tales to his lordship over her mistress' complaints on being inserted into it. Jadzia twinkled at Irene and whispered a suggestion which had Irene blushing and giving a throaty chuckle at the idea.

She was glad to be in such finery to match her husband. Wojciech had sorted out court clothes and was clad in silk and velvet, in shades of red, much embroidered in gold. His kontusz was darkest claret velvet, richly frogged on the chest. The lining was red and gold brocade and his sash was gold brocade. The żupan under it was scarlet and his boots and breeches black. But it was his face her eyes sought, and a shared look which meant they would have married in linen and nettlecloth to be together. The display was mostly for the villagers.

The villagers certainly cheered after the priest pronounced them man and wife, and Irene put up her face for a kiss. Wojciech obliged.

The happy couple slipped away from the wedding feast and Wojciech swept Irene into his arms and kissed her as though he was never going to stop. Irene found this a most agreeable occupation, and leaned against him, kissing him back. She reached up to bury her hand in his curls, and absently threw his hat into the corner to give greater scope to this operation. Wojciech clung to her.

"I can hardly believe we can be together at last," he whispered.

"Believe," said Irene, "And stop talking."

He laughed and kissed her again, hands wandering. Irene also enjoyed letting her hands wander, but spent some of the kiss undoing his kontusz sash and kontusz. She slid her hands inside the kontusz to slide it off his shoulders. This effectively trammelled Wojciech somewhat so he assisted with its removal in order to go back to the task of holding his wife. A wife who had too many clothes on.

"Undressing me is all very well, but how do I get you out of a gown? You have an unfair advantage, woman," said Wojciech.

Irene gave a gurgle of mirth.

"Intelligence is the greatest part of a battle; you taught me that."

"I yield," said Wojciech.

"Then watch, and learn," said Irene. "This is how one gets out of the *robe Anglais* I am wearing."

She proceeded to strip a bit at a time, telling how it came apart and making him repeat the lesson before she would go on to the next bit.

"First you must undo the tapes in the skirt of my gown, and unpin it from the bodice," she said. "Then it comes off like a kontusik. Mind the pins; the bodice is pinned on too."

"What is this obsession with pins? Where do I put them?" grumbled Wojciech. Irene laughed.

"Now do you see why I prefer to dress as a szlachcic?"

"Oh, yes," said Wojciech. "The English style is very decorative though, and – ow! No, now I have them all out, and I took out the ones for the bodice too."

"You are doing it out of order," said Irene. "I might have to put it back on to teach you how to do it properly."

"You will not," said Wojciech. "And then the skirt ..."

"Petticoat, it's called, my lord. Which ties at the back," said Irene.

"No wonder they say Englishmen are cold lovers, they have died of old age by the time they have undressed their wives," said Wojciech.

"Are you impatient, my lord?"

"Impatient enough to consider taking my sabre to it," said Wojciech. "Good grief another skirt beneath it?"

"The top under-petticoat," said Irene.

"Did you put on extra on purpose?" he demanded.

"No; indeed you will not have to unlace me as I use my new garment, and nor did I put on pockets," said Irene.

The uppermost under-petticoat pooled on the floor.

"Why are you wearing a horse-collar for ploughing?" demanded Wojciech.

"It's a padded roll to shape the skirt, and I have one I used to smuggle out a lot of clothing, when I ran away," said Irene. "It just unties."

"And another petticoat under that, your ...chest thing ... and then shift? Enough, woman! Get down to your shift or I'll go sleep in the stables!"

Irene gave a squeak at this awful threat and hastily wriggled out of the quilted under-petticoat, and her support garment.

"Now you take off your żupan; fair's fair," she said. "Then you may untie my stockings and take them off."

"Now that I can look forward to," said Wojciech, relieved, pulling off his żupan. He picked her up and tossed her onto the bed, and ran a hand up her left leg to find the ribbon which tied her stocking. Slowly he untied it and rolled down the stocking, very, very slowly, his fingers drifting on her skin. Irene moaned.

"I can tease too," he said.

"Your turn to take something off," said Irene.

Laughing they completed undressing each other, and regarded each other solemnly.

"Just make it up as you go along, you said?" said Wojciech, kneeling over her. Irene chuckled low in her throat.

"I'm sure we'll figure it out," she said. "My lord, I am in need of kisses".

"I ... I am afraid of hurting you," he whispered.

"Just come here," she growled, reaching up to him.

It might be noted that they figured it out very well indeed.

Sarah's other books
Sarah writes predominantly Regency Romances:

The Brandon Scandals Series
    The Hasty Proposal
    The Reprobate's Redemption
    The Advertised Bride
    The Wandering Widow
    The Braithwaite Letters
    Heiress in Hiding

Wild Western Brandon Scandals
    Colonel Brandon's Quest

The Charity School Series
    Elinor's Endowment
    Ophelia's Opportunity
    Abigail's Adventure
    Marianne's Misanthrope
    Emma's Education/Grace's Gift
    Anne's Achievement
    Daisy's Destiny
    Libby's Luck

    Spinoffs:
    The Moorwick Tales
    Fantasia on a House Party

Rookwood series
    The Unwilling Viscount
    The Enterprising Emigrée

The Wynddell Papers
    Lord Wynddell's Bride

The Seven Stepsisters series
Elizabeth
Diana
Minerva[WIP]
Flora [WIP]
Catherine [WIP]
Jane [WIP]
Anne [WIP]

One off Regencies
Vanities and Vexations [Jane Austen sequel]
Cousin Prudence [Jane Austen sequel]
Friends and Fortunes
None so Blind
Belles and Bucks [short stories]

The Georgian Gambles series
The Valiant Viscount [formerly The Pugilist Peer]
Ace of Schemes

Other
William Price and the 'Thrush', naval adventure and Jane Austen tribute
William Price sails North
William Price on land
William Price and the 'Thetis' [wip]

100 years of Cat Days: 365 anecdotes

Sarah also writes historical mysteries

Regency period 'Jane, Bow Street Consultant 'series,
a Jane Austen tribute
    Death of a Fop
    Jane and the Bow Street Runner [3 novellas]
    Jane and the Opera Dancer
    Jane and the Christmas Masquerades [2 novellas]
    Jane and the Hidden Hoard
    Jane and the Burning Question [short stories]
    Jane and the Sins of Society
    Jane and the Actresses
    Jane and the Careless Corpse

Spinoffs:
The Armitage Chronicles

'Felicia and Robin' series set in the Renaissance
    Poison for a Poison Tongue
    The Mary Rose Mystery
    Died True Blue
    Frauds, Fools and Fairies
    The Bishop of Brangling
    The Hazard Chase
    Heretics, Hatreds and Histories
    The Midsummer Mysteries
    The Colour of Murder
    Falsehood most Foul
    The Monkshithe Mysteries
    Toll the Dead Man's bells
    Wells, Wool and Wickedness
    The Missing Hostage
    The Convenient Saint and Other stories
    Sell-sword Summer

Children's stories
Tabitha Tabs the Farm kitten
A School for Ordinary Princesses [sequel to Frances Hodgson Burnett's 'A Little Princess.]

The Royal Draxiers series
Bess and the Dragons
Bess and the Queen
Bess and the Succession
Bess and the Paying Scholars
Bess and the Gunpowder Plot [wip]
Bess and the Necromancer [wip]

Non-Fiction
Writing Regency Romances by dice
The Regency Miss's Survival Guide to Bath

Fantasy
Falconburg Divided [book 1 of the Falconburg brothers series]
Falconburg Rising [book 2 of the Falconburg brothers series]
Falconburg Ascendant [book 3 of the Falconburg brothers series, WIP]

Scarlet Pimpernel spinoffs
The Redemption of Chauvelin
Chauvelin and the League
Chauvelin and the Lost Children

Other Baroness Orczy spinoffs
Lady Molly – Married

Made in the USA
Coppell, TX
20 February 2021